A power[...]
hard in he[...]

So hard, it was painful. Brandt Stryker was a man with depth and compassion. He'd been hurt inside and out and was scarred because of it.

Dalilah needed to hold him, love him, and it scared her. Then she did something she didn't think through: she kissed him.

Brandt melted into the sensation of her lips on his. He kissed her softly, so gently it hurt every nerve in his body. He wanted her—all of her.

Then a slow prickle started up his neck—a hunter's instinct. A sense of being watched, preyed on. He froze.

"Don't move," he whispered against her lips, his hand going for the gun. He breathed in, then whipped onto his back, spinning the rifle around to face their attacker.

Dear Reader,

As you may have noticed this month, Harlequin Romantic Suspense has a brand-new look that's a fresh take on our beautiful covers. We are delighted at this transformation and hope you enjoy it, too.

There's more! Along with new covers, the stories are longer—more action, more excitement, more romance. Follow your beloved characters on their passion-filled adventures. Be sure to look for our newly packaged and longer Harlequin Romantic Suspense stories wherever you buy books.

Check out this month's adrenaline-charged reads:

COWBOY WITH A CAUSE by Carla Cassidy

A WIDOW'S GUILTY SECRET by Marie Ferrarella

DEADLY SIGHT by Cindy Dees

GUARDING THE PRINCESS by Loreth Anne White

Happy reading!

Patience Bloom

Senior Editor

LORETH ANNE WHITE

Guarding the Princess

HARLEQUIN®

entertain, enrich, inspire™

Recycling programs
for this product may
not exist in your area.

ISBN-13: 978-0-373-27808-4

GUARDING THE PRINCESS

www.Harlequin.com

Printed in U.S.A.

Books by Loreth Anne White

Harlequin Romantic Suspense

Silhouette Romantic Suspense

★Shadow Soldiers
★★Wild Country
‡Sahara Kings

Other titles by this author available in ebook format.

LORETH ANNE WHITE

was born and raised in southern Africa, but now lives in Whistler, a ski resort in the moody British Columbia Coast Mountain range. It's a place of vast wilderness, larger-than-life characters, epic adventure and romance—the perfect place to escape reality. It's no wonder she was inspired to abandon a sixteen-year career as a journalist to escape into a world of romance fiction filled with dangerous men and adventurous women.

When she's not writing, you will find her long-distance running, biking or skiing on the trails and generally trying to avoid the bears—albeit not very successfully. She calls this work, because it's when the best ideas come.

For a peek into her world, visit her website, www.lorethannewhite.com. She'd love to hear from you.

To Norma Beswetherick, for making a Botswana safari come true.

And to Susan Litman, for all the editorial support and encouragement along this writing road.

Prologue

A plume of yellow dust rose along the horizon, carrying like spindrift over Mopani trees eaten squat by elephants. High above in a haze-white sky, vultures wheeled on thermals—drought had this southern region of Zambia in a death grip.

Amal Ghaffar raised his binoculars and studied the approaching vehicle. It was a jeep, drab olive-green, stark against the dry earth. As it neared, he recognized the hulking shape of Mbogo at the wheel. Amal lowered his scopes and resumed cleaning his AK-47 with his right hand. The sleeve of his khaki shirt hung empty where his left arm used to be. Heat pressed down on the shade cloth over his head, sweat trickling from his sideburns.

Amal didn't bother to look up when the jeep drew to a stop outside the camp and the door slammed. He listened to the crunch of Mbogo's combat boots approaching.

"What is it?" Amal said.

Mbogo slapped a newspaper onto the small table in front of Amal.

"Page nine." His voice was a deep baritone and it carried the resonant rhythms of Africa.

Amal's gaze slid slowly over to the newspaper.

"It's a British paper, a week old."

Mbogo remained silent.

Amal finally glanced up, then pulled the paper toward him and opened it to page nine. For an instant he was paralyzed by the black-and-white photograph.

He leaned forward for a closer look, to be certain. But there was no doubt—it was *her*. All flashing black eyes, thick dark hair, a broad smile across her exotic features. She was, as usual, exquisitely dressed. Standing beside her was a tall, dark-skinned man with hooded eyes and pitch-black hair. Her left hand rested on the man's arm and the diamond on her ring finger was large enough to feed a small nation.

Amal's attention darted to the text below the photo. A date had been set. The wedding of Princess Dalilah Al Arif of Al Na'Jar and Sheik Haroun Hassan of Sa'ud would take place in the Kingdom of Sa'ud nineteen months from now, as per the contract negotiated between their fathers almost twenty-three years ago. It would marry two oil-rich kingdoms, one in the Sahara, the other across the Red Sea in Arabia.

"According to that article she's in Zimbabwe right now," Mbogo said quietly. "And in two days she'll be staying at a lodge near Victoria Falls."

Amal stared at the photo. It was a sign—a gift from God, delivered right to his very hand. For two long years he'd been forced to live like a wounded rat, scurrying around the dry hills and plains, hiding in the insect-infested jungles of this dark continent with a rogue band of fugitives, eking out a living by doing mercenary jobs for corrupt men in power, thwarting the international agencies hunting him. The Al Arif family had taken *everything* from him, including his left arm, and his father. They had forced him into this existence.

Now, suddenly, he could taste revenge.

"We leave before nightfall," Amal whispered. He got to his feet, his empty sleeve flapping in the hot breeze. "And in case we don't reach her in time, put out word that I want her. Alive. Although dead will suffice as long as I am brought her head on a plate. Let it be known I'll pay—very well."

"And how will you pay?"

Amal's eyes flared to Mbogo. "Her brothers will. Ransom. While they think I have her alive." He grabbed his gun, a new fire burning in his gut. "The world will see what happens when you dare cross a Ghaffar."

Chapter 1

The screeching monkeys in the branches above the lodge patio forced Dalilah Al Arif to lean forward in order to hear what the shorter Chinese diplomat was saying. She smiled and nodded encouragingly, not wanting to ruffle any feathers tonight—this deal that would see Zimbabwe ceding platinum-mining rights to China was unprecedented in scope. For her part, Dalilah was in the country to ensure the provision of clean-water points for the impacted villages was firmly entrenched in the deal when it was signed in Harare tomorrow. ClearWater, the New York–based nonprofit agency for which Dalilah volunteered, would handle the installations over the next five years.

She'd been working on securing ClearWater access in Zimbabwe for almost four years now, and it would be her swan song. Because when she married in nineteen months, she'd be leaving Manhattan, along with her foreign-investment consulting career and charity work, to live in Sa'ud. There she'd be expected to work at her new husband's side as queen when Sheik Haroun Hassan took the throne from his ailing father. This had been her destiny from the day she turned five. She accepted it, but tonight, on the eve of her success, Dalilah was having trouble with the idea of letting go of the things that had come to define her, of losing her freedom.

But the marriage would forge a powerful political and economic alliance between the two oil-rich kingdoms, one in Al Na'Jar in the Sahara, the Sa'ud across the Red Sea in Arabia. It would boost her own country's economy. It would help her brothers, one of whom was king.

It's what her dead father had wanted.

And at least, after this deal was signed tomorrow, she'd be leaving a legacy for hundreds of villagers. It would be a tribute to the freedom she'd enjoyed, and in which she'd prospered.

Most of the serious talks with China had been conducted over the past fortnight in Harare, and now the delegates, including Dalilah, had been flown to a high-end game lodge near Victoria Falls as part of the president's show of hospitality. His largesse stuck in her craw when she thought of the country's starving and disenfranchised citizens, but dealing with the devil was a necessary evil if she truly wanted to help. It was like this in much of Africa, and Africa was her speciality. Having been raised in the Sahara, Dalilah understood the precious commodity that was water on this continent, and she understood the complexities of government and corruption.

As she listened to the Chinese delegate, she sipped sparkling water from a glass held in her carefully manicured hand. The evening air was warm against her bare shoulders, the sun sinking to the horizon in a blood-orange ball, colored by haze from surrounding bushfires brought on by drought. The acrid scent of smoke tinged the air, and she could hear drumming from a nearby village. It carried an undercurrent of foreboding, something primeval that lurked under the layers of feigned civility.

"The fires smell close tonight," said a delegate from the Czech Republic as he sidled up to Dalilah and the Chinese representative. The Czech's pores sweated the smell of metabolized booze. He mopped his forehead with a kerchief and pointed his glass of vodka out toward the treed gardens where sprinklers threw graceful arcs of water over lush lawns. A family of warthogs grazed on the grass near the river, and tiny white lights pricked their way through the dusk, marking pathways to the thatched guest cottages, each of which was decorated in different African themes. Lanterns hung in trees where the monkeys chattered.

"At least the wind is blowing away from us," he said. "Our guide said it'll turn tomorrow, but we should be gone before that." He tossed back the last of his vodka, standing too close to her now. "At least we will be safe."

"Yes," she said. *Too bad about all the villages and wildlife in the path of the fires.*

"It's incredible to think it's so dry out there when Victoria Falls and the massive Zambezi is just a few miles away. All that water."

"It is," Dalilah said, swallowing her real thoughts. The Czech Republic was a cosigner with China on the deal—she had to play nice, only until tomorrow. Once this was signed, she was going to take a long hot shower and scrub the schmooze off her skin.

"A most spectacular waterfall," the Czech said as he waved for a waiter to bring him more vodka. A man in a red fez and white button-down shirt approached quickly with his silver tray and filled the man's glass.

The Czech raised his full glass to the darkening sky.

"Here's to Dr. Livingston for discovering the falls!" Then he tossed back the entire glass.

"The locals call the falls *Mosi oa Tunya*," Dalilah responded quietly. "It means the smoke that thunders. They called it that well before Livingston ever arrived."

He shot her a sharp look, and she cautioned herself. *Be nice. Tomorrow it will be a done deal.* But the stress of the week was taking its toll on Dalilah. Earlier in the day, after a game drive, a whirlwind visit to the falls and a lavish lunch, she'd tried to steal a few moments alone, seating herself on a bentwood bench along the high riverbank that ran along the lodge property.

The riverbed was dust-dry, apart from a few deep, lingering, brown pools, and to her delight, a family of elephants had come down on the opposite bank to drink from one of those pools.

Dalilah had watched them for almost an hour, stress easing from her neck and mind, until a crocodile broke the muddy surface and latched onto the baby elephant. The ensuing fight, the raw violence of it, had grabbed her by the throat.

As she'd been held fixated by the death struggle, this same Czech had approached her from behind, his footfalls rustling through the tough grass. He'd stood over her shoulder and made some inane comment about the spectacle unfolding in front of them as he offered her a sweating glass of gin and tonic, ice chinking in the oppressive heat.

He'd stood beside her, watching, sipping his own cocktail, cheeks flushed and eyes bright with the thrill of his own personal reality show.

And something cold and disturbing had settled into Dalilah's chest on that riverbank this afternoon, something she couldn't define. A sense of change coming. Something dark.

Whatever it was, her mood altered the color of the afternoon. The shadows in the trees across the bank had grown a little darker, the shapes of the leaves more prickly, The sun too harsh. The insistent, sad *Qwa-waaaaee* call of a gray lorie seemed even sadder. *Go-a-waaaay. Go-a-waaaay.*

The locals called it the go-away bird. It was one of several Botswana birds that issued an alarm call when a large predator came near, although it was difficult to tell whether the lorie was warning of a human in the area or a lion stalking out of sight in the long grasses.

"The danger is everywhere out here," the Czech said at her shoulder. "Always a predator in the shadows, lurking, waiting to kill. You go about your business, then *suddenly,* it strikes." She heard him sip his drink, ice knocking against crystal, and she couldn't help flicking a glance over to where her two bodyguards stood, watching her discreetly from the shadows of nearby lucky bean trees.

"We're put on this earth to eat or be eaten," he intoned. "To kill or be killed, except with us humans, it's not always about food or water. Sometimes it's just for fun, or revenge. Sometimes an attack comes indirectly through commerce, greed…" He trailed off, his words slurring, his philosophical idea blurring around the edges.

Dalilah fingered the mammoth pink Argyle diamond on her ring finger as she thought of the elephant kill that afternoon, of the Czech's ominous words. The diamond was a symbol of her call to duty, her looming future. Was she going to be confined to a life of polite talk and diplomatic function, feigning civility with the likes of this Czech boozer for the rest of her life?

As the sun slid below the escarpment the cloak of darkness was sudden and thick. Small bats flitted out from under the lodge's thatched eaves and a fish eagle cried somewhere along the river. She could hear the rising whoops of hyenas—the sounds of the bush night shift, and violence, beginning.

The dinner gong boomed suddenly and lodge staff politely began to usher guests across the lawn toward the *lapa,* a fenced-off circular dining area where a huge fire crackled inside a stone circle at the center. Pulsing embers had been raked to one side. Upon them rested several three-legged African cast-iron pots, simmering with traditional game stews, one with a vegetarian selection for Dalilah.

Delegates took their seats at long tables decked with white linen, candles, polished silverware. Wine flowed, and the entertainment began—xylophones and softly throbbing skin drums, voices that sounded like the land itself. Dancers shuffled out from behind the branch fencing, stomping bare feet, nutshells and bottle caps clicking in bracelets around their ankles as they swayed and hummed to the beat. A lone voice rose above it all, a cry, in song.

Goose bumps chased over Dalilah's skin, and she had to resist the urge to close her eyes and just drink in the sounds. Instead, she nodded politely at a representative from Bangkok who'd taken a seat at her side, instantly feeling crowded, which, she suspected, had little to do with this occasion and more to do with her future.

By the time the first song ended and the guests applauded, the night was thick as velvet, stars spattered across the vault of African sky. Nature seemed to be encroaching on the periphery of the camp, closing in with mysterious night sounds. Fatigue slammed down on Dalilah, and her mind turned to her guest suite, the cotton sheets, the hot tub. Sleep. A warm wind gusted, rustling the nyala leaves above, and Dalilah suddenly felt as if she was being watched. She glanced up into the branches, saw the glow of a tiny white owl looking down at her.

Slowly Dalilah turned her attention to the armed and silent bodyguards lining the six-foot-high branch fence, watching. The security detail had been provided by the president to watch over the delegates. Her own men stood behind her at a comfortable distance. Yet the chill of foreboding deepened and she shivered.

Brandt Stryker checked the name attached to a small plate on the bungalow door—Dalilah Al Arif, delegate, ClearWater. He knew about the nonprofit that helped bring fresh water and farming aid to impoverished communities in Africa. They did good work. He hadn't known the Saharan princess was involved with that work. He knew very little about her other than she was a high-maintenance, high-society player with looks to kill.

The lock was easy enough to pick. Brandt edged open the bungalow door. Inside, the air conditioner hummed, cooling the air. White cotton sheets on the canopy bed had been turned down; a foil-wrapped chocolate nestled on the pillow alongside a miniature bottle of cream liqueur made from the fruit of the African marula tree.

The princess's cell phone lay atop the covers. It was buzzing.

Brandt went over to the bed, the soles of his boots squeaking slightly on highly polished stone. The buzzing stopped. He picked the phone up. Eight unanswered calls, probably from her brother, Omair, trying to alert Dalilah, let her know that he was coming for her.

Irritated, Brandt tossed her phone back onto the covers. Now the job of convincing her to come peaceably would fall to him.

Using the barrel of his rifle, he edged the muslin drapes

aside slightly and peered out the window. Down the pathway, under the branches of huge nyala trees, firelight winked through gaps in the branch fencing surrounding a *lapa*. He could hear drumming, singing, ululating. The dinner would go on for a while yet, he suspected.

His plan was go down to the *lapa* and identify his target from the shadows. Once he had confirmation Dalilah was among the guests, he'd head back to this bungalow as festivities began to wrap up, and wait for her here.

He opened her closet. Cocktail dresses in exotic and gauzy fabrics hung in a rainbow of colors. He trailed the muzzle of his gun through sequins, sparkles, shimmering scarves. At the bottom of the closet was a high-end luggage set and five pairs of sandals with ridiculous heels. The princess's saving grace was a lone pair of sturdy hiking boots, a pair of khaki pants, two T-shirts, a longsleeved button-down shirt and a sun hat. He tossed those onto the bed. His intention was to gear her up properly before he took her out into the night.

Brandt opened one of her drawers, looking for thick socks—once she returned to the bungalow he didn't want to waste a second getting her changed and out of here. He stalled suddenly at the sight of a black bra and small pile of G-strings—mere scraps of silk. And he couldn't help touching them, the fabric snagging on the rough pads of his fingers. He hadn't seen, or felt, really expensive feminine underwear in years, and the silky sensation of it stirred something in him, a deep rustling of memories. An unspecified longing.

Then he cursed sharply, slamming the drawer shut.

He'd had his fill of women, of deceit. He liked things the way he had them now. He lived solo in the bush for weeks on end, and when his piloting jobs did take him to Gaborone, he found sex. No fuss, no foreplay, no commitment, just pleasure straight up. Until recently he hadn't felt bad about it either—but lately, even the mindless sex had left him feeling hollow, unsatisfied, uneasy.

He found the princess's purse, checked the passport picture in her wallet. His heart beat a little faster at the sight of her thick hair, her dark, almond eyes, her exotic features. Her looks alone pushed his buttons. He needed to get this job done fast—this was not a woman he wanted to linger around. She reminded him too much of someone else, of a past he'd worked for ten years to forget, but still couldn't quite shake.

Brandt's mind went to the phone call and the man who had coerced him into this mission—Sheik Omair Al Arif.

"I won't do it," Brandt had informed Dalilah's brother. "I'm done kidnapping damsels in distress—you know what happened last time."

"Which is why you're going to do this for me now, Stryker, please—you owe me. My sister's life is in danger and you're the only guy in a position to get her out quickly. You'll be in and out in seventy-two hours. Fly her over the border into Botswana, take her to your place out in the bush, let me know she's safe, and I'll send someone out there to bring her home."

"You really trust me?"

"You sober?"

"For the moment."

"Stay that way and I trust you. You'll be well compensated."

"Look, I don't want your money, Sheik." But truth was, Brandt did. He needed cash. He'd sunk everything into his farm, and to make ends meet he was forced to fly tourists out to game lodges across Botswana. A solid injection of capital would enable him to turn down the piloting work and stick to his land.

And he knew Omair would pay handsomely.

"Do this for me, Stryker, and next time I'll owe *you*. Anything you want."

Brandt laughed and hung up.

But he wasn't laughing now. It was a restiveness he felt, a sixth sense of something bad closing in. Brandt had learned to trust that sense.

Quietly he left the bungalow and moved down through the shadows toward the *lapa*.

The fencing along one side of the dining area was open to a low rock wall that dropped down into a grove of trees. Brandt crouched among the smooth roots of those trees, gun in hand as he scanned the group. He saw her instantly. Princess Dalilah Al Arif. An exotic bird in cocktail gold among a group of mostly middle-aged men gone soft around the center and flushed with booze.

She turned her pretty, dark head to listen attentively to a squat, lantern-jawed man at her side. In her left hand she held a drink and a diamond as big as a plum caught the firelight. If that was an engagement ring, where was her fiancé in shining armor now? Brandt wondered.

The firelight caught her face as she turned in his direction—dusky skin, smooth, her eyes like black shining pools made even darker and bigger with eyeliner. She gave the poor schmuck beside her a full-wattage princess smile.

The man held his drink up in a mock toast and Dalilah tossed back her mane of curls and laughed, showing the long column of her throat, the low cut of her gold cocktail gown, the outline of breasts that were small and firm looking. And as she crossed her legs, the slit in her gown fell open, exposing taut thighs, slender ankles, ridiculously high stiletto sandals in gold to match her dress.

She was a glimmering flame among these dull male

moths bumping fruitlessly, and dangerously, against her fire. A tease, engaged to another man.

Brandt disliked—and distrusted—her immediately.

He studied the security detail behind her—two men, likely her own. His attention shifted to the Zimbabwe soldiers lining the fence.

He'd seen those same men sharing dark beer and a joint when he'd cased the lodge and outbuildings earlier. Their eyes now gleamed yellow in the firelight, skin shining, postures showing boredom. They wouldn't be sharp. Even so, he had no intention of engaging these goons. They were most likely trained to shoot and kill on sight, no questions asked.

Shifting on his haunches to ease the stiffness of old injuries, Brandt moved his attention back to his target. She was still laughing, seductive. A temptress. The way Carla had been. He wondered why the men couldn't see the calculated precision, the tightly scripted choreography of her movements. Bitterness filled his mouth. He'd been one of those blind men once. It wouldn't happen again.

The food plates came and went. Drink flowed. Chatter grew loud. Stiffness cramped his limbs. Brandt cursed softly to himself—this could go on all night. Very slowly he reached into the side pocket in his cargo shorts and slipped out a silver hip flask. Cautiously, he unscrewed the cap, took a deep swig, relishing the hot burn of scotch blossoming through his chest as he settled in for the long haul, his back pressed against the smooth bark of the tree. And he told himself—seventy-two hours more, and his hands would be washed clean. His debt to Omair finally paid.

The music, the drumming, grew louder, faces more flushed, voices raucous. Vervet monkeys began to mimic the humans from the branches above, swooping in closer, hanging by their tails and using their long arms to steal food. And somewhere out in the veldt Brandt heard the first soft rumblings of thunder. Surprise rippled through him—this hadn't been in the forecast. With his surprise came tension. A spring thunderstorm could bring early rain, flash floods, lightning and more fire.

He wanted to be up in the air and over Botswana airspace before any weather hit.

After-dinner liqueurs were now being poured. His patience grew thinner. He took another swig from his flask, pooling whiskey in his mouth, but before he could swallow, Brandt sensed something.

He held dead still, listening.

A crunch of flinty stone. The crack of dry twig. A softer warning chitter passing through the monkeys above.

All instincts sharp as razors, muscles primed, he concentrated on the ambient sounds under the bacchanalian clatter in the *lapa*.

Another slight shuffle. Then a birdlike call, soft.

Human.

Slowly he swallowed his mouthful of booze, his mind sharp and clear as morning. He rose. And he could sense them approaching, surrounding. Hunters. Experienced.

Clicking the safety off his rifle, he felt for the hilt of the panga sheathed at his hip—a blade that widened and curved upward toward the tip, the weapon of choice during the Rwandan genocide—a common tool of African violence.

Then on the far side of the *lapa,* a crack of gunshot.

It echoed through hot, black air. Then followed an almost imperceptible moment of dead stillness as everything quieted and the *lapa* became a freeze-frame—shadows against flame as liqueur-addled minds tried to compute what was happening.

Another shot, and a yell. Then it erupted—men in black balaclavas wielding AK-47s, knives and machetes stormed the *lapa*. Bodyguards returned fire as guests screamed, diving for the ground, crawling under tables and through upturned chairs and over broken glass.

Brandt held back, quickly computing. The attackers numbered upward of a dozen, and they were mowing down everyone in their wake, blood flowing freely. But one man among them stood slightly apart from the others. He seemed to be searching for something, controlling the team. As the man turned, Brandt saw he had only one arm.

Amal Ghaffar.

The man laid eyes on Dalilah, pointed and yelled.

All attention seemed to turn to the princess, who was crawling under a table.

Brandt swung himself up over the low rock wall and, using tables for cover, ran toward her in a crouch. He ducked under the tablecloth. She was kneeling beside a prone man, pressing her hand tightly against his neck, her eyes wild with terror as the man's blood pulsed thick through her fingers. Even in danger, she was trying to help.

She glanced up, saw Brandt, and a raw kind of rage twisted through her features as she reached for a fallen carving knife. Brandt raised his finger to his lips, shook his head. But her fist curled around the knife even as she pressed her other hand to the man's neck.

Brandt crawled closer. "Leave him," he whispered harshly. "He's gone."

Her gaze shot to the fallen man's face and a shudder ran through her body. There was another volley of shots, screams, orders being barked in Arabic. Someone started to pull the table away. Bodyguards returned fire. A fresh burst of adrenaline kicked through Brandt's blood.

No time to waste. He grabbed her arm, but she lashed at him with the carving knife, almost slicing across his biceps.

"Dalilah! Listen—"

Shock flashed through her face at the sound of her name, but she lunged at him anyway, this time the blade coming right for his heart. Jesus. Brandt rolled sideways, twisting her arm sharply back until the knife dropped from her fist and her cheek was forced flat against the ground. He hooked his arm around her neck. Squeezing tight, he held her head in position with his other hand until he felt her go suddenly limp. Then quickly he dragged her across the rough paving and rolled her over the low wall. Her body thudded softly onto grass on the other side.

But as Brandt began to scramble after her, a man in a balaclava dived at him. Brandt swung round, unsheathing his panga, and sliced the man clean across the throat. He saw the gaping maw of red and black where the neck had been, the white of spinal column. Hot blood gushed onto him as the man's body slumped forward into his arms. Bile rose in Brandt's throat and for a moment he was unable to move.

A fresh volley of gunfire shocked him back. Brandt pushed the man off, clambered over the wall and bent to pick up Dalilah. Slinging her limp body over his shoulders, he ducked into the shadows, disappearing into a night black and thick with the smell of fresh death and smoke.

As he ran, thunder rumbled again along the distant horizon, a little louder now.

Mosi oa Tunya, he thought—the smoke that thunders. He repeated the mantra in his head as he ran through the bush, his burden heavy across his shoulders. He'd killed a man. He'd broken his vow of ten years.

She'd made him do it.

The princess reminded him of a woman from his darkest past, and now she was hurtling him right back into the terrible black nightmare of it all. Nausea roiled. With it came rage.

Mosi oa Tunya. Mosi oa Tunya. Mosi oa Tunya.

But it was not enough to keep his demons at bay. Not enough to stop her assailants from coming after them.

And it was not enough to stop the storm he could now smell in the air. Thunder growled again over the Zimbabwe plains and a hot wind began to gust in a new direction. The fires would turn, too, now. He realized suddenly his GPS and sat phone were missing from his hip. Must've lost them in the tussle. No time to worry about it now. His only goal right now was to reach his Cessna, get up into the air and over the border before the weather—or Ghaffar—hit.

Something told Brandt he was not going to make it.

Chapter 2

First there was only blackness, pain. Then as consciousness filtered back, Dalilah realized her head was hanging down, hair swinging, blood filling her cheeks, her body rhythmically bumping against something...

She was being carried over a man's shoulders.

A twig sliced across her brow as her abductor began to descend a steep hill, stones clattering ahead of him. She tried to pull her vision into focus. It was night—dark, apart from moon and starlight. She could see the ground below, parts of her abductor's body. His legs, boots. He was wearing safari shorts, thick socks, a machete at his hip.

Panic struck like a hatchet as memory slammed into her—the attack at the lodge. Men in hoods. Shooting, blood, screams. Barked Arabic commands. The delegate lying under the table, blood spurting from a gunshot wound in his neck. She realized with horror her fingers were still sticky with the man's blood.

Leave him. He's gone—the fierce whisper of her attacker, his ice-blue eyes drilling into hers. Eyes so pale
and luminous against his darkly tanned face it had frightened her. She'd tried to stab him with a carving knife,
but he'd grabbed her around the neck, and her world had
gone black.

He'd taken her!

Dalilah squeezed her eyes shut, trying to gather herself. Fight? Flee? But where to? She opened her eyes again
and tried to carefully lift her head in order to assess more
of her surroundings, but he felt her body stiffen because
he said, "Don't even try it. Don't move. Fighting me will
make it worse."

His voice was rough, deep, and he spoke English with
the flat, guttural accent of an Afrikaner. She knew the
sound well—had spent several months in the country and
had worked with an Afrikaans-speaking South African
in New York.

"What do you want with me?" Her voice came out
hoarse, her throat hurting where he'd strangled her.

"Hold still. My Cessna is just down there, on the plain."

Fear spurted afresh through her, and she struggled
wildly against his grip. "Who are you? Where are you
taking me? If it's ransom you want, I can—"

"Jesus, woman. I don't want to hurt you—"

But she kicked at him hard, grabbing a handful of his
short hair, twisting. He cursed viciously, swinging her
forward and tossing her to the ground with a thud. Stones
stabbed sharply into her back as breath whooshed out of
her lungs with the impact. Dalilah's eyes watered, pain
sparking through her ribs.

"You bastard!" she hissed as soon as she managed a
breath. "What do you want with me?"

"My name is Stryker—Brandt Stryker. Your brother

sent me to get you." He bent forward, hands on knees, struggling to catch his own breath. He was big. Well over six feet. Even in the milky starlight she could see he was fair. Square-jawed, broad-shouldered. Built. A rifle was strapped across his chest. His pale khaki shirt was dark with sweat, his sleeves ripped off at the shoulders, and she saw blood smeared down his arm.

Something in Dalilah stilled.

"My brother?" she asked quietly.

"Omair."

"You *know* Omair?"

"Yes. I owe the damn sheik. Come on, get up. They're going to be here any second."

"Who!"

"Amal Ghaffar. Bloody one-armed jackal and his wild pack of dogs."

Ice slid through her veins. *"Amal?"* Her voice came out a whisper. "The Moor's son—he's *alive?"*

Her assailant threw her an odd look and was silent for a beat.

"You didn't know?"

Dalilah stared at him, thinking of the Arabic words she'd heard back at the *lapa*.

He gave a snort. "Figures your brothers might keep that from you. Amal Ghaffar has been hiding in Africa for the past two years, ever since your other brother Tariq shot off his arm in France and he got himself onto the world's most-wanted list. Omair has been hunting him via an underground mercenary network, but every time Omair's men get close, Amal and his pack move first."

Her abductor held his hand out to her.

Dalilah stared at it, anger curling into her chest.

"You're saying my brothers knew all this time that Amal was out here, alive?"

"That's exactly what I'm saying, Princess. Look, we need to move. They're going to be up our asses as soon as day breaks and they find our tracks."

Dalilah got awkwardly to her feet. He caught her arm as dizziness spun her world and she stumbled. She held on to him, steadying herself as pain sparked through her head. She realized her cocktail gown was ripped up to her hip, her legs scraped. One of her stiletto heels had broken in half. But all paled in face of the words he'd just uttered.

"Why would they keep this from me?"

"Why don't you ask them yourselves once we get out of here." He tried to usher her forward, but she yanked free.

"Those other men—"

"They're all Amal's, a band of rogue mercs, and they want your blood, Dalilah. Omair got wind via the underground that a bounty has been put on your head. Amal wants it, literally, on a plate if he can't kill you himself."

Blood drained from her face. "How…how do I know you're telling the truth, that you're not—"

"You don't," he said brusquely. "But make up your mind fast, Princess. Because it's me or those men, and I'm not waiting." With that he spun around and started marching down the ridge alone, not even bothering to glance over his shoulder to see if she was coming.

Fear propelled her after him, her lopsided stiletto heels spiking deep into soft, drought-dry sand and making her stagger wildly. Thunder clapped suddenly overhead and Dalilah ducked, wincing as the sound reverberated right through her bones. Black clouds were beginning to blot out the stars—the storm was closing in.

"Wait!" she yelled, trying to run faster, floundering even more on her uneven heels. But he kept moving ahead of her at a clip.

"Storm's coming," he called over his shoulder. "Need to get the Cessna up and over the Tsholo River before it hits!"

"Where are we going?"

"Botswana."

"I—" She lurched forward suddenly and slammed to the ground. She cursed, eyes watering as she scrambled back to her feet and ran after him again. "I need to go to Harare! You've got to take me to Harare!"

He stopped suddenly, spun round. "*Got* to?"

"I have to sign a major deal tomorrow." She was panting now, breath raw in her throat. "For ClearWater. I need to—"

"You don't get it, do you, Princess?" He pointed back up the ridge. "At first light—if not before—Amal and his men are going to find our tracks, and they're going to follow them right here! If we don't get into the air and over the border before that storm hits, or before they arrive, we're outnumbered and outgunned, and you're dead. I'm here to see that isn't going to happen, which means the only place you're going right now is to Botswana where I can protect you until Omair or his men come and take you off my hands."

Anxiety, fear, desperation, failure—it all swamped through Dalilah at once, overwhelming her. "This deal," she said softly, all the fight going out of her. "I've been working on it for four years now. If we don't sign tomorrow…I…the villagers won't get water…." Her voice cracked and tears spilled down her face. She sunk to the ground and buried her face in her hands.

Something seemed to shift in him, because he crouched in front of her and touched her arms, his palms rough against her skin.

"Dalilah," he said quietly, "Those delegates aren't signing anything tomorrow. They're all dead."

She couldn't breathe. She started to shake as it truly sunk in what had just happened at the lodge.

"They died because they were there with you—those men mean business. Come, we need to move. Now."

"Clean water," she whispered. "Those people *need* water. This mining-rights deal was our way in to get it to them. It was the one thing—the *last* thing I could give them. My last mission."

"Hey, look at me." He tilted her face up, forcing her to look at him. His eyes were ghostly in the darkness.

"Get up onto those pretty, long legs of yours, and you'll live to fight another day, because there *will* be another day, another deal."

She wanted to say there wouldn't. She'd be getting married. This had been her very last fight. Her swan song. And she'd lost. She'd lost it all.

"My Cessna is down there, see?"

She looked where he was pointing. Over the grassland in faint moonlight the fuselage of a small single-prop plane glinted. Then a cloud passed over the moon and darkness was complete—the plane seemed to vanish as she felt the hot breeze stiffen. Carefully she got to her knees, and then to her feet. He steadied her by the elbow as wooziness and nausea swept through her again.

"You ready?" he said.

Dalilah nodded. He regarded her for a moment, then said, "Stay right behind me, okay—that's an order." He clicked on a flashlight and started to walk.

She stumbled after him in the darkness, her brain reeling as she tried to process it all. For two full years she'd naively believed that peace had finally come to the Al Arif family and their desert kingdom of Al Na'Jar.

Now this.

The thought that her brothers had purposely misled

her infuriated Dalilah beyond words. It had been like this all her life—the older alpha males in her family always trying to coddle and protect her, supposedly for her own good. Did they give her absolutely no credit? Did they not understand she could take measures to protect herself? That she held the same fierce allegiance to country as they did—and that she was marrying Haroun because of it?

Now Amal was after her blood and they'd dispatched this brusque brute of a male to "save" her.

"Hurry up!" he yelled over his shoulder as she began to lag behind.

She muttered a curse in Arabic, slowing even further in softer sand.

He stopped, spun round. "Jesus, Princess, do you want me to carry you, or what?" Frustration cut through his voice.

Refusing to dignify him with an answer, she stopped, bracing her hands on her hips as she tried to catch her breath.

"Okay, this is it." He reached forward to grab her arm, but she jerked free of his grip, standing her ground. "You're a patronizing misogynist, you know that?" she snapped. "Call me Princess one more time and I'll take my chances with Amal and his men! Screw you and my brothers!"

She caught what looked like the glint of a smile crossing his face.

Her anger spiked. "They had no right to keep this from me!"

"Yeah, but they're also paying my bills—and my job is to get you home alive."

"I swear it, if you call me Princess one more time, you'll be sorry."

Brandt grabbed her hand. "Believe me, you'll be more sorry if you stand here worrying about my manners."

He began to drag her at a clip through the long grass toward his plane. But as they neared, Brandt felt a sudden prickling down the back of his neck. He stilled, stopping her. Something was off. Then as he squinted into the darkness, the sliver of moon broke momentarily through the clouds and he saw what his subconscious had already noticed—the propeller was gone. A cold dread sank through his chest.

Thunder growled softly over the plain, and a fork of lightning stabbed with a loud crack down to the earth, briefly and starkly illuminating the plane. Static raised the hair along his forearms.

"Get down to the ground," he said quietly to Dalilah, eyes fixed on his plane as he doused his flashlight.

"Why?"

"Because you're a lightning rod right now."

Apparently sensing the shift in him, she acquiesced, crouching quietly to the soil in her torn gown. Brandt unhooked his rifle, clicked off the safety and just watched the Cessna for a few moments. Another flash of lightning forked over the grassland, and in that moment of brightness Brandt saw the Cessna's doors and tail flaps were gone, too. But he could detect no movement around the plane.

"Wait here," he said. "Don't move."

He slowly approached his little craft, wind beginning to buffet him, hot and full with the promise of rain. As he neared, his worst fears were confirmed. His craft had been stripped.

Another bolt of lightning cracked to the earth, and thunder boomed, echoing over and over again as it rolled into the distance. Sheet lightning glimmered behind clouds.

Climbing into his craft, Brandt used his flashlight to pan the interior. Seats had been ripped out, stuffing taken, the instrument panel denuded, the first-aid kit gone... Every piece had been ripped from the Cessna like meat from a carcass.

Now he had no navigation equipment, no form of communication. No water, food or first aid. No gear for his principal. Something in Brandt froze as he realized he was thinking in the terminology of his old profession. His stomach turned oily and he closed his eyes, starting to shake internally as he recalled the gaping maw that had been the throat of the man he'd just killed.

Murdered.

Another human.

It used to be so easy. Simple. He used to fight with such clear purpose.

With a trembling hand Brandt reached for his hip flask, took a deep swig, then another. He stayed crouched in his stripped plane like that for a moment, eyes closed, letting the whiskey flush through and calm him. Then his eyes flashed open.

He would not let it happen again. He could not lose another principal. Another woman in his care. Especially one who reminded him so sharply of Carla, of his mistake, of his spiraling descent into pure madness. It would kill him this time.

That left him with only one option—forge ahead and get this mission over with. But it sure as hell wasn't going to take a mere seventy-two hours now. They would have to trek on foot to the Tsholo River, which lay at least twenty klicks to the west. And they'd never reach the dry riverbed before the rain hit. If the storm was bad, or if it was already raining heavily farther upriver, it could mean dangerous flash floods as the seasonal waters came down.

Then if they did manage to cross the Tsholo, on the Botswana side they'd face miles and miles of hazardous terrain populated with all manner of wild animals. Bushfire could also become a hazard, given the shifting winds. Plus, they'd have to stay ahead of Amal's pack, and Amal likely had a combat tracker on his team.

This part of Africa was rife with expert military trackers trained guerrilla-style under the infamous Selous Scouts of old Rhodesia. Probably some of the best in the world, men who didn't need modern GPS or infrared, or topo maps with contour lines. Hunters who knew the bush like the backs of their hands.

He should never have taken that damn phone call from Omair.

Brandt sucked it up, the whiskey helping a little, and jumped lightly down from the plane. Clouds had thickened and the sky was black as pitch now. The air had a heavy, crackling weight to it. Brandt used his flashlight to make his way back to the woman crouching in the long grass.

He panned his beam over her, taking a good study now that they were going to be forced to walk. Her stilettos were a ridiculous height, and the heel of one was broken in half. She couldn't go any real distance in that footwear, and he could only piggyback her for so many klicks at a time. There was no way his boots would even begin to fit her. He might have to carry her the whole goddamn way. Conflict twisted through Brandt as he considered his options. Then it hit him—there was a satellite bush camp run by one of the safari lodges about fifteen kilometres to the north. He knew it was still there because he'd seen it while flying over this afternoon. It would mean a big detour on foot, one that would cost serious time and might lose them any window to cross the Tsholo before the river came down. But it could mean supplies and survival in the long run.

It was a risk he had to take.

Brandt crouched beside her. "Here's the deal, Dalilah. My Cessna has been stripped. We need to make a detour to—"

"Stripped?"

"Just the bones left."

"By who?"

"Could be anyone. Leave anything in the wrong place for too long, and Africa's recyclers will find it and get to work. There's not one part of that plane that won't be used to make everything from shoes to furniture or toys and cooking utensils. I reckon whoever did it will be back at first light with equipment to drag off the rest."

"But you do have a cell phone, right?"

He snorted. "Cell reception out here? You must be joking. And even if there was, who you going to call—Mercs-R-Us?"

"You're telling me you left your phone on the plane?" Anger sparked through her voice. "Because that's damn stupid—at least we could've tried to call my brother for help when we got closer to a cell tower or something!"

"I lost my sat phone and GPS in the battle to save your life."

She went silent, her black eyes glistening in the dark.

"You coming?"

She didn't move. He began to walk without her, exasperation sparking through him.

"I don't believe this!" she yelled behind him.

"Welcome to Africa, sweetheart," he called over his shoulder.

"Speak for yourself," she snapped, coming after him. "I was born on this continent. It's mine as much as it's anyone else's. I don't need *your* welcome, and you call me sweetheart, I'll—"

He spun around. "You'll what?"

She glowered at him. Thunder crashed again, and he saw her flinch. Under her bravado, the princess was scared. She was feisty, though. If he could keep her angry, it might help keep her focused. The main trouble was her gear. He hoped he'd find some clothes for her at the camp.

"We have a long way to go, Dalilah. Save your breath, okay?"

"You mean we're actually walking to Botswana?"

"Unless you have a better idea," he replied, raising the beam of his light, watching her face, her flashing eyes, trying not to think how stunning she was, even in this light, even disheveled like this. A honey badger, he decided, fierce in spite of fear—he liked her this way. Not exactly the pampered, whining princess he'd expected her to be.

But he didn't want to dwell on this thought. Mostly he wanted to keep her alive, then get her the hell out of his hair. ASAP.

"We need to cross the Tsholo into Bots before the rains flood the riverbed. If the waters come down suddenly, we could be trapped on the Zim side for a full day or two. We'll be safer in Botswana. Even so, it'll only be a brief respite, because I don't doubt Amal will try to cross and come after us there."

"How far is the Tsholo?"

"Too far in those shoes. We need to make a detour to the north first where we can liberate some supplies from a bush camp."

Silence hung thick and swollen with electrical-storm energy rustling between them as she challenged his gaze.

He could feel her mind computing as she tried to accept her situation. Begrudgingly, he could only admire that.

"You're from South Africa?" she said quietly.

"Originally."

She shot a glance out over the veldt, then she looked up at the lowering, black sky. He could see her figuring her odds.

"Which way is north?"

He jerked his chin into the distance. "That way. The detour will cost us time, but it might buy us mileage for the long haul if we can find you some boots, water, food. And it *is* going to be a long haul now."

"How long?"

"Several days, if we're lucky."

She pushed a fall of dark hair off her face. "And you have no compass, no GPS, there are no stars visible."

"I have my wits, sweetheart."

She muttered something darkly in Arabic.

Brandt held up his palms. "Sorry. Habit."

"Yeah, I'm sure you have a whole truckload of habits. All good ones, too." She brushed past him and hobbled off on her lopsided stilettos in the direction he'd indicated, leaving him behind this time.

"And don't whine that I'm going slow," she yelled over her shoulder. "You have better shoes."

Another smile tempted his lips and Brandt trotted up behind her. Grasping her arm, he turned her back to face him. "That's why you're going to ride on my back."

"You're not going to *carry* me."

"Why not?"

"You…can't."

"Piggyback. Just the detour. Come, hitch up that frock and hop on up." He held his hand out to her.

She stared at his hand, then lifted her eyes. "You're some piece of work, you know that?"

"That's exactly why your brother sent me."

She pulled what was left of her dress to her hips and Brandt swung her around onto his back. Her thighs were firm and smooth, her body lean yet full in the right places. He swallowed as she settled against him, hooking her arms around his neck and gripping his hips between her thighs. Her massive diamond engagement ring butted against his chin, rubbing her nonavailability right into his face, even as he could smell the shampoo in her hair, her expensive perfume, feel her breasts pressing against his back.

And as he began to jog, Brandt forced himself not to focus on the friction of her pelvis against his hips, but all he could think about suddenly was the scraps of silky G-strings he'd seen, and touched, in her drawer. And what she might be wearing now. A scrap of that same sensuous fabric was probably all that separated him from the most intimate parts of her body.

Brandt inhaled, readjusting the rifle across his chest, his tiny flashlight panning the ground. He figured Amal and his thugs were probably ransacking the lodge in search of Dalilah right now, not anticipating someone had whisked her away. As far as he could tell, only one man had seen him trying to rescue the princess. And he'd killed that man.

But come daybreak, they'd see his boot tracks. They'd come at a clip.

Brandt began to move at a faster trot, wanting to reach the escarpment and descend into thicker riverine foliage as soon as possible. They'd be less visible there. The locals had already spotted—and stripped—his plane, which meant there was a chance he and Dalilah might be seen, too. Although he hoped the looming storm would keep most humans battened down in villages.

Dalilah readjusted her position on his back, finding a better grip with her thighs. Desire swelled hot and sudden in his groin as her body rubbed against his. Brandt cursed softly to himself—physically, this woman really did it for him, in every way. She was his type, as Carla had been. And look what had happened to Carla.

It hit Brandt hard right there—no matter what dangers the next hours, days or weeks brought, his biggest personal challenge was going to be proximity to the princess herself.

He had a feeling she was going to be a little too hot for him to handle, and Brandt had zero intention of getting burned again.

Chapter 3

Dalilah felt herself slipping down Brandt's back and once again tried to maneuver herself higher, squeezing her thighs tighter around his body as he trotted through long dry grass. But he was big between her legs and the strain of holding on was making her muscles burn. The back of his shirt was damp from exertion and his neck smelled very faintly of aftershave. It made her wonder about him—who he really was, where he'd been going before he'd suddenly been diverted into this mission. She wondered if he'd had any idea it was going to turn into this—a manhunt.

Thunder grumbled again and the wind felt hotter. She peered into the darkness trying to get her bearings, but there was nothing to orient her, just shadowed shapes of trees, scrub, rocky outcrops.

He stopped suddenly, breathing hard.

"What is it?" she whispered near his ear.

"Elephants," he said as he set her gently down to the ground. "Over there." He pointed.

Dalilah heard the crack of a branch, and a crunch. Then a monstrous, ghostly shape seemed to materialize out of the darkness itself. More followed, big hulking forms moving slowly across the land, ears silently flapping, curved tusks gleaming ghostly white. A sense of awe washed over her skin and she rubbed her arms, instinctively moving closer to Brandt, knowing at the same time a small machete and rifle were nothing against these beasts.

Neither of them spoke, just watched in humble silence as the ghostly gray Goliaths moved quietly in single file across the plain. There was a baby behind one and Dalilah's thoughts turned to the vicious crocodile fight she'd witnessed back at the lodge, the Czech with the gin and tonic, the strange portent of danger. She glanced at Brandt. It was a feeling she should have given more weight to.

The matriarch leading the herd paused suddenly and turned to face Dalilah and Brandt, lifting her trunk as she sniffed them, her ears flaring out wide. Brandt reached for Dalilah's hand, and he brought his mouth close to her ear.

"Whatever you do, don't run," he whispered, breath warm against her skin. "Out here, only food runs. Besides, there is nothing here that you *can* outrun."

She swallowed, heart banging against her ribs. He gave her hand a squeeze, reading her fear, just letting her know he was there, and Dalilah moved closer to him. His air of confidence made her feel safe.

Satisfied that the humans posed no threat, the giant pachyderm turned, and lumbered on. Her tribe followed.

"Wow." Dalilah exhaled after the night had swallowed the animals. She realized she was shaking.

"See how all the Mopani trees here are short and

squat?" Brandt whispered. "They're eaten like that, by the elephants."

Dalilah realized she was still holding his hand tight, and she awkwardly extracted herself but stayed close, her body almost touching his. She was suddenly acutely aware that any number of creatures were probably watching them from the darkness right now, assessing threat, waiting for opportunity.

The Czech's words filtered back into her mind.

We're put on this earth to eat or be eaten. To kill or be killed, except with us humans, it's not always about food or water. Sometimes it's just for fun, or revenge.

Like with Amal. Watching, waiting all these years. Dalilah rubbed her arms again, cold suddenly in spite of the heat.

"You ready to move again?" His voice was a little kinder, gentler. He'd been as affected by the animals as she had, Dalilah noted. He might be experienced, but not jaded, not when it came to something like this.

"Come, hop on."

"I'm walking, Brandt."

"You'll hurt your feet, then we're done for."

"Forget it, you can't carry me all the way. I th—" Abruptly he grasped her by the hips and swooped her round onto his back. As he did, his fingers caught on the thread of her G-string, and she felt him stall. It made her suddenly conscious of the intimacy of her position on his back, and it clearly hadn't escaped his notice, either.

He started to move again, this time at a faster trot, his small flashlight bobbing in a little yellow circle on the ground immediately in front of them. Lightning forked again over the horizon. The terrain began to change, thorn trees getting taller. After several miles he was breathing hard, his body wet with exertion.

The smell of smoke grew stronger. He coughed.

"Brandt, put me down."

He kept going.

"I'm going to hurt you if you don't put me down—you can't keep going like this."

He gave a snort.

"I mean it."

He trotted faster.

She gripped his hair, pulled. "Put me down!"

He dumped her to the ground, hard and sudden.

"Dammit, woman. I should leave you out here for the bloody jackals!"

"Give me that machete," she demanded.

"What in hell for?"

She took off her shoe. "Please, just give me that blade," she said, holding her hand out.

He met her gaze, the paleness of his eyes unnerving in this light. Caution snaked through Dalilah. She didn't know how far she could push him. She knew nothing at all about him other than Omair trusted him. Which wasn't necessarily a good thing. Her brother knew some rough and dangerous people.

Slowly he unsheathed his blade, handed it to her by the hilt, and in the faint beam of his flashlight she caught what looked like a twist of amusement on his lips. Irritation spiked—he was humoring her, waiting to see what she was going to do. Well, she'd show him.

She crouched, and balancing her stiletto against a rock, Dalilah raised the blade into the air. As she brought it down, he caught her wrist midmotion.

"Don't be a fool!" he growled. "You're going to slice off your goddamn fingers like that!" He pushed her aside and lopped off the heel in a clean swipe.

"Other one," he said, holding out his hand.

She gave him her other shoe. He matched what was left of that heel to the other with a neat slice of his blade.

Dalilah put the decapitated sandals back onto her feet. Gritting her jaw in determination, she stood. The shoes were uncomfortable, but the soles had enough give so that she could walk, and it was better than having lopsided stiletto heels pinning her into the ground with each step.

He resheathed the blade. "Fine. Walk then. But there are three rules. One—we walk single file. You stay right behind me. Two—I give an order, you jump. Three—you keep pace or you're back on my shoulders. Got it?"

Before she could retort he strode off, his flashlight a tiny yellow beam on the ground. "And it's a panga, not a machete," he called over his shoulder.

She hobbled after him, immediately struggling to match his pace.

"You're going faster to spite me, aren't you?" she said after a few minutes, already breathless.

"Believe me, if I wanted to spite you I'd do a lot more than walk fast," he grumbled.

"Look, I didn't *ask* to be rescued," she retorted. "Especially by some pigheaded brute with a massive chip on his shoulder."

"I didn't ask to rescue you, either, sweetheart."

"What's your problem under it all—you don't like women? Where'd you earn that chip on your shoulder anyway?"

He didn't bother to reply.

"What did Omair do for you that you owe him?"

He was quiet for a moment. "If it wasn't for your brother I'd be dead."

Surprise chased through her. "What do you mean?"

"Save your breath, woman, you'll move faster."

"Dalilah! My name is *Dalilah!*" Tears of frustration

pricked at her eyes as she tried to run faster behind him, fear crackling at the corners of her mind. The scent of smoke was growing stronger and she could feel static in her hair—electricity quietly rustling everywhere in the dark. And her feet were already hurting, stones hard under the soles, grass cutting her skin.

He picked up more speed as the clouds seemed to lower even farther, and she felt a bullet of rain hit her shoulder. Big marbles of water suddenly began to bomb into the dry, dusty earth, the scent of soil was pungent, and she heard him curse ahead of her.

"Run," he called out, breaking into a trot himself. "This is going to be a mother of a storm. We need to get gear and make for that river, stat!"

Gathering up what was left of her cocktail dress, feet sending sparks of pain up her legs, Dalilah ran as best she could. Raindrops were attacking them now, crashing into the earth, slamming into her head, onto her shoulders, wetting her hair. Wind gusted, thick with smoke from a nearby bushfire. Her hair was quickly plastered to her face.

Brandt reached a slope of smooth stone and began to descend rapidly ahead of her. But the rock was slick with water, and with no grip on her soles, Dalilah went down hard, smacking onto rock as her shoes slid out from under her. Her arm caught in a small crevice and torqued against her weight as she slid. She cried out in pain.

He spun around instantly, and swore. Dalilah couldn't hold back the tears of pain that pooled in her eyes and ran with the rainwater down her face.

Frustration licked through Brandt as he aimed his flashlight at her face—it quickly changed to worry as he saw her complexion was bloodless, her eyes black, shimmering holes of shock and pain. Quickly he panned the light over the rest of her body. She was hunching over her left arm, her gold dress wet and glittering against the red rock.

"You should've let me carry you," he said, crouching beside her.

"You were getting tired," she snapped.

"That's not for you to decide. Let me see your arm."

But she kept her arm tight against her stomach. "It's fine." Rain pelted down and thunder crashed right above them. They hadn't seen the brunt of the storm yet, and in his mind Brandt could visualize the rivers filling, their window to cross the border closing. Urgency bit at him.

"Dalilah—give me your arm."

She glanced sharply up at his use of her name, and she met his gaze. Something punched through his stomach, low.

"Let me see," he said softly, taking her arm in his hands.

Her skin was slick with water as he felt carefully along the bone. She sucked in air when he neared her wrist.

"It hurts there?"

She nodded, biting her lip.

Brandt concentrated on the area, detecting a slight grinding feeling under her skin—crepitation. She had a fracture. *Damn!*

"Can you wiggle your fingers, move your hand?"

She wiggled, but not without obvious pain.

"I'm pretty sure you've fractured it."

"I'm sorry," she whispered, looking truly frightened for the first time since the ambush at the lodge.

His tone grew gentle. "Hey, it's okay. We'll get you somewhere we can splint and bandage you up properly. There should be some first-aid stuff at the camp, maybe even some painkillers." As he spoke, Brandt squinted through the sheen of rain, scanning their surroundings. "See that cluster of baobabs down there, below the cliff?"

She nodded.

"I'm going to leave you down there, with my rifle, while I run the rest of the way to the camp. Those trees are over a thousand years old—they'll protect you from the worst of the storm. That cliff reaching up behind the baobabs—it's the highest point of this terrain and it will take any lightning strikes. You'll be safe there, okay?"

As safe as one can be out here.

"Brandt—"

Something in her voice cut through him.

"What is it?"

"I've been difficult, I'm sorry. Thank you—for coming, for saving me. I...I don't think it's really all sunk in until now." She sounded beaten suddenly.

He nodded, instantly erecting his own emotional walls. He should be the one apologizing for being so brusque with her. But he wasn't going to. He needed to maintain distance, and if she disliked him for it, so much the better. Because he needed her to focus. He wasn't going to lose another principal.

His big mistake had been falling for Carla all those years ago. And because he'd become vested, because he'd lost focus, she'd died the most horrible death one could imagine.

He took Dalilah's good arm, helped her to her feet. They began to move down the rest of the rock slope, carefully this time, him holding her by the elbow and steadying her around the waist, rain drenching them.

"Do you think there'll be people at the camp?" she asked as they neared the prehistoric-looking trees with branches that resembled roots upturned to the sky.

"It's a satellite bush camp. I know the outfit that runs it—I've flown for them before. They might have a party of guests there," he said. "If not, there might be someone sleeping there to guard the place."

"They could help us."

"No, they can't. We don't know who's heard of the bounty on your head and this is a hungry country—life is cheap. I'm not trusting anyone. We've got to look after ourselves."

They reached the grove, the ancient trees dwarfing them, and Brandt was relieved to find they were in the lee of the cliff and protected from the real teeth of the wind.

"How much is this bounty on me, Brandt?"

"One million dollars. For your head. Five million if you're brought to Amal alive."

He felt the spark of shock run through her body.

"My *head*?"

"Yes."

She swallowed, staring at him.

"How...can he promise so much?"

"Omair expects that Amal will try to extract a large ransom from your family, and he's intending to use this to pay the bounty if need be."

"They won't do it—my brothers will not pay that bastard. They will *not* negotiate with the devil!" A sudden defiant anger crackled through her words and Brandt felt a spurt of relief. Anger was good. It would keep her sharp, ward off the real shock he figured was yet to fully hit her.

"I know your brother, Dalilah. Omair will do *anything* to save you." He gave a dry laugh. "Including trust me."

"You say that like it was a mistake."

"His options were limited. Come, we need to get you up onto that fork between the trees, off the ground, out of the worst of the rain."

Brandt lifted Dalilah up by the hips and set her into the crook where two baobabs joined. He chambered a round into the rifle and held the gun out to her. "You know how to use one of these?"

"Probably better than you do."

"How so?"

"There's a lot you don't know about me, Brandt."

He laughed, then quieted at the seriousness in her features, the air of mystery deepening around her, his prejudices tumbling one by one, hour by hour. "Any other surprises up your sleeve?"

She gave a weak smile, her almond eyes huge black pools. She looked frightened, vulnerable, brave and even more beautiful. It twisted some unused muscle in Brandt's chest. He gave her his flashlight and spare rounds. "Use the torch only if necessary—we might need to conserve the battery."

She nodded.

"Sit tight, okay? I won't be long." As he withdrew his hand, the backs of his fingers brushed against her ring. He glanced down at the rock.

"Engagement?" he said—couldn't help himself.

Her mouth flattened, and she nodded. He caught something strange in her eyes as she met his gaze, and it made him hesitate. "You'll be fine," he said, more for his own benefit than hers. Then Brandt turned suddenly, and disappeared into the storm.

Dalilah watched the darkness swallow him, wondering if part of Brandt Stryker's bluntness was his way of keeping focus, or if his jabs were actually designed to make her angry so she'd keep hers. Because it had worked.

Thunder exploded right above her head and she winced, crouching farther back into the crook of the trunks. Rain splattered into a sheet of water collecting on the packed earth below the trees. It began to run like a river.

After what seemed like an hour, she grew stiff, and

fear began to sink deep and cold into her chest. The night seemed to grow even darker, the pain in her arm more intense. She thought of Amal wanting her head, and her pulse quickened.

What would she do if Brandt didn't come back? Try to make it to that bush camp on her own? She had no idea where, or how, to find it. And he was right about the bounty—anyone in the country could turn on her, law enforcement and military included. It was a starving and denuded nation under a long, corrupt and brutal regime. Her mouth turned dry and she began to shiver. Images slammed through her mind—men in balaclavas, shooting, screaming, the sound of breaking glass, cutlery.

Dalilah squeezed her eyes tight, but she couldn't shut out the memory of the dead man under the table, blood welling from the small black hole in his neck. His blank, dead gaze. She opened her eyes and fingered the rifle trigger, drawing some resolve from the feel of the weapon in her hands. Then she heard a noise, somewhere above in the tree.

Her nerves twitched and she peered up into the darkness. Dalilah couldn't see anything, but she could feel it—a presence, something close, watching. She flicked on the flashlight, panned the branches above. A pair of green eyes glowed back—the forward-facing eyes of a predator. Heart jackhammering, she panned the flashlight farther to the left.

Ice slid through her veins as she registered what was sharing her tree.

Brandt crouched in the shadows, assessing the camp, oblivious to rain washing over his face and soaking through his clothes. A covered game-viewing jeep had been backed in beside five Meru-style tents. That meant there were guests here, a fully equipped camp. And if there was one good thing about this weather it was keeping both guests and guides battened down inside those tents.

This deluge would also wash away most of the tracks he and Dalilah had made from the safari lodge. But if Amal did have a skilled combat tracker on his team, Brandt had no doubt that come daylight they'd still find enough trace to pursue them.

His gaze went to the food-storage shed—it was constructed of metal, a padlock on the door. The padlock hung open.

Brandt had already checked out the jeep. The keys were inside, and it was equipped with GPS, radio, four-wheel drive, first-aid kit, blankets for night game drives. There were emergency flares in the glove compartment, along with a lighter and waterproof matches and map. A jack and spare tire were secured in a compartment at the rear. There was also a spare can of diesel fuel and a large water container that had been freshly filled. Brandt ran in a low crouch toward the shed, ducking around the side wall. He waited, his hand hovering near the hilt of his panga.

No one stirred.

From this vantage point he could see a pair of hiking boots behind the mosquito netting in the enclosed entrance area of one tent. They looked as if they might fit Dalilah. Even if they were too big they were better than the getup she was in now.

Quickly he edged round the front of the shed, unhooked the padlock, pushed the door open. Metal creaked loudly. He stilled, muscles taut. But the rain drumming on the tin roof was loud, and branches creaked and moaned in the wind.

He moved fast, filling a plastic cooler with food— tinned goods, dried meat, stuff that would last. He found a box of ammunition, then he reached up, snagged a large bottle of whiskey off the top shelf, tossed it into the cooler. Might take some edge off this mission.

Brandt hefted the chest into the backseat of the jeep. The vehicle had three rows of pew-style seats, the last one slightly higher than the others. The roll bars were topped with canvas but the sides of the jeep were open. The vehicle was far bigger than they needed, and it was going to be a little cumbersome, but a godsend given the loss of his Cessna. He was still bitter about that.

He jogged quietly back and hunkered down next to the tent that contained the boots. He listened for sounds inside, heard someone snoring. Rain pattered loudly on canvas.

Slowly, he unzipped and opened the mosquito flap, reached in for the boots. That's when he saw a backpack with a sleeping bag tied to the bottom leaning against the back of a camping chair.

Brandt snagged the pack, slowly edging it toward himself. He opened the flap and saw shirts, pants, socks, bush hat, bug repellent, headlamps. He almost smiled. Some poor bugger was all set for a safari hike tomorrow. Feeling in the side pocket, he pulled out a wallet. Inside was a German driver's license and wad of greenbacks. The cash might come in handy.

Gathering up the gear, Brandt jogged back through the rain to the jeep. The vehicle had been parked facing a sloped dirt track that quickly turned into a steep decline.

He climbed into the driver's seat, geared into neutral, released the brake, got out and pushed. It took three hefty attempts, but once the wheels released from their indentations in the mud, it trundled easily toward the slope. Brandt steered with one hand on the wheel as he ran alongside. When the vehicle gathered speed and started down the incline, he jumped into the driver's seat.

The jeep lumbered wildly down the slope, gathering more speed. Brandt didn't fire the ignition until he neared the bottom. The jeep growled to life as thunder clapped overhead, then echoed down the valley. A gust of wind drove rain through the open sides, soaking him. He'd bet the people back at the camp hadn't heard a damn thing and would only discover their transport missing after daybreak.

"Good girl." He patted the dash. "You're a real beauty." The diesel tank registered full, too.

Brandt drove fast over the rough terrain. As soon as he felt he was far enough from the camp, he reached for his hip flask and took a deep swig, almost emptying the thing. At least he had a refill now, several times over. Brandt grinned. Things were most definitely looking up.

Within minutes he could make out the dark silhouette of the cliff in the distance, then the baobab grove at the foot of the rocks. But as the jeep mounted a last small incline and Brandt swung his headlights over toward the trees, he saw a strange pile in the mud at the base.

It took a split second to realize what he was seeing.

Dalilah—leopard!

His heart exploded into his throat as he slammed on the brakes. Leaving the headlights shining on the terrible sight, Brandt lurched out of the jeep and raced through the mud toward the pile of animal and human tangled in the water at the base of the trunks.

Chapter 4

Mbogo shoved a wiry old man dressed in khaki bush gear toward Amal.

"He's the best tracker the lodge has. The other staff said so."

Amal regarded the man. His hair was frosted with white and his face was wizened and craggy. But being old wasn't necessarily a bad thing out here. This was a land still ancient enough to value the wisdom of elders, and out here in the bush a good tracker was one who'd hunted for food as a child, learned from his forefathers.

Slowly, Amal walked around the man, who lowered his head and stared at the floor. Amal was using the safari lodge's curio shop-cum-office as a temporary command center. The room was filled with racks of postcards, shirts, hats, wood carvings and batik fabrics. Against one white-washed wall stood a locked cabinet containing silver and copper jewelry and semiprecious stones. On another wall hung photos of lions, elephants, rhinos, buffalo drinking from a water hole. Another shot showed a leopard draped over a branch in front of a sinking sun. The Big Five, the most dangerous animals in Africa to hunt on foot.

But it was the hunt of human that excited Amal. He had Dalilah Al Arif's scent now, and blood on his hands. Adrenaline coursed through his veins.

He was not a sophisticate like his father, the billionaire industrialist who'd wanted to rule an empire. No, Amal was a hands-on fighter who liked the trenches. Amal *liked* the gore on his hands, the intimacy of a kill, seeing fear in his quarry's eyes. He was fueled by simpler things than his father. Revenge. Hatred. A need for cold hard cash.

"Is that you?" Amal pointed to one of the photos showing a guide standing behind a fat white hunter proudly holding up the dead head of a Cape buffalo.

"Yes, sir." The old man would not meet Amal's eyes.

Deference. Amal liked that.

"It's a very dangerous animal, the buffalo."

"Yes, sir."

"My man here, his name is Mbogo. It means big bull buffalo. He's dangerous like the buffalo."

The man said nothing.

"What's your name?"

"Jacob."

"How long you been tracking, Jacob?"

"I hunted with my grandfather from when I could walk."

"You from around here?"

"My village is near the Zambezi. You can hear the drums at night."

"You work with the lodge a long time?"

"More than twenty years, sir."

Amal nodded. He'd brought his own tracker, but local knowledge was invaluable. He stopped in front of the man.

"Look at me."

The man's eyes lifted slowly, wide and white with fear. Sweat gleamed on his ebony skin.

"I want the woman who was with the guests. Do you know which woman I mean?"

"There was only one woman in the delegate party, sir."

"Dalilah Al Arif—the princess. We came all the way from Zambia for her. But now—" he clicked his fingers under the old man's nose "—she's gone, like that! We've searched the lodge, the grounds, everywhere. How can a woman like her disappear, Jacob? Do you think she ran into the bush by herself, in those shoes? In that dress?"

Jacob said nothing.

"She had help, that's what! My tracker found sign in the dry sand under the trees next to the *lapa*. A man was waiting there. A big man. Do you know who he was, Jacob?"

Sweat glistened down the old man's face. "No."

"Are you certain? Because you do know what happened to the lodge owners and the rest of the staff when they didn't cooperate with us—they're all dead."

The old man swallowed. "I don't know who this man is, sir."

"But you're the best tracker—you can help me find him."

"Sir, I have a wife—"

Amal glanced at Mbogo. "We know."

Sweat trickled down the old man's brow and he began to shake.

"Now, listen to me carefully, Jacob," Amal said, leaning forward. "You find this man and princess for us, and your wife will be safe. You'll be my lead tracker. My own guy will work as your flanker. You'll both go ahead of the horses and jeeps, understand?"

Thunder boomed overhead. The lights inside the thatched bungalow flickered and the masks on the wall seemed to come alive in the shadows. Outside, monkeys screamed.

But before the old tracker could answer, there was another sound right outside the door. A snarling and clacking of teeth—a human scream. Yelling. A thud. A whimper.

Jacob's gaze shot to the door.

Through the door came one of Amal's men, his arm dripping with blood. With him he dragged a reddish-brown dog by a rope tied tightly around its muzzle and neck. The dog frothed at the jowls and its tail was tucked in tight. Jacob went wire tense, his eyes narrowing.

"You know this dog, Jacob?"

"Jock. He's the master's dog. I've been using him to track game."

A slow smile curved over Amal's face.

"Kill it."

"No!" barked Jacob.

All stilled. Pearls of sweat trickled down from Jacob's sideburns, his face a sheen of perspiration.

"That…is a good dog. He can track. He's fought a lion."

"Are you lying to me, Jacob?"

"Jacob doesn't lie, sir."

"Give him the animal," Amal said quietly to Mbogo while watching Jacob's face. "You start now—use the dog."

"Dalilah!" Brandt yelled as he ran through the rain. Lightning cracked overhead, sharply silhouetting baobab branches that clawed up to the sky. His mind twisted in on itself as he registered that she was sprawled over the

leopard, not under it, her long wet hair trailing in the river of mud. Neither she nor the animal moved.

He dropped to his haunches at her side, fear choking him as he felt for a pulse. But as he touched her skin, she raised her head. Haunted eyes met his, mascara trailing a harlequin's black tears down her cheeks.

"Brandt?"

"It's okay, I'm here."

"I killed her." Her voice came out in a cracked whisper. "I shot her."

He touched the animal. Its fur was warm.

"She was above me, in the branches, coming down, hissing…I shot her before she could kill me. I… There was a… I didn't… I…" She began to shake, unable to form words.

"Hey," he whispered, gathering Dalilah into his arms. "It's okay." She folded into him, resting her wet head against his chest. Brandt just held her for a moment as she sobbed with great big wrenching heaves. A reciprocal emotion swelled hot through his chest and he put his face up to the rain, the enormity of his responsibility suddenly overwhelming. He knew that failing this woman would be the end of him.

Inhaling deeply, he smoothed her wet hair back off her cheek. "Dalilah," he whispered, looking deep into her eyes. "We can talk about it later, but now we need to move."

He picked up the rifle lying in the mud and lifted her to her feet. Leading her to the jeep, he helped her into the passenger seat, the canopy protecting her from rain. Brandt quickly rustled through the pile of gear he'd loaded in the backseat, found a heavy gray blanket and wrapped it around her shoulders. Her eyes caught his, held, then she looked away, drawing the blanket tighter around her shoulders, shivering, her face bloodless.

Brandt was fully aware that the physical and mental effects of shock were often underestimated. It was a medical condition that could become dangerous, and fast. He needed to watch her closely, make sure she stayed warm. But their immediate priority was crossing the border or they'd be trapped on this side and facing Amal by morning.

"We'll get you into some dry clothes as soon as we get over the river, okay?"

She wouldn't meet his eyes.

"Then I'll splint your arm, get some food into you." He placed a water bottle beside her. "Stay hydrated, okay? There's probably aspirin in that kit there at your feet. Take what you need."

But she just sat, staring wide-eyed into space, jaw tight.

Brandt ran back to the leopard sprawled in the mud. She was right, it was a female. She'd shot it in the throat. Then he saw the enlarged teats on the animal's belly. Glancing up into the tree, he panned through the branches with his flashlight. And his heart just about cracked—a cub, mewling, the sound drowned out by the storm.

That must have been what truly shattered Dalilah.

He crouched and shunted the dead leopard onto his shoulders. It was heavy and blood washed with rain down his arm as he made his way back to the jeep.

Horror widened Dalilah's eyes as she saw Brandt approaching in the headlights with the animal draped over his shoulders.

"No! Oh, God, no, what are you doing?" She spun round as he heaved the dead animal into the far backseat.

"Can't leave it lying out there," he said brusquely, coming round to the driver's-side door. "This storm will cover a good deal of our trace. But leaving that leopard with a bullet hole lying under the tree like that—might as well leave a flag with a note telling Amal's men we came this way."

He climbed, secured his rifle into a bracket on the dash beside a hunting spotlight.

"Brandt—"

He shot her a glance as he put the vehicle in gear.

"There was a baby, a cub."

"I know." He pressed down on the gas, tires whining in mud as the vehicle kicked forward.

"We can't leave the cub."

"We have to. I'm not killing it."

"Something else will." Her voice was filled with desperation.

"Dalilah," he said softly, jaw clenched, eyes focused on the terrain illuminated by the twin yellow beams of his headlights. "We can't take it. We have to let nature take its course here."

She pushed herself back into the seat, fighting something inside. Then a flash of anger burst through. "I didn't sign up for this!"

You and me both.

But he said nothing, concentrating instead on negotiating a rocky escarpment as he worked the jeep toward the banks of the Tsholo. With the dash-mounted GPS came increased confidence. He told himself they'd be over the river, hopefully, within an hour or two. Once across the border he'd treat her injury, get some food into her, then they could start the trip across Botswana veldt. They'd travel along a giant rift valley until they could find a route up to the plateau, after which they'd head for a paved road that bisected the eastern region of Botswana. They'd drive south for several more kilometers, the paved road hopefully hiding their vehicle tracks, then the plan was to veer offroad again into a controlled game area from which there'd be another day or two of driving across Botswana bush to his farm where he'd get on the phone to Omair. And then the princess would be history.

"I'm a vegetarian," she said. "I don't kill things."

He continued to drive in silence. The ground was dangerously rutted, flowing with water. The storm crashed around them, and branches were going down. Water was building into small rivers. Brandt needed full attention on his four-wheeling skills, and she needed space to lash these things out in her head herself, so he let her at it.

But his silence just seemed to egg her on.

"On principle," she reiterated a few minutes later, as if he hadn't heard. "I don't kill animals!"

"You're looking to get a rise out of me," he said.

"*You* brought me here!"

"Look, Dalilah, I get that you don't kill animals. Me, I don't kill humans. On principle—I made that vow years ago. And now look at me—"

She shot him a hard look.

"I was forced to kill a man back at the lodge to honor a promise I made to your brother, a promise to get you out of here alive. Because of *you* I was forced to break that goddamn vow never to kill another man—" his voice came out more strident than he'd intended, and he gripped the wheel harder than he meant it to "—or woman."

This time she stared at him in silence. Good. He'd hooked her out of her thought loop.

"So we're square, okay? I didn't want this any more than you did. That leopard was a case of kill or be killed. Survival."

She continued to stare at him, and he knew what she had to be thinking—*what woman had died at his hand?*

Brandt gritted his teeth, swinging the wheel too hard to the right to avoid a boulder that appeared abruptly in his lights. The vehicle slid sideways in mud, tilting almost onto its side as they traversed the escarpment.

Dalilah gasped, clutching on to the roll bar.

Brandt cursed and stopped the jeep. *Focus, dammit.* But this woman was messing with his head and his memories. And his anger had pushed him to take chances with the terrain. He wiped sweat off his brow, then slammed the vehicle back into gear.

Slowly he coaxed the wheels forward, crawling out of the tight spot. He sped up when they hit flat ground. There was little scrub now, mostly grassland. Rain was whipping sideways under the canopy, and the wet grass made a clacking noise under the carriage as he gunned forward.

Brandt could smell smoke again, getting stronger as they got closer to the river. Not good.

Fisting her blanket tight around her neck, Dalilah turned away from him and glared ahead.

They'd been driving in silence for maybe half an hour when she said, "Would you like me to hold the hunting spot so you can see better?"

He cast her a glance. "I didn't think you'd even noticed there was one."

"I'm not totally useless." She reached for the game spotlight on the dash. With her good hand, she fiddled with it, clicked it on, held it forward. Stark white light illuminated terrain to the periphery of their headlights.

"Thanks. Makes a big difference."

After a few more kilometres, he said, "I don't know many people who could bring down a leopard at close range with a broken arm. You were right, you are good with a gun."

She snorted, but said nothing. Brandt knew it must

be killing her to have that dead leopard, evidence of her skill, on the backseat right now. He stole another sideways glance at her.

Even with the muddy, wet hair, the leaked mascara, the ripped outfit, her profile was aristocratic. Chiseled cheekbones that flared sharply under her almond eyes. The full mouth, determined set of her chin. Yeah, she was regal, even now, shivering under a blanket. And she was holding that spotlight steady like a trouper in spite of the pain and fear she must be feeling.

A grudging admiration curled through Brandt. Not only was the princess blessed with killer looks, she was a survivor—this woman had what it took. She pressed all his buttons and she was not averse to giving him a run for his money.

That made him like her, against his best effort. It made him care.

And Brandt knew then—he was in more trouble than he'd thought.

Almost an hour later they crested a ridge and saw a deep, dark line of vegetation snaking across the plain.

"The Tsholo," Brandt said, halting the jeep. "Douse the spotlight."

Dalilah looked at him. "Why?"

"Too bright. There could be people down there— illegals trying to cross from Zimbabwe into Botswana before the waters come down. I want to keep as low a profile as possible in case Amal comes this way and starts questioning stragglers."

Nerves bit into Dalilah. She killed the light with one hand, her other arm too painful to move.

"What about our headlights?" she said, replacing the spot on the dash.

"I'll cut them when we get closer, drive in the dark. We'll go slow."

He began to take the jeep down a precarious, rocky drop.

"So the riverbed is dry?" she asked, peering ahead at the dense vegetation snaking across the plain.

"I sure as hell hope so."

The jeep jolted suddenly and pain sparked up her arm. Dalilah's eyes watered and she clenched her teeth. She'd felt a sense of foreboding when she'd sat on that riverbank and that crocodile had come from nowhere, but not in her wildest dreams had she imagined this—being attacked, knocked unconscious, kidnapped and hauled off on the back of this man into the African wilderness.

Dalilah stole a sideways glance at Brandt. Her abductor and rescuer.

Mostly rescuer, she hoped. Because there was something scary about him. Perhaps it was his sheer physical size, his brutal capacity for analysis in a dire situation. She wondered what woman he'd killed. And why. Who was Brandt Stryker when he wasn't paying back a debt to her brother, and what had Omair done for him?

If it wasn't for your brother I'd be dead.

Dalilah was hit by another spike of anger—as soon as she got to a phone, she was going to call Omair and demand answers. How on earth could she take efficient measures to protect herself if she didn't know what dangers even lurked out there?

The anger spread through her chest. Her whole life had been spent trying to break out of the overbearing, protective shadows of her brothers. Ever since she was a kid she'd strived to prove herself as capable, or better, than them. It had become her driver, and that passion had forged habits in Dalilah that had taken her to the top of her profession as a foreign-investment consultant based out of Manhattan. She'd come to believe her brothers had finally accepted her independence, her capabilities.

Yeah, right. Look at her now. On the run in a starving country, being hunted by a bloodthirsty rogue who literally planned to cut off her head, and her only hope of survival laid squarely in the hands of this rough Afrikaner merc, because yes, Dalilah figured Brandt *was* a mercenary. It was likely how he'd come into contact with Omair in the first place.

Brandt slammed on the brakes abruptly and Dalilah jolted forward.

"What is it?"

"Fire." He jerked his chin. "In those trees—exactly where we were headed."

"Why are we headed there?"

"I know the riverbed is hard sand there, and it's a narrow crossing with low banks on the Botswana side." He spun the wheel, turning sharply northwest. "We'll have to cross higher, but the higher upriver we go, the steeper the bank on the Botswana side, and the wind is going to drive those flames upriver, fast." He hit the gas, wheels skidding beneath them as they blundered through scrub, racing away from the smoldering fire in the trees.

"What about the headlights?" she called out, hanging on to the roll bar.

"Got to risk it now!"

Dalilah gritted her teeth, pain shooting out from her arm as they jerked and bashed over rocks and bushes. As they neared the fringe, the trees seemed bigger, darker. Leaves clapped in the hot wind that would bring the fire to them. They entered the trees and in the glow of the headlights the wet bark glowed yellow-green. Panic licked softly through Dalilah's stomach, fueled by the tension she could feel rolling off Brandt as he negotiated the gaps between the trunks.

Suddenly ahead of them stretched a wide swath of silvery-white sand. The Tsholo. And as their headlights hit the far bank, Dalilah saw a cliff of sand on the far side. How they were going to get up that cliff once they crossed, she had no idea.

"Hold on!" he yelled, gunning the jeep down an incline toward the dry riverbed. They hit soft sand and the tires began to spin, but he kept going, steady, the rough diesel engine growling.

*Go, go, go, keep going...*she willed the jeep to keep powering through to the other side. But it was a big vehicle, heavy, and the sand was soft.

Wheels started to spin deeper, then the left front wheel on the driver's side suddenly dug right in, tilting the front of the jeep forward and pressing the running board against the riverbed.

Brandt cursed in Afrikaans as he grabbed the game spotlight and hopped over the driver's-side door. He panned the far side of the river, and swore violently again as the beam glinted off water moving below the sandbank cliff.

"Water's starting to come down already. A full flash flood could hit in minutes. Get out, now!" he ordered. "Go back to the Zimbabwe side and climb to higher ground under the trees. Get as far away from the river's edge as you can without losing sight of me. And take the rifle!" He ran around to the back of the jeep and opened the compartment under the rear seat.

Dalilah spun round to look at the bank from which they'd just come. A few hundred yards downriver orange flames were already crackling fast and furious through foliage along the bank, coming directly toward them. Wind was blowing hot into her face, full with the smell of the fire, smoke stinging her eyes.

She turned back to see Brandt had put on a headlamp and was hauling out what looked like a massive jack, which he threw onto the sand in front of the sunken tire. He returned for a shovel, began digging sand out from under the front chassis of the vehicle. Adrenaline mushroomed through Dalilah.

She ran up to the vehicle, removed a second, smaller shovel from the tool compartment. Using one hand she began digging awkwardly next to him.

"What are you doing?" he yelled, water sheening over his face.

"Helping—what do you think I'm doing?"

"I said move, dammit! You want to be a sitting duck in a flood, or what! Get the hell out of this riverbed."

"No!" she yelled, rain plastering hair to her face, her dress to her body. She could hear the crackle of the fire now. She dug faster.

"Dalilah, you agreed to do as I say. I came here to keep you alive." His voice vibrated with fierce energy.

"No, Brandt, ultimately I am responsible for myself. My decision. My life. We work as a team or we don't work at all."

He cursed. "Just because you've ordered people around your whole life—"

She raised her good hand, pointed her finger at his face, blinking into the glare of the lamp on his forehead. "You know *nothing* about me. If you want to get us out of here, quit picking on my title, stop being such a prejudiced ass and dig before the river comes down or the damn fire swallows us." Her voice was pitched high with fear, and she was using words she never ordinarily used, but she didn't care. She *was* afraid. And she sure as hell wasn't going to stand on that riverbank while Brandt was swept away without her. She was sticking right at his side come hell or high water. Or fire and crocodiles and leopards. Or Amal.

"Dalilah—"

"Shut up and dig! I'd rather face a flash flood than be raped by Amal's men and have my head cut off!"

Brandt spun away from her and angrily jabbed his spade into the sand. "You're something else, you know that?"

"Yeah, I am. And so are you!"

Brandt stilled, and glared at her for a moment, then a wry smile curved his lips. He gave a quick nod, then resumed digging. He had to hand it to her—Princess had won his admiration.

Chapter 5

Jacob gently fingered the swelling on Jock's muzzle, looking for the cut where he'd been kicked in the face. Jock whimpered as Jacob found the wound. It wasn't too bad, and the bones didn't appear broken.

"It's all right, boy," he whispered in his local Shona dialect, the love in the touch of his gnarled hand conveying all to the animal—he was not alone, even though his owners had been murdered. Jacob was also certain the attackers had slain his wife. He and the dog were in this together now. Both afraid. But not broken.

"Soek," he whispered softly, holding his palm down to the soft red earth that was still dry under the fat branches and old canopy of the nyala tree—it was his indication for Jock to start a search.

Amal shot Mbogo a quick glance and raised an eyebrow.

"Lodge owners were Afrikaners," Mbogo said quietly. "Guess they spoke to the dog in Afrikaans."

In his peripheral vision Jacob was keeping an eye on the one-armed Arab and his big bull of a comrade, Mbogo. Jacob was a skilled hunter, trained to observe, to listen, without appearing to do so.

Mbogo cradled an AK-47 in his meaty hands. Bandoliers filled with ammunition crisscrossed his broad chest and a giant panga was sheathed down the side of his tree-trunk-size thigh. In contrast, the Arabic man at his side was slender with a narrow face and wild eyes. Even so, Jacob felt the Arab was the more dangerous one. He spoke English with an American accent and he also carried a panga, the blood of the delegates and lodge employees still black on his blade. A smaller curved and bejewelled dagger was hooked into his belt.

At Jacob's boots, Jock sniffed the soft indentations in the earth where the man who took the princess had crouched. The dog was circulating air through his nasal passages with soft snorts, cataloguing the scent. Behind where Amal and Mbogo stood on the raised wall of the *lapa,* bodies lay among overturned chairs, broken glass. The fire in the circular pit had died, food in the pots burned, the scent of it all pungent. Ants had already found the slain. There would be flies later, and when the sun rose, the cadavers would begin to rot fast. Vultures would circle up high and silent on thermals above the camp as the heat of a new day pressed down.

Jacob was going to kill that one-armed bastard and his big bull. He'd kill them or die trying. But if he was going to stay alive long enough in order to make the attempt, he had to prove his worth and lead them close to their quarry. Jacob could do this. He was one of the best. The dog would help him—they were both born of a land that knew hardship and betrayal. They knew how to be patient.

"Good boy," he whispered to Jock as the dog locked

onto the scent of his quarry and began snuffling toward the outer fringe of the nyala grove, heading toward thick kikuyu grass wet with rain.

"Boss, over here!" Jacob called as he moved quickly after the dog into the grass.

"Bring the lights!" Amal yelled to his men.

Two men came running with game spots taken from the lodge. White light flooded the ground where Jock worked, shadows darting around the periphery.

"Do you have his scent?" Amal said, appearing behind Jacob's shoulder.

"Yes, boss." He moved faster after Jock, who was heading out onto the lawn. But as the dog entered more dense vegetation, he lost the track, began scouting for it again. He got it, and tail wagging like a metronome he snuffled forward.

"Good boy," Jacob whispered, running after the dog again. But out near the high riverbank where there were no trees and rain fell heavily, pooling on sand and running in little rivers, Jock lost the scent again.

"Too much running water in the grass over here, boss," Jacob said as he crouched, motioning for a handheld spotlight to be brought closer. A man handed him a spot, and Jacob put his cheek almost to the ground, shining the light at an angle. He saw faint depressions under the water—the man's tracks. By the depth and spacing between his prints, the man who made these was big—over six feet. Strong. Moving fast. There were no woman's tracks nearby. He was still carrying the woman at this point.

Jacob doused the spotlight and peered silently into the raining darkness.

"What is it?" Amal snapped impatiently.

"They went that way," Jacob said quietly. "Toward the Tsholo."

"The border!" Amal said to Mbogo. "They're heading for Botswana!" He turned abruptly and barked at his men. "Saddle up the horses! Get the jeeps fueled! Take whatever supplies we need from the lodge. We start moving within the hour!"

The air was growing thick with smoke. Brandt wiped rain from his eyes and quickly positioned the jack under the front bumper of the jeep where he'd dug out sand. Dalilah stood at his shoulder, rifle in her good hand as she nervously watched the advancing fire. He began jacking fast. Rain hammered down relentlessly, pocking the sand. Across the riverbed on the Botswana side, brown water was beginning to flow faster and deeper.

"Get some of that driftwood," he barked at Dalilah, jerking his chin to a pile of bone-white branches in the center of the river. Brandt hated asking her. She had to be in serious pain, but she was right about one thing—they'd get out of here faster if they worked as a team. And she'd shocked him with her ability, her resilience. Instead of being the whining, pampered hindrance he'd expected, Princess was a trouper, and he could use her.

The flip side was that if the Tsholo did come down in a flash flood, as he'd seen happen before at the beginning of the wet season, they'd *both* be swept to their deaths.

I'd rather face a flash flood than be raped by Amal's men and have my head cut off...

She was right about that. It would be better for her to die with him than be left alone at the mercy of Amal and his men. Determination fired into Brandt at the thought of what that jackal and his band of rabid dogs might do to Dalilah, and he held on to that, pumping the jack fiercely, shirt plastered to his back. He'd tear those bastards apart limb from limb before he allowed them to lay one hand on her.

The image of another woman slammed suddenly into his mind—her throat slit. Her body brutalized. And for a nanosecond Brandt was blinded. He froze, hearing Carla's screams in the wind.

No. Not now. That was the past. History did *not* have to repeat itself. And it wouldn't—not if he stayed focused, if he refused to allow himself to get too emotionally vested, or distracted.

He bit deeper into his determination as he continued to work. Thunder boomed above, the sound rolling into the kloofs and hills. He could hear the crackling of fire in branches now. Smoke burned the back of his throat and his eyes watered.

Finally the jeep chassis began to lift from the sand.

Dalilah returned with a bundle of dry wood under her right arm. She dropped the driftwood to the sand at his feet, exhausted, hair sticking to her cheeks as she bent over to cough and catch her breath. Compassion speared through Brandt. He quickly started packing the wood under the front wheel then he lowered the jeep, removed the jack and tossed it into the backseat. He hopped into the driver's seat and fired the ignition. Slowly, he pressed down on the gas. The front wheel turned, whined, almost edging up onto the wood, but the vehicle fell back into the ruts

"Dalilah, can you push? We need something extra so the wheel can find purchase on the wood."

Shoving wet hair back from her face, she went round to the rear of the vehicle. Again, he carefully pressed down on the accelerator. The wheels whined as Dalilah leaned into the rear, using her good arm.

"Easy, easy," Brandt whispered as he felt the jeep beginning to move. "Please, baby, come on, come on, you can do it." The headlights panned ahead, illuminating the white river sand. Brandt had no idea whether the rain was packing it hard, or turning it into quicksand—soft and dangerous. Even if they did get the jeep unstuck, they still might not make it across all the way now. But it was the rising pools on the far side that really worried him. Then there was the steep wall of a bank. He glanced at the dashboard clock—3:23 a.m. If this didn't work—if they couldn't get this jeep over the Tsholo border and into Botswana within the next fifteen minutes, he was going to abort the attempt, take what he could from the jeep and hightail it out on foot. But that would lower their odds of survival on the other side tenfold.

Suddenly, the front tire bit. Brandt's heart lurched as the jeep kicked forward. Dalilah fell with a smack to the sand as the vehicle shot out from under her. She let out a cry of pain as she hit the sand, then scrambled to her feet and ran after the jeep. Brandt could not apply the brakes now. They'd sink. So he kept going, slow, steady as he leaned over and flung open the passenger door.

"Run, Dalilah! Jump in!"

She leaped in, scrambling up onto the seat as he increased gas, steady, steady, until with relief he felt the sand turning solid beneath the tires. Behind them on the Zimbabwe side from which they'd come, the riverine fringe was now completely ablaze. Even if they wanted to return, they couldn't. There was only one way, and that way was forward.

He blew out a breath, dragging his hand over wet hair, his heart thumping. He shot her a glance. "You okay?"

She nodded, but she was white with pain, her eyes huge. Brandt felt a sudden punch of affection. Quickly he turned away, concentrating instead on driving. They were reaching the brown pools and water was flowing in widening streams between them. Tension wound tighter.

"How deep do you think that water is?" she said.

"Don't know." He entered the narrowest part of a stream between two of the deep-looking pools. Water swirled dark in his lights. The front tires went into the water, then the back ones. As he drove, the jeep went deeper, water coming up over the wheels now. Brandt kept the forward motion steady. Then suddenly the jeep plunged abruptly forward, water sloshing up over the running boards and flowing in under the door. He could feel it soaking into his boots. His mouth turned dry and he quickly changed direction, steering upriver instead, trying to keep the jeep level and keep it from becoming immersed even more deeply. Water churned around the wheels.

"You know how to swim?" he said.

She gave a snort.

"That's a yes?" He was worried now.

But she didn't reply, her gaze fixated on the water still rising around them, her knuckles white as she gripped the top of the door. A wave rolled suddenly over the bonnet. Water leaked under the fold-down windshield, wetting their knees.

The engine burbled strangely and Brandt swallowed. He knew as long as he could maintain forward momentum, the diesel engine would be fine. But if the sand turned to mud, and the wheels slipped just once, the engine would take in too much water and seize. He wondered about crocs—these pools were a lot deeper and bigger than he'd thought.

The engine gurgled again, and Dalilah shot him a hard look. He said nothing, kept his attention on driving. Suddenly he felt the jeep wheels levelling out. The tires found harder purchase and they shot up the other side of the pool.

He kept revving until they slid onto firmer ground, then he gradually eased up on the accelerator. Slowly Brandt breathed out the air he'd been holding in his chest—they were out of the water.

But now they were sandwiched in a V of sand between the rising flood on one side, and the high-bank cliff, and the only way was north, even farther upriver, where the bank seemed to rise even higher.

"We'll keep going," he said. "Until we find a way out."

Ahead in their headlights the rain was silvery, and the strip of white sand between cliff and water grew narrower and narrower as the river continued to swell. Urgency bit into Brandt.

They could be trapped.

"If a full flood comes down," he said, trying to keep her positive, "it'll keep Amal and his men on the other side for at least a day or so until they find a way to cross."

Dalilah's gaze flicked to the high bank on the Botswana side. "Yeah, and at least we'll be driving head-on into the wall of water if it does come down," she said. "Always nice to face what's coming."

Brandt laughed, a great big booming release of tension. He loved that Princess had a sense of humor on top of her bravado.

"Hold tight, Princess!" he yelled as he veered left and zoomed through more water that was closing them in. It splashed up the sides of the vehicle, higher, higher. Then something hit them with a hard thud.

Oh, Jesus.

"What's that?" she hissed.

Then he saw—the carcass of a bloated cow, floating down. For a minute he'd feared it was a croc. Relief rushed out his chest once more and he laughed again. But this time she remained wire-tense, her fist clutched with a death grip on the bar.

Brandt drove fast, denying the first stirrings of panic licking through his gut as his headlights kept illuminating more and more cliff. The clock was ticking—they had to get out of here.

Dalilah reached suddenly forward, grabbed the hunting spot off the dash, flicked it on. She panned up the river, farther than his lights reached. All caution about being seen was now completely overridden by a desperate urge to get out of the riverbed, away from rising water.

"Over there!" she yelled. "A gap!"

Sweet heaven—she was right. A break in the cliff wall, a gentle incline up onto the high bank. Sweat dripping into his eyes, Brandt raced for it, water chortling at the wheels. He swung the jeep up onto the banking incline, and the jeep stuck. He revved, hard, tires spitting out wet sand. The engine cut, and they stalled. Brandt cursed viciously as he tried to restart it, praying there was no water damage somehow. The engine coughed, turned, then died again. He tried again, slower on the gas. The jeep growled to life. He said a silent prayer as he began carefully edging the four-wheel drive up the bank, all the way up. They shot out over the top onto hard grassy ground fringed with tall fever trees.

He hit the brakes. Put his head back and inhaled deeply.

"Oh, God," she said at his side.

He shot her a fast glance, worry spurting through him.

"I don't believe it," she said, tears of relief pouring down her face, and she smiled. "We made it," she whispered. "We actually made it!"

Her emotion made his eyes prickle, too.

"Yeah," he said, placing his hand on her knee, his throat

going tight. "We bloody well did. We make a good team, Princess."

She bit her lip to stop it from trembling, and nodded.

Brandt maneuvered the jeep a little higher onto the hard ground and into a grove of tall fever trees, where he parked under the canopy. They sat for a few minutes in silence, mentally regrouping as drops of water from the leaves plopped onto the canvas above their heads. There was a sudden shaking of the ground and an explosive roar. In their headlights they saw a wall of chocolate-brown water streaked with foam come crashing down the river, swallowing up logs, fallen trees spinning, dead cattle bobbing, along with an old tire and other unidentifiable debris. Waves licked and churned and danced up the banks, pulling in great blocks of sand that crumbled away into the flood. On the far side of the river, the flames ate at the blackened trunks of trees, the orange glow of the fire casting a coppery sheen over the churning brown water.

Finally Brandt doused the headlights.

Neither spoke as they listened to the roar of the floodwaters, watching the strange interplay of ghostly orange light on the raging river. A few more minutes and they would have been swallowed by it, too.

In silence, Brandt reached into the backseat, found the whiskey bottle, uncapped it. He held it out to her. Dalilah hesitated, then took the bottle from him. She took a deep swig and coughed, eyes watering.

She handed the bottle back to him, and he took a deep drink himself.

For another few seconds they sat like that, stunned, the adrenaline still humming through their bodies as the severity of what had almost happened sank in. She reached for the bottle, took another sip, put back her head and laughed. Husky, deep, real gut-laughter, a little crazy.

"Dalilah?" He touched her, worried. "You okay?"

She wiped tears from the corner of her eyes. He wasn't sure whether they were tears of laughter or not. Or both.

Then she looked at him, really looked at him, her eyes black and luminous in the faint coppery light being cast by the fire on the opposite bank.

"I don't think I've ever felt so alive as right now. Even though the pain is killing me." She took another swig, handed him the bottle, wiped her mouth. Then closed her eyes as she let the whiskey do its thing.

Brandt was startled by a dawning realization—this woman was fired by adrenaline, adversity. It fueled instead of cracked her. He got this. He got *her*—she was like him. And the knowledge gave him a deep twisting feeling in his chest, a sense of kinship. A bond he didn't want. With it came a whisper of fear—they had a long way to go yet.

She laughed again, softly, more sadly, her eyes still closed. "God, when did drinking get to be so good?"

And now all he wanted to do was kiss her, so badly he thought he'd burst. He wanted to feel her lips against his, rip her out of that torn, wet cocktail dress, hook his fingers into that scrap of a G-string and just bury himself in her, have those firm dusky thighs wrapped around him. Become one. Defy death, affirm life—an urge as old as time.

Her eyelids fluttered open as she sensed a shift in him, and something in her features stilled as she registered the look on his face. Their gazes held as something dark swelled between them, the pent-up emotion almost tangible. Raindrops plopped onto the canopy above. Brandt could smell the smoke, the mud in the churning water, the heat of the jeep's engine. And he leaned forward, inexorably pulled toward her by some undeniable force. He could detect the faint scent of coconut in her wet hair. Their mouths were so close he could taste the whiskey on her breath. Her lips opened.

The water rumbled and there was a dull boom as a tree thudded into the bank below. Another grumble of thunder growled far over the plains.

He began to throb, ache, in places so deep he didn't know they even existed anymore. His vision narrowing, he leaned in closer and gently cupped the side of her face. She tilted her chin to him.

Their lips touched, brushed, lightly as feathers. A volcano of lust erupted fierce into his belly, molten desire firing into his chest, quickening his breathing. She arched up into him, her hand touching his waist as he pressed his mouth to hers and her tongue found his. Brandt stroked his palm down the length of her arm, his fingers softly covering hers, kissing her harder, deeper. Then he felt the rock on her hand, the diamond. Christ, what were they doing!

He jerked back, shocked.

She stared into his eyes, just as stunned. Silence— heavy, loaded with crackling tension—filled the space between them. Words defied Brandt.

Sorry didn't cut it. Because he wasn't sorry. He'd do it again in a heartbeat.

And that's when fear plunged its blade really deep into his heart—this woman scared him. She made him want. In a way that was raw and deep and very dangerous. A way that he hadn't wanted in years, not since a time when life still held possibilities and dreams. She'd reawakened a part of himself he thought long dead. Dalilah really was too hot for him to handle. And for the next few days, it was going to be his job—to handle her.

"Brandt," she said.

"Don't," he said. "Please, don't say anything, Dalilah. It… Nothing happened."

Her mouth went tight, and he saw something heavy and sad in her eyes. He also saw her complexion was suddenly wan, and she was starting to shiver again.

He cursed himself, resenting the erection still hard and hot in his pants—a mocking reminder he was a damn fool. He was supposed to be taking care of her, not satisfying his own lust.

Self-recrimination slicing like ice through him, he flung open his door. "Let's find you some dry clothes, take a look at that injury, get some food into you."

He put the Petzl headlamp back onto his head, clicked it on, and rummaged around in the back for a second headlamp, which he'd taken from the bush camp. He looped the strap of the second lamp over the roll bar, under the jeep's canvas roof, so that it cast its light down into the interior of the vehicle.

Survival lust. That's all it was, he told himself as he tossed things out of the backpack. It was normal. Survivors could become euphoric in the face of cheating death. Humans were hormonally primed to jump each other's bones after times of war. This ensured propagation of the species, survival of the tribe. There was a design to nature, and that's all this was. Humans, at the base level, were programmed no less than other mammals.

Focus. Get over it.

But Brandt knew he was fruitlessly trying to justify his actions. Actions that were inexcusable, the same kind of actions that had gotten Carla tortured, raped and murdered while he'd been forced to watch helplessly.

He tossed a pile of clothes into the front seat beside Dalilah. "Put those on." His words were brusque, and he knew it. He saw a glimmer of hurt in her eyes, but he didn't care—couldn't afford to. It was best this way. She gathered up the clothes, and her gaze held his for several beats.

"What?" he snapped.

"Nothing." Her words were just as terse.

"Dalilah," he said, then hesitated. "It was a mistake. It won't happen again."

She bit her lip and turned away from him.

Brandt cursed again to himself as he dug a kikoi out of the backpack. He held up the woven African sarong. It looked brand-new—those poor German tourists must have bought it at some market recently. He draped it over the roll bars that divided the front from the backseats, making a curtain to afford Dalilah some privacy while she changed.

From behind the curtain he said curtly, "If you need help changing, tell me."

"I won't," she said crisply. "I'm fine."

Silence.

Brandt scrubbed his brow and blew out a chestful of air. He'd crossed the line, but she was just as guilty. She was engaged to another man, and Brandt held on to that. Women could not be trusted. They broke promises.

Especially women like her.

Chapter 6

Dalilah tried to sort one-handed through the jumble of clothing Brandt had thrust onto the seat beside her, but she was shivering badly now. Temperatures had dropped, but she knew the kiss had shaken her more than the cold. She didn't want to articulate what that really meant to her, or her future. But she sensed a seismic shift had taken place somewhere deep down within her and it had all started with this last ClearWater mission to Zimbabwe. Dalilah suddenly had no idea what she was doing anymore. After all these years of knowing with crystal clarity that it was her royal duty to marry Sheik Haroun Hassan, after knowing she had to come to the marriage a virgin, as per the contract her father had signed, Dalilah had gone and kissed a virtual stranger—and liked it. A lot. Too much.

She'd barely ever kissed a man in her life.

Stupid, she muttered to herself. *Damn stupid. You're drunk, stressed and in shock and in pain, and it'll all look different in the morning. Just shut it out, like it never happened. In daylight you'll be able to see your path again.*

Dalilah struggled out of her torn gown and into the light safari pants. She pulled a long-sleeved cotton shirt over a T-shirt, and fumbled to get her feet into the socks and hiking boots Brandt had given her. The dry clothes were deliciously welcome, if a little big.

As she tried fruitlessly to do up the buttons on the shirt, Dalilah glanced at the sarong Brandt had used to partition off the driver's seat from the back of the jeep. He might be a brutish, scarred lion of a man, but there was a gentleman buried deep inside that tawny brawn somewhere. And the tenderness in his touch had not gone unnoticed in spite of the way he'd shut her down—he was struggling with something inside himself, also. It made her even more curious about him.

Cursing as a button refused to slide through the tiny opening, she glanced again at the curtain. Behind it she could see Brandt's shadow moving as he organized things in the back.

If you need help changing, tell me.

No way on this earth was she going to ask him for help dressing, not after what his touch had already done to her body. And her mind.

While she struggled, Dalilah could hear Brandt going around to the rear of the jeep. The vehicle began to bounce around as he hefted and grunted. Then she heard his boots crunching through twigs as he left the vehicle. Quickly she leaned forward and peered around the sarong curtain.

He was carrying the stiff leopard carcass across his shoulders, the headlamp lighting his way toward a cluster of trees. With a grunt, he lowered himself to his haunches and tilted the leopard's body onto the dirt. It landed with a soft, dull thud. Dalilah closed her eyes.

She'd forgotten for a moment the leopard was still on the backseat. She'd forgotten, too, in their struggle to get out of Zimbabwe alive, about the little cub left behind in the tree. Emotion ballooned painfully in her chest.

It had all been too much. She breathed in deeply, steadying herself as she opened her eyes and watched Brandt.

He was on his haunches, his forearms braced on his muscular thighs for balance, as if he was just sitting there, thinking. Then he reached out and laid his palm gently on the animal's fur, something reverent in his gesture. Something very private. Then as if sensing her watching, he suddenly spun around.

Dalilah ducked quickly back behind the kikoi. She heard him returning, opening the tool compartment at the rear. Then she heard a clunking sound as he removed something, and his boots crunched over to the leopard again. Once more she peeked round the curtain.

He had the shovel in his hand. The blade chinked against small stones as he thrust it into the soil—Brandt was digging a grave for the female leopard.

Dalilah's chest hurt as she watched him gently roll the dead animal into its resting place. He began to cover it, his muscles rolling under his soaked shirt, and it struck her how tired *he* must be. How long he'd been at it since flying his plane into Zimbabwe, hiking up to the lodge to rescue her. Finding all this equipment and getting them both across the river. Now he was taking time to bury the leopard in a way that revealed a respect for life.

Compassion washed through Dalilah. And for a brief moment she wished she hadn't witnessed this vignette. It was bad enough falling in lust with this man, but feeling this kinship, this compassion—it complicated things she was already struggling with in her own head.

Omair might have sent the right man to save her life. But on some level Dalilah sensed Brandt was a game changer—he'd unleashed something in her that wasn't going to be easy to put back into its box. Perhaps Omair had actually made a grave mistake.

She should never have kissed Brandt back. But she had. Dalilah's gaze lowered to the massive diamond on her swollen finger, a stone that could probably feed an entire Zimbabwean village for a lifetime. A stone that could buy access to clean water resources, to solar power. A stone that could help her do the good she craved. And Dalilah was suddenly overwhelmed. She felt like a hypocrite and it all came crashing down on her now, rapid-fire chunks of thoughts, images. Her life. Her duty. Her freedom. Why she'd been in Zimbabwe in the first place...how this had been her last big deal. How her brothers had lied to her by omission, trying to protect her by not informing her that they knew their family's arch enemy—Amal Ghaffar—was still alive.

How she felt nothing at all for Haroun—hardly knew him at all.

And suddenly she was spent, in pain, beyond thinking, analyzing, didn't even want to. She just wanted to get through this. Alive.

Exhausted, Dalilah sat limp, staring at the coppery glow of the flames on the churning and swirling river, listening to Brandt moving in the shadows as he finished covering the grave.

"You done yet?" he called out as he returned with the shovel.

"I'm surprised you went to the trouble of burying it," she said. "Why did you?"

"Trackers would have seen it," he said, voice clipped

as he marched around to the rear of the truck, where he replaced the shovel.

"They're going to see our tire tracks here under the trees, anyway," she said, reading more into his actions than he was admitting.

Choosing not to answer, he sullenly dusted his hands off on his shorts and re-angled the headlamp on his head before reaching for the first-aid box. "So, are you done?"

"Apart from the buttons and the bootlaces. I can't do them with one hand."

He grunted as he ripped open a pouch containing a pad soaked in disinfectant and cleaned his hands with it. Then, climbing into the front seat next to her, Brandt regarded her, assessing her condition. Under the light coming from the lamp on the roll bar above, Dalilah noticed for the first time a tattoo of a lion on his shoulder.

"Clothes don't fit too badly," he said, opening the first-aid kit.

"Good thing the pants came with a belt." Dalilah offered a tremulous smile, but he did not return it. A strange little sinking feeling went through her stomach.

All business now, Brandt took her arm, felt for a pulse, before cutting off the sleeve above her elbow. Feeling carefully along her radius, he lingered, closer to her wrist, gently palpating where there was swelling. She winced, and immediately he released pressure.

"Seems to be a fairly straightforward fracture. Best we can do is splint and stabilize it until we can get medical attention. Your fingers are quite swollen," he said. "If you swell any more, Dalilah, we're going to have to cut that thing off, okay?" He jerked his chin at her engagement ring.

She moistened her lips, nodded, tears of pain and emotion filling her eyes. He glanced up at her face, forcing her to squint against the sharp light from his headlamp.

"Sorry." He lowered his head, averting the light from her face.

"I'm okay. Just…tired."

He inhaled slowly, deeply, as he opened a packet containing a blue-and-orange splint. "SAM splint," he explained. "Made from malleable aluminum lightly padded with foam on either side. It can be molded and shaped for various splinting tasks."

He bent the splint to form a long channel, which he wrapped around the back of her elbow, sandwiching her arm down to her fingers, which he left free. He bound the splint firmly into place with a bandage, his movements deft and smooth.

"You've done this before," she said.

"A couple of times."

"Are you a mercenary, Brandt?"

"Ex. I'm going to do up your buttons, then make a sling." His hands moved between her breasts and he kept his eyes averted from hers. "Now, hold your splinted arm against your abdomen like this," he said, showing her. Then, lifting the damp hair away from the nape of her neck, he tied a sling fashioned from one of the triangle bandages.

A shiver chased down her back as the rough skin of his callused hands brushed against the tender skin on the back of her neck. She felt him pause briefly at her reaction. The tension between them was still thick and sexual.

"There," he said, packing up the first-aid kit. "That should do it."

"Did you work with Omair, with the Force du Sable?"

"You need to eat something," he said, ignoring her question. "I've got some tinned food, biltong, apples."

He moved the curtain aside and reached into the cooler at the back as he spoke. "We'll get something into you, then you must sleep. We've got about an hour left until first light. The flood buys us some time, and it's better not to move into unknown terrain while dark if we can help it. But when we do move, we'll need to go fast because we'll be leaving a trail in the mud that even a blind man could track." He held up three tins. "Bully beef, ravioli or chili con carne?"

She glanced at the tins. "You said you had apples?"

He frowned, handed her a green apple.

"Thanks." Dalilah took a bite. It was sour, and she felt nauseous.

"You need something more substantial than that," he said, reaching up to click off his headlamp.

She said nothing, just chewed, focusing on making the fruit go down. He watched her intently, then his gaze slid back down to the diamond ring poking out of her splint.

"Who's the guy?"

Dalilah swallowed her mouthful of apple. He was probably thinking about the fact she'd kissed him back while she was promised to another man.

"Sheik Haroun Hassan of Sa'ud," she said.

His eyes flashed up to hers.

"The *Kingdom* of Sa'ud?"

"Yes."

His jaw tightened and he leaned back into the driver's seat, facing the front. He stared at the churning river as he spun a can of ravioli round and round in his hands.

"You have an issue with the Kingdom of Sa'ud?" she said quietly, watching his profile, the tension in his hands.

"I know the House of Sa'ud is stinking oil-rich." His words were abrupt, and he didn't look at her when he spoke. "I also know the Sa'ud royal family is fiercely traditional, and that the old king is not expected to live long. It's creating some uncertainty in the Middle East."

She nodded. "Haroun is his only son. He'll be king soon."

"And then you'll be queen." His tone was matter-of-fact, yet spiced with distaste.

"And you disapprove."

He just snorted.

"Brandt—what is it?"

"Two years ago," he said quietly, watching the water, "there was a big to-do in the news about a sheik from the House of Sa'ud. He was accused of having his fiancée murdered while she was visiting Dubai. The king used his influence, made the charges go away."

Dalilah swallowed, the apple sticking in her craw. "Yes," she said quietly. "The sheik was—is—a very distant cousin of Haroun's. But the Dubai incident had nothing to do with Haroun."

He spun suddenly to face her. "The woman was his *fiancée,* Dalilah."

"She was killed by two Egyptians. It was a robbery gone wrong in her hotel room. The Egyptians were caught."

"The BBC claimed the Egyptians were hit men—"

"There was no proof, no evidence. No—"

"There were rumors the hit men were hired after the Sa'ud sheik found his fiancée was cheating on him, that it was an honor killing, because she was unfaithful, tainted goods." He turned to face her and his ice eyes were suddenly ice-cold and fierce under the white light of the Petzl lamp above.

A chill sunk into Dalilah. She held the half-eaten apple in her lap, her own insecurities about the case welling inside her again.

"Do you believe everything you read?" she said.

"I believe in this case, where there's smoke, there's fire."

"The truth is not always what it seems at first blush, you know. This guy—Haroun's cousin—was prejudged because of his culture, because he's a wealthy oil sheik."

"Is *that* what you think this is? Prejudice?"

"Yeah, I do. Just like you prejudged *me* for being royalty."

He glared at her, a muscle working along his jaw.

Dalilah pushed a fall of hair off her brow, self-conscious now. And she realized her hair was thick with mud, and that she was too darn tired to argue or explain anything. Or even think about how Haroun had sidestepped the issue when she'd tried to discuss the case with him last year. She put her head back, the unfinished apple resting uneaten in her hand.

"So, when is the wedding?"

She looked away. So far away, it all seemed. She got a sinking, claustrophobic feeling in her chest at the thought of it all.

"Nineteen months."

"You'll get married in Sa'ud?"

She nodded.

He blew out a breath.

Dalilah turned her head toward him. "What exactly is it that you don't you approve of, Brandt? It's not like you're getting married—my choice has nothing to do with you."

He met her eyes. "You're right, it doesn't."

Guilt sliced through her—she'd kissed him. And a need rose in Dalilah to make him understand that she wasn't a cheat, that she had values. That this momentary indiscretion was bothering her intensely.

"Tradition decrees we marry in his kingdom," she explained.

Several beats of silence filled the space between them, and his gaze lowered slowly to her lips. Dalilah swallowed.

"I suppose," he said slowly, still focused on her mouth, "that your guest list reads like a United Nations who's who. I mean, who doesn't want to rub shoulders with Sa'ud royalty, in spite of who they are. Did you send an invite to the White House, too?"

"You *do* have a problem."

"Lady, I've got a lot of problems. Acquired over a lot of years. You don't even want to go there. Let's just deal with what's at hand, okay. Why don't you lean your back against the door, get your feet up on the seat here so I can lace up your boots."

She put her feet up and he tied her bootlaces, his jaw tight, his movements brusque, tension still rolling off him. He yanked the laces tight. Too tight.

"Ouch."

"Sorry." He didn't sound it. He loosened the lace, tried again.

"Is it Haroun's wealth, his power that you don't like?" she said irritably. "Or you don't respect tradition or what? Or just the Sa'uds and their power?" She was pushing. She knew it, but now she needed to know, maybe because she was struggling trying to justify it all to herself.

"I guess I'm wondering where Haroun is right now," he said. "And why Omair, not your fiancé, is paying me to save your royal tush." He leaned forward slightly, lowering his voice to a dark whisper. "And you know what else is worrying me, Dalilah? It's what Haroun might do if he finds out you like to kiss strange men—because Sa'ud sheiks seem to have a bad reputation handling that sort of thing."

Blood drained from her head. "Brandt, it's not what—"

He held up his big hand, stopping her dead. "Forget it, Dalilah. I don't want to know."

"You lie," she said softly. "Or you wouldn't have asked otherwise. You owe it to me to allow me to explai—"

"Here." He abruptly peeled the top off the can of ravioli in his hands and stuck the fork end of his army knife into it. "Get this into you."

Frustration burned through her. "I told you, I'm vegetarian."

"Not on my watch you're not," he snapped. "I'm getting you out of the bush alive, whether you like it or not. We have no idea how long this will take. And when the jeep's fuel runs out, we could be trekking on foot for days. You need energy to survive and there's precious little lettuce or tofu you're going to get out here, so you'd better adjust." He took the half-eaten apple from her hand and replaced it with the tin.

"Eat."

Defiance set her mouth and she glared stubbornly ahead.

He grabbed the rifle, flung open the door and went to stand on the riverbank, a dark silhouette against the fading glow of bushfire.

She glanced at the tin. In spite of herself hunger was gnawing into the acid burn of whiskey and sour apple in her stomach. Dalilah carefully tested a mouthful of cold beef ravioli. It didn't taste half-bad. She tried to put her principles aside and took another mouthful.

Brandt began to pace along the bank, rifle in hand, staying close enough to ensure she was eating. And she did eat, suddenly overcome by ravenous hunger. The last time she'd had food, she realized, was part of a green salad at lunch yesterday. Finishing the contents of the small tin, she set it on the dash and within minutes, was asleep on the front seat.

Brandt glanced up to the vehicle. Under the faint bluish-white glow of the Petzl, Dalilah was slumped, head to the side, her dark, muddy hair splayed across the top of the seat. He blew out a heavy breath of air and stood for a while longer on the bank.

A predawn cold descended on him as the fire across the river began to die down to embers. He stared at the twisted black silhouettes rising out of the glowing coals, the carnage they'd escaped. Dawn was imminent, and with first light would come Amal. Brandt figured he'd let Princess sleep for maybe thirty more minutes, then they needed to move.

He returned to the vehicle, untied the sleeping bag from the bottom of the pack and, unzipping it, he draped it gently over her, tucking in the edges.

Unable to stop himself, he carefully studied her face in repose, taking time now to note the arch of her lips, the density of her impossibly long, black lashes, the angle of her cheekbones. Brandt's skin heated as he thought of her kiss, her taste, her hunger, how he'd acted completely apart from logic.

Hell, he *still* wanted her—physically. Which went against the grain. His idea of commitment these past ten years was staying the whole night.

But this woman was in another league.

And she was promised to a man soon to be king, a sheik richer than the bloody queen of England. This knowledge had starkly redefined the boundaries of his mission. And yeah, maybe it was jealousy in part that made him feel a little bitter, that had made him attack the Sa'ud royal family like that, but there *was* something darker at play here. Haroun Hassan and the House of Sa'ud were dangerous.

Brandt knew this for a fact—he had inside information about those two Egyptian killers. While doing covert intelligence work in Libya, he'd seen proprietary photos of the two men, and in intelligence circles, those men had both been known assassins.

This gave him a whole other reason to keep his hands off Princess Dalilah Al-Arif—it was for her own protection. Because he had little doubt that if Sheik Hassan found out Dalilah was messing about with some hot-blooded, bush-addled ex-merc, it could be the death of her.

And him.

Oddly, this realization also stirred a protectiveness in him, which didn't make sense. He glanced down at her again, and softness stole into his heart in spite of himself. There was something so gentle and vulnerable about her in sleep, her fiery energy blurred. He wondered why she'd actually chosen to marry Sheik Haroun Hassan in the first place, why she wanted to give up her independence, the charity work she was doing in Africa. Probably prestige, he thought. The Kingdom of Sa'ud was far more wealthy and politically influential than the Kingdom of Al Na'Jar—Haroun was a catch. With these thoughts came a whisper of disrespect.

For whatever reason Princess Dalilah had promised herself to the future king of Sa'ud, it *was* the choice she'd made. And in wearing that ring she'd made the man a promise.

A promise was something Brandt took very, very seriously.

He'd been burned himself by broken promises—he knew what that could do to a man. Brandt reached for the bottle of whiskey and took a hard swig. As the burn flushed through his chest he glanced down at Dalilah again, and this time he managed to feel nothing. She was just a principal. A package. He'd deliver her to her brother, and he to her prospective husband. No coddling. Talking only when absolutely necessary.

Just a job—for more reasons than he could count now.

Jacob held up his hand, calling the hunt party to a halt. A hint of light was creeping into the sky and he could just make out the glint of a small plane on the grassland below.

He and Jock had been leading the hunt posse through the night, assisted by Amal's tracker and followed by four men on horses and six men in jeeps, including Amal. Jacob crouched to quietly watch the plane from the ridge and assess the situation.

But as Mbogo caught sight of the plane he whooped, hitting the accelerator of the jeep he was driving. Swerving around Jacob, Mbogo barreled his vehicle down the ridge and out over the plain toward the aircraft. The other jeep and three of the men on horseback bombed after him. One man on horseback remained to guard Jacob, his gun ready lest the tracker tried to take the gap and flee.

These men were stupid, thought Jacob as he began to proceed after them, slowly on foot, watching Jock carefully as he moved. They would miss signs by going straight for the plane. As he got to the bottom of the ridge, Jacob noticed Jock alerting to scent. He followed Jock until the dog alerted again.

Crouching, Jacob examined the ground with his flashlight, the man on the horse behind watching him. The rest of the party was circling the plane and he could hear snatches of voices carrying over the grassland. But his interest was in a series of holes in the ground. In some of the holes were tiny flecks of gold that reflected in his beam. The marks of gold stiletto heels, he thought. And one of the heels had been broken.

The princess had been here, crouching. There was a faint handprint, too. Jacob cut for more sign around this area and found a boot depression pooling with water. Slowly he glanced up and studied the plane in the distance. In the increasing light he saw it had no propeller, no doors.

The man who took the princess must have been planning to take to the air. But his plane had been robbed. No supplies, no transport, broken shoes on the woman. They would not get far. If the pilot was sharp, he'd go first to look for transport, food, water, before moving on.

Jacob looked up into the sky. If the pilot came over the Tsholo River in his plane, like a bird he would have seen the bush camp that lay to the north.

"*Soek,* Jock," Jacob whispered to the dog, showing him the ground to initiate another search. The dog soon led him to what he was looking for—a set of tracks heading northward, toward the camp. He patted Jock, gave him a piece of biscuit from his pocket, then started toward the plane and the men. As he got closer, he saw, painted on the tail, the word *Tautona*.

Jacob knew immediately whose plane it was. A person could not be in Africa long without being given a nickname, something that described his personality. *Tautona* was the Setswana name given to a legendary bush pilot from Botswana named Brandt Stryker who sometimes flew guests over the border to the safari lodge where Jacob worked. Tautona was one of the few pilots who would still fly into Zimbabwe. Now look at what had happened to his plane—that's why people didn't come here anymore. The country was too hungry.

Jacob did not tell Amal what he'd seen, or knew. He just watched as Amal's tracker started gesticulating west toward the river. The tracker was saying the plane had

Botswana registration. It meant their quarry would probably have continued on foot directly west, making for the Tsholo River.

Amal glanced suddenly at Jacob, and he tensed inside.

"Jacob, come!" Amal pointed west. "They went that way—find their tracks!"

"I think they went another way, boss."

"What?" Jacob pointed north. The men shook their heads and murmured in dissent.

"Get over here!" Amal ordered. Jacob just lowered his head. This angered Amal, who marched up to him and unsheathed his dagger. He shoved the tip against Jacob's neck. "You messing with me, old man? You trying to send me on a wild-goose chase?"

"No, sir."

Something flickered in Amal's oil-black eyes. "We'll see. If my tracker is right, if we find their trace at the river, I cut your guts out and leave you for the hyenas, understand?"

"Yes, sir, boss."

Amal resheathed the dagger.

Jacob moved silently behind the posse of men as they headed straight for the line of dense foliage in the distance. Behind him the man on horseback followed, and Jacob knew the rifle was continually trained on him.

But he was biding his time. He had good information—he now knew how to find Mr. Stryker even without tracks, and he'd use his knowledge when it would serve him best.

Chapter 7

Dalilah came awake slowly, surfacing from some dark and terrible nightmare. Her head was spinning, images slicing through her brain. *Automatic gunfire. Blood. Massacred bodies strewn under tables. Broken glass. Being carried on the back of a brutish man into the black African night.* An awful dream...then her eyes jolted open.

Faint, gray light filtered into her field of vision. She turned her head slowly. Branches dripped onto the drab, olive-green canopy above her head. She was covered by an unzipped sleeping bag, warm, and she could smell mud, foliage like hay. The sound of a churning river filled her brain.

Panic licked suddenly through her and Dalilah tried to push herself into a sitting position on the front seat of the jeep before remembering her arm was broken. Gingerly, she edged fully up on the front seat. Through the dirty windshield the brown river swirled with yellow foam.

The scent coming from wet, burned trees across the river was strong. Her heart started to pound. It wasn't a dream.

The nightmare was real.

She held dead still, trying to orient herself, recall the sequence of events that had brought her here. But her arm hurt and her brain was fuzzy. Carefully she moved her head, neck stiff, taking further register of her surroundings.

She was alone in the front seat. Rain had stopped. The jeep was parked under a cathedral-like canopy of tall trees with lime-colored bark, leaves moving like silvery fish in a warm breeze that stirred up cooler pockets of air; the sensation of both warm and cold against her face felt strange.

Her heart beat faster, something akin to dread licking into her belly as she wondered where Brandt was, and then she recalled his kiss, the taste of him. Her own hot well of desire.

Oh, God.

She inhaled deeply, spun round in full-blown panic now, then sucked air in sharply as she saw him standing in the shadows, silent, rifle cradled in his arm. He was watching her, his pale eyes glacial-cool slits against darkly tanned skin, his features hard in this cruel light of dawn. Had she imagined it all in the night—the compassion in his touch, the warmth, the ferocity and tenderness of desire?

"How're you feeling?" His Afrikaans accent sounded as gruff as he looked this morning.

Dalilah brushed a tangle of knotted hair back off her forehead. "Terrible, thanks."

She disentangled herself from the sleeping bag as he started toward the jeep.

"Do you need to stretch your legs, or can you wait?"

She took his question as euphemism for bathroom break. "I can wait."

"Good, because we need to get moving—I already let you sleep too long."

He climbed into the jeep beside her, and the weight of the vehicle shifted. He secured the rifle on the dash and folded down the spattered windshield.

Brandt started the ignition and the diesel engine purred to life. He began to reverse from their spot beneath the trees. Swinging the wheel around, he checked the GPS and set a course directly perpendicular from the river. Dalilah saw him glance at his watch. Tension whispered through her.

Sharp grass stalks clicked and rustled under the carriage as they negotiated the space between trees and already temperatures were increasing. Dalilah glanced at Brandt's profile, taking her first proper study of him in the unforgiving light of dawn.

He had a fighter's face. The bridge of his nose had a bump, as if it had been broken more than once, and he had a fine scar across his jaw. He was not handsome, but arresting—there was something mesmerizing about the broad strokes and aggression of his features. This was a man who wouldn't shy away from confrontation, who'd physically stand up for what he believed, or wanted.

His mouth was also powerful—wide, well-defined lips, the lines bracketing them etched deep. She liked the character in his face, a rugged map of his past experience. The memory of the taste of him, the sensation of the feather-soft brush of those powerful lips against hers filled her mind and Dalilah swallowed, her gaze lowering to his strong neck muscles that flared into broad shoulders which she knew from experience were strong and hard like iron.

Dalilah glanced at his hands on the wheel. Firm, sure. Big. Knuckles also scarred.

She knew the palms of those hands were rough, and his fingers callused, but that his touch could be as gentle as he was dexterous. This was a physical man who spent a lot of his life outdoors, a man shaped, most likely, by wilderness, the sun, the space and freedom. And violence.

Dalilah wondered again about what he'd said about killing people, about how he knew her brother. He could feel her studying him, she was sure of it. But he didn't glance her way. The sky turned soft gold as the first rays of sun crept over the land. Heat and humidity peaked instantly. She loosened her shirt, feeling thirst.

"Why a lion?"

Now he looked at her. "What?"

"Your tattoo."

He gave a soft snort. "My African name—Tautona. That's what the locals call me. It means old lion."

"Why an *old* lion?"

A wry smile twisted over his lips. "Guess they figured I'm like those scarred old males that have been ousted from their pride and live alone on the fringes of the veldt. Have to hunt all by themselves—no females to do the job for them."

"Is it true?"

He shot her another glance, and the brackets around his mouth deepened, but he said nothing.

"Where are we going?" she said finally.

"First, west. Then north, then southwest."

"I mean, what is the plan, our destination? How long is it going to take?"

He inhaled, his grip firming on the wheel, as if irritated by having to explain things.

"Look, it might help to share the plan," she said. "I

helped you back at the river, remember? You might need me again. We made a good team last night."

A muscle began to pulse at his jaw. And when he didn't bother to dignify her with a reply, she lowered her voice and said irritably, "Brandt—"

He muttered something in Afrikaans she couldn't understand, then said, "I want as much distance as possible between us and the Tsholo, okay? Then we turn northward to find a route up onto a plateau. Once up on the plateau we'll head for a paved road, hopefully lose tracks while driving south along the tarmac for a while, then we'll cut back into the bush and make for a safe place and phone your brother." His tone was terse. "However, if by the time we reach the plateau tonight there is no sign of them following us, we might stop and rest for the night at an old airstrip I know, move again at first light."

"How will we know if they're following?"

"We should be able to get a good view of the land all the way to the river from up on the plateau." He reached into the giant cooler on the seat behind him as he spoke, his eyes fixed on the terrain ahead. He came out with another apple and a bottle of water.

"Breakfast," he said, dumping them in her lap. "I'll make you some tea later."

"Tea?" A sudden craving for the strong, warm sweet liquid filled her with a kind of desperation. "How?"

"Found a gas burner and kettle in the back with the shovel. Tea bags come from the bush camp."

She positioned the water bottle between her knees and unscrewed the cap with her good hand. "I'm impressed that you got all this stuff," she said, raising the bottle to her lips. "We could go for days—"

"Hope not," he said crisply.

She paused, bottle midair. "Me, too. I was just—"

"Eat," he said brusquely. "Drink."

Dalilah glared at him, something immediately resisting inside her. She wasn't accustomed to being ordered around. Her brothers tried, but she fought them every step of the way. It had become a reflex—her life was dominated by too many alpha men trying to push her around for her own damn good.

In spite of her thirst, Dalilah's mouth flattened and she recapped the water bottle. She set the bottle and apple on the seat next to her.

He cast her a sideways glance, the sun's rays filtering through the trees making his eyes an even paler blue.

"You really should eat."

"I will when I'm hungry." She was drawing her own little line in the sand, for whatever that was worth. But it made her feel stronger.

He was about to argue, but stopped himself, a whisper of another wry smile ghosting his lips. He found her rebellion amusing. Her blood began to boil.

As the sun climbed higher into the sky, the air grew humid and blisteringly hot. The jeep bumped and bounced over increasingly rocky terrain. Trees went from green to a blackish-gray, leafless, sharp. Strips of bark hung from trunks. Surprise rippled through Dalilah as she became suddenly aware of silvery monkeys in the branches around them. The troop was watching them pass. Silent. Menacing.

Qua-waaaaee—Go awaaaaee. Qua-waaaaee—Go awaaaay. The sad call of a gray lorie again.

Brandt glanced up into the trees, and she could sense a renewed tension in him. In spite of the heat, a ripple of coolness trickled down Dalilah's neck.

Soon they were out on a plain again, this one dotted with the iconic acacia trees of Africa. White thorns as long as her middle finger and fat as a pencil stuck out from the branches.

"Keep your arm inside the jeep," he ordered as one of the tree branches scraped down the side of the jeep. "Those thorns will shred skin to ribbons."

Dalilah removed her elbow from where she'd been resting it on the door.

"You didn't say where we were actually going after we get up to the plateau," she said, wiping sweat from her brow with the back of her hand.

"A safe place."

"Like, where?"

"Like, you don't need to worry about it."

Exasperation flushed through her. "Anyone ever tell you you were short on both words and manners?"

"Get down!" He swerved as a branch whipped inside the jeep, and Dalilah flung herself onto his lap.

He grinned as she looked up at him in shock.

"You did that on purpose!" Dalilah snapped as she shoved herself back into a sitting position. The brackets around his mouth creased and fine lines fanned out from his eyes, but he said nothing.

"I know what you're doing, Brandt! You're being a cantankerous boor to keep me all worked up. You think if I'm angry, I'll focus on survival and won't wimp out on you!"

"If you've shown me one thing, Princess, it's that you don't do wimpy."

She glowered at him. "Is that a compliment or insult?"

"Fact." He chuckled low and throaty, but without the sound of real mirth. "And you got that right. I am a *Boer*—come from good old Dutch-Afrikaner farming stock."

"I said boor, not *Boer*."

He chuckled again and she muttered a curse in Arabic, grabbed the bottle of water and took a big angry swig as she turned her body away from him and sat in simmering silence.

The veldt stretched endlessly to the horizon, just rocky outcrops, thorny trees, dry, dead grass, dun soil. The wind died, and heat began to shimmer in oscillating waves off the land. Dalilah lifted her thick hair off her neck, wishing she had something to tie it up with, but there was no way she was going to ask Brandt Stryker for help.

Abruptly Dalilah felt the jeep slow, then stop. She swung round in the seat, instantly worried.

"Look…over there," he said softly, pointing into the distance.

About a hundred yards out, as if materializing from the interplay of shadow and light in the trees, two graceful giraffes stood side by side, looping their necks around each other. Brandt cut the engine.

Heat pressed down, the engine ticking as it cooled. The sounds of the bush seemed to rise from nowhere to envelop them—the slight rustle of grasses, the clicking of grasshoppers. The faint chorus of a million birds that exploded suddenly into the sky, swarming in unison, alighting on a tree, then bursting up from the branches in a riot of movement as the flock moved to another tree.

Dalilah shaded her eyes, and as she watched the towering animals swinging their necks, everything else seemed to slip into the far reaches of her mind. No Manhattan. No Haroun. No looming wedding. She felt a shift in Brandt's energy, too, and glanced up into his face. He met her gaze for a brief moment, and Dalilah saw something dark and hungry. But his eyes narrowed abruptly and he turned away. That's when it really hit Dalilah—Brandt was fighting an attraction to her. He was angry with himself for overstepping the line, and with her for enabling him.

"Two males," he said, nodding toward the animals.

"You can tell by the lack of hair on top of their horns—they rub them smooth by fighting. And see over there?" He pointed, and Dalilah was conscious of the golden hairs on his strong, tanned forearm. "In the trees to the right—there's the female they're fighting over."

"That's fighting?"

He nodded.

They watched for a few seconds longer as the giraffes, torsos pressed together, did a sidestepping movement, like a dance, gangly legs moving in perfect choreography. Then suddenly, the giraffe with the darker markings swung his neck down low then slammed it hard up into the other male's neck. A slapping sound carried over the veldt.

Dalilah's stomach clenched. The light-colored giraffe seemed stunned by the blow and stumbled as it tried to sidestep away from the aggressor. But the larger, darker giraffe stepped in time with him, keeping his torso pressed against his opponent.

"The one on the left, the lighter-colored, younger male is trying to get away now," Brandt explained as the older one looped his neck down again and swung it hard up against the other animal with another resounding crack.

Dalilah gritted her teeth, her hand fisting.

The younger giraffe staggered and its long legs buckled slowly under its body. It hit the ground in a puff of red dust, the tawny rise of its torso just visible through the gold grasses. The older giraffe hovered above the fallen animal, leg raised, hoof poised to kick, his head held high. When the fallen animal struggled to stand, the old male kicked hard, and its opponent went back down.

They waited. Grasshoppers clicked. Heat shimmered. "What's going to happen?" she whispered.

"The young male will die if it's fallen flat and can't get up," Brandt explained. "These animals have hearts as heavy as a human head, so they can pump blood all the way up those long necks, but lying down too long will send too much blood to their brains and they'll pass out and die. It's why they sleep standing up."

She swallowed, a strange desperation clawing up inside her. So much beauty in this land, even in this graceful fight. Yet it was combat. Harsh and deadly. Over a female, the right to mate. To create life.

The palette of this bushveldt—the stark reality of it, was just so in-your-face raw, life and death at its purest.

Hunt or be hunted, kill or be killed.

Just as she and Brandt were being hunted now, and could be killed.

When the fallen giraffe failed to get up, Brandt started the ignition and they began to move away. Dalilah turned in her seat, hoping. But he didn't rise from the grass.

"You okay?" he said gently.

She bit her lip, nodded, thinking that even while on the run, Brandt had stolen a moment to stop and point those animals out to her, that he'd stayed to appreciate this world he inhabited, this Africa that she, too, loved. Curiosity about him deepened within her.

"Your name, Brandt," she said quietly. "It comes from an Afrikaans word, doesn't it?"

"Dutch. It means burned, or to burn."

"Figures," she said with a wry twist of her mouth.

He raised his brow, glanced at her.

"You were born in South Africa?"

"Yeah." But he offered nothing more. Dalilah figured it was as much as she was going to get right now.

The early-morning sun had turned the raging floodwaters of the Tsholo River a burnished, seething chocolate color.

"There's nothing here!" Amal snapped at his tracker. He could feel time bleeding through his fingers and he was not prepared to lose the Al Arif princess's trail. Not when he'd gotten so close, had almost tasted his revenge.

Sweat beaded along his tracker's brow as the man once more tried to cut for sign along the riverbank. But there was no trace of them at all along this stretch of the Tsholo. Horses whinnied and his other men shifted on their feet.

"Mbogo," Amal yelled. "Fetch Jacob!"

Mbogo went to get the old man and pushed him in front of Amal.

"Why do you think they went north from the plane and not down here?"

"If they came by the sky," said the old man, "then they probably have a long way to go. And now they have no more transport. If they are to go this long way on foot, they'll need water, food, some shoes for the lady. Maybe they'll want some more transport. From the sky the pilot would have seen a safari bush camp that lies north of here. A smart man would go to the camp first for supplies, and then try to cross the river before the flood. I think they're on the other side already."

Amal's body vibrated with rage.

"Get my tracker," he growled quietly to Mbogo through his teeth, then he turned back to Jacob. "Are you certain?"

"No, boss, but a hunter must track with his eyes and his head and his heart. This is what things are telling me."

Amal inhaled deeply as Mbogo brought forward the tracker he'd enlisted in Zambia.

"Get on your knees," Amal commanded as he unholstered his pistol. The man looked shocked.

"Now!"

He knelt before Amal, who pressed the nose of his gun to the man's forehead and looked at Jacob. "This is what'll happen to you if you mislead me." Amal curled his finger round the trigger.

Jacob closed his eyes, turned his head away.

"Watch!" Amal yelled.

Slowly, Jacob met the Arab man's eyes. In their depths he saw the Devil. Amal fired.

His tracker slumped forward to the ground.

"We try it your way now, Jacob. Find that pilot and the princess for me, and you'll live."

Not for one moment did Jacob believe this Devil would allow him to live once he'd found his prey. From the bottom of his soul, Jacob understood he had to kill this man before the man killed him. But first he would have to lead him close, very close, to what he was seeking. Then it would be Jacob's chance.

Quietly the old man clicked his tongue for Jock to follow him and started back across the grassland toward Tautona's airplane.

They passed through an area of tall trees where baboons swung, limb to limb in the canopy above them. The animals stopped and stared as they drove under the branches.

When they left the trees, all the birds seemed to fall mysteriously silent apart from one. *Ha! Ha! HaaHaa!*

Dalilah swatted at a cloud of insects, tension coiling tight inside her.

HaHa-di-Daaaa!

Brandt flicked open the glove compartment, took out a plastic tube and tossed it to her.

"Bug repellent."

Silently Dalilah opened the tube and patted the white cream around her neck, the chemical scent making her feel queasy.

Hah hah haaaa! Di daaaaaaa...Ha! She willed the bird to shut up as she scanned the trees for sight of it. But she couldn't locate it.

HahaHaHaaaa!

Again, that ominous feeling of being observed by unseen eyes came over her. As if their progress was being communicated and telegraphed ahead of them as they went, as if the bush was a whole sentient thing, merely allowing them passage. But always watching.

"Do you think they've found our tracks on the Zimbabwe side yet?" she said.

"Yup. But they'll be held up by the river for a day or so. Once they cross and find our camp, however, they'll come fast."

Dalilah's thoughts turned to their campsite the previous night. The leopard. The baobab. Him.

"What did you mean, Brandt, about a vow never to kill again?"

"It's nothing."

"It's not noth—"

"It's *not* your business, okay. Don't worry about it." His words were clipped.

"I was just wonder—"

"Forget it, Dalilah. I just said it to drive home a point, to get your mind back on track. It's got zip to do with you."

Irritation spiked through her. Every now and then it was as if his guard came down, and she felt she connected with this guy, felt that they shared a bond. Then it was as if he flicked a switch.

"It's got everything to do with me," she snapped. "You said as much yourself—that rescuing *me* forced you to kill a man back there at the lodge. You said *I* made you break a vow not to kill another man, or woman. Did you kill a woman, Brandt? What woman?"

Any hint of congeniality vaporized instantly as a cold hard anger altered his features and his hands fisted around the wheel. Right away Dalilah knew she'd hit *the* nerve in Brandt Stryker. He *had* killed a woman.

Part of her brain screamed to drop the subject right here. But she couldn't.

"Who was she, Brandt? What happened ten years ago?"

"Dalilah," he said very quietly, "I'm not looking to make friends, nor tell my life story. My mission is to get you to a safe place, and to call your brother. He will either come fetch you, or send someone to take you off my hands."

"So I'm just a package to be picked up and dropped off."

"Yes," he said. Then, as if he couldn't stop himself, either, he said, "And then you can be nicely handed over to King Haram."

"Haroun!"

"Whatever."

She glared at him, her blood starting to boil, her face going hot. "Where do you know my brother from, anyway?" she demanded.

"I told you, Omair and I used to work together." His voice was going tighter, lower, even quieter. Warning flushed through her. But she was like a runaway train now, unable to pull the brakes, heading downhill no matter the cost.

"And you said you owe him—why?"

Brandt flashed her a fierce look, his wolf eyes like slits, warning her to back down. "I *told* you already. Omair saved my life. So let's drop it."

"How did he save your life—what happened?"

He fixed his gaze dead ahead, fists clenched on the wheel, as he negotiated a particularly rocky section.

"Look, Princess," he said, the jeep swaying, "save your energy, because you're going to need it. This is not a social trip. You don't need to know me, and I don't need to know you. Let's just get this over with."

She muttered in Arabic, repressing the urge rising in her to punch him, to beat out the information, make him drop the damn barriers. One trait she'd never managed to outgrow was curiosity and dogged determination to ferret out the truth, especially if someone tried to thwart her from doing so.

He swerved sharply as the jeep cut too close to another acacia tree and the branches raked down the side of the vehicle, slapping inside. She ducked back, but not in time. A thorn ripped through her sleeve, splitting open her skin. Blood welled. Dalilah's eyes burned with pain and frustration.

"I told you to keep your hands in!" he snapped.

"I did! You're doing this on purpose. You're a pig!"

"Yup."

"I know you care—I *felt* you care!"

His gaze shot to her, eyes crackling. She was getting to him, rattling his cage. Things were shaking loose inside— she could see it in his eyes, in the set of his features, the tension in his neck.

"You know *nothing,* Dalilah, and it's none of your goddamn business what happened in my past. I don't know what you hope to achieve by pressing me like this."

"I'm pressing because I want to know what happened to the nice guy who rescued me last night. The guy who fixed my arm and helped me through the darkest hours of dawn. Who..." Her voice cracked. "Who kept my morale up. Who...who kissed me."

Angrily she swiped the tears pooling in her eyes.

"You want to know why I kissed you, Dalilah? Is that

what this is about? I'm a red-blooded male, that's why. And you looked pretty damn hot in that body-hugging cocktail gown. I carried you on my back, and it felt good—it gave me an itch I needed to scratch."

"Damn you," she spat at him.

"You did a bloody good job of kissing me back," he countered crisply.

Her cheeks went hotter, a fire burning into her stomach, embarrassment twisting through her chest.

"Why did you do that?" he said.

But as Dalilah opened her mouth, she realized the stupidity of what she was trying to say—that she'd kissed him because he...what? Had awakened something in her? Lust? A need she didn't know she even had? Because in spite of his overbearing attitude she'd been drawn to the tenderness underneath all that brawn, and that he was sexy as all get out himself. Rough. Raw. Ready. And she hadn't realized how much she liked that, or what she might be missing for the rest of her life. She inhaled deeply, scrubbed her hand over her face.

"I must have had an itch of my own," she said quietly.

"Touché," he said. "Next time save your itch for your fiancé."

"Oh, you're a real bitter piece of work, you know that," she whispered, turning away from him, humiliated.

The humidity and heavy silence that weighed down between them became almost unbearable as they traversed an endless plateau of smooth rock that trapped the sun's heat and radiated it back at them. A snake, long, black with a yellow stripe, slithered out of their way and into a dark crevice. Dalilah worried her engagement ring, turning it round and round her swollen finger, angry at herself for starting the argument, and for the need she felt now to defend herself. But no matter how she thought about coming at a defense, she knew this tough-ass mercenary who'd been around the block more than a few times would not understand.

How could she explain that she'd been in Haroun's company a total of five times in her life? She could count the occasions on one hand. And each time had been in the presence of a royal chaperone, as per traditional decree. The wedding contract stipulated the couple follow a traditional courtship, and as per Sa'ud custom, once a woman had met with a man in this manner, this many times, it constituted an engagement anyway, contract or not.

But she'd never kissed Haroun, barely even touched him, apart from posing for official engagement photographs. It was decreed she come to the marriage utterly pure.

Dalilah had been raised to accept this. It was her royal heritage, and her duty to her kingdom, to fulfill this political contract. And it was a relatively small price to pay compared to what the rest of her family had sacrificed and endured for their kingdom. Da'ud, her eldest brother, had been assassinated on his yacht in Barcelona as he slept. Her parents had also been assassinated—throats slit in their palace bed. Zakir, next in line to the throne, had been forced to give up his career to take the throne at a time of violent unrest while he'd tried to hide the fact that he'd been going blind. Omair in turn had been doomed to hunt the globe in an attempt to unveil the assassins and exact revenge. And pulling the strings, creating all the problems that had plagued the Al Arifs, had been the Ghaffars, led by Aban Ghaffar, aka The Moor.

To learn that his son Amal was here, in Africa, alive— to discover that this violent battle for their lives and kingdom was not over—was terrifying. Overwhelming.

The least Dalilah could do was forge ahead and fulfill her marriage obligations with Haroun. The political alliance would strengthen the Al Na'Jar army and economy. Sa'ud and other Middle Eastern allies would come to their defense if needed.

She *had* to do this even more so now to protect her brothers, their growing families. And the innocent people of her nation.

This was not a time for inner conflict and selfish desire.

Dalilah stared out over the dry scrub, the red rocks of the Botswana plains, and wished she could return to the clear convictions she'd once held.

It shouldn't feel as difficult as it did—Haroun was a striking and likable man. He seemed kind, smart, easy enough to be with. But there was no chemistry at all. How could she tell Brandt what his kiss had truly done to her? Or why she *had* even kissed him, or how it all fed into the mounting insecurities and fears over her own future with Haroun?

Sure, she might come to feel something for Haroun. But the idea that she might never, ever experience true love, the giddy highs of real passion—the stuff of films and great books, emotions that drove people to fight wars, create magnificent art, build soaring temples—depressed her.

As much as Brandt mocked her for being royal, it wasn't easy. She couldn't have the things normal people aspired to, even though her needs as a woman might be just as deep and real as the next woman's.

He reached into the backseat suddenly, yanked out the whiskey bottle, held it between his thighs as he unscrewed the cap, took a deep swallow. She watched his Adam's apple working, and slow fingers of desire tickled down inside her…she couldn't help it. Even now.

He held the bottle out to her.

"Want some?"

"No."

He took another sip, then recapped it.

"What are you seeking alcoholic relief from? Me?"

He gave a hard, dry, hard laugh. "I'm not seeking relief. It's the breakfast of kings. Oh, wait, not *your* kind of king."

Her jaw dropped. "You're *jealous?*"

He barked another laugh, pressing down on the gas, and bouncing the jeep in a way that forced her to grab the roll bar for balance.

"Jealousy doesn't suit you, you know."

"Suits me just fine."

"I thought you'd want to stay sharp, not drunk," she said.

"This is me being sharp, sweetness."

She cursed at him in Arabic again and he drove faster, jouncing her around in the front seat.

"So that's it—you despise me because I'm engaged to a man with more money and power than you'll ever have, yet I still kissed you."

"Jesus, Dalilah, give it up, will you? It's just a freaking kiss."

"You think I'm promiscuous, cheating on him, betraying him, is that it? Is it that simple?"

"I'm a simple guy."

"Oh, *that's* amusing! Simple is the last thing you are. You're a…a cantankerous bull with issues over your past and…God knows what else."

He snorted.

"See? You even sound like one."

He spun abruptly to face her, and she recoiled slightly at the sudden ferocity in his features. "You want the truth,

Dalilah? Here it is—" he turned back to face the terrain "—I don't do commitment and I like to be with women who don't do commitment, either. No promises. Just straight-up good sex. Both sides understand the equation and want nothing more. I do *not* have a problem with promiscuity."

Blood flared hot into her face. "So what is the problem?"

"The problem is you. *You* do commitment. *You* made the choice to marry Haram—"

"Haroun!"

"You made him a promise by wearing a rock big enough to feed a small goddamn country, and you know what? While I don't do commitment as a matter of routine, when I *do* choose to make a promise, that's everything in my book. Believe it or not, I do have honor, and I'm loyal to a goddamn fault. Just ask your brother. It's why I went to work with men like him—men who promise to leave no man behind, and know how to keep that promise. And it's why he came to get me out of a hellhole in Nicaragua— he wouldn't leave me behind. And that, Princess, is why I owe Omair. That's why I'm here saving your pretty little ass right now, because Omair knows I owe him, and that I'll die before I let you get hurt." He clamped his mouth shut as he swerved sharply round a steep rock, almost tipping the jeep onto its side.

"Doesn't mean I have to be nice about it," he muttered as he gunned the jeep into an expanse of sand dotted with squat Mopani.

Dalilah stared at his rugged profile, assimilating this new information, her heart thudding wildly in her chest. "You think I have no honor? You think *I* don't keep a promise? Because that's not true! You have *no* idea what I'm prepared to give up for a promise not even made by—"

"Just stop talking, okay."

Her eyes widened. "Where in hell do you get off—"

"I was in that other man's position, Dalilah," he snapped angrily. "Not once, but twice. Call me a fool, but I didn't learn from the first time around and a woman just like you burned my ass. Then got killed for it."

Her mouth dropped. "That's not…you don't understand. I—"

"I don't want to understand."

He drove faster, harder, sending up clouds of fine gray dust that coated the trees, giving them a ghostly air of menace in the heat. Vegetation closed in again, as if the bush was deliberately trying to block their way.

Brandt swung round a thick clump of Mopani, and dead ahead in the track, hemmed in by trees on either side, loomed a large bull elephant with crooked tusks.

He slammed on the brakes.

Silence descended as dust rose in soft billows around them. Time stretched, warped, shimmered in the heat. The elephant was so close Dalilah could see individual hairs poking out of its leathery skin. Two egrets rode on his shoulders and tracks of dark moisture leaked like tears from behind his eyes.

The bull raised its trunk, catching their scent, and his ears flapped out wide. The egrets took flight.

Her heart began to slam against her ribs.

"Don't. Move," Brandt whispered.

She couldn't if she tried. She was paralyzed with fear. Her attention shifted to the animal's tusks, then to the moisture tracking through gray dust on the inside of the bull's back legs. His penis arced almost to the ground.

The bull flapped his ears in and out, swayed his tusks.

Slowly, carefully, Brandt shifted the gears into Reverse. But before he could even touch the gas, the bull's ears suddenly flattened against his head and he curled up in his trunk, lowering his head.

"Oh, hell," Brandt whispered, hitting the gas. *"He's coming!"*

Chapter 8

The elephant charged in a thundering cloud of boiling dust. Brandt floored the accelerator, one hand gripping the steering wheel, his other arm over the backseat as he tried to keep an eye on both the advancing bull while blasting the jeep backward at full throttle through thick sand. He swerved round a clump of trees, tires whirring up dirt, brush catching under the chassis.

Bang!

The jeep jarred as something hit underneath. *Crap.* And the bloody bull was still coming. Swinging the wheel hard, sweat drenching his shirt, blood pounding in his ears, he fishtailed backward around an outcrop of red rock.

The bull slowed near the outcrop, then stopped, his ears fanning in and out from his head. Brandt kept going, engine whining—he wasn't certain the charge was over—but his heart sank as, in the sand in front of the jeep, trailed a black swath that was pouring out from under their vehicle like blood from a severed artery.

He brought the jeep to a stop in soft sand, his attention riveted on the animal as he carefully read the bull's body language, the position of his ears, trunk. The elephant's ears flared slowly out then in once more, as if deciding whether to charge again, then he turned and loped slowly into a copse of trees in the distance. Leaves began to shiver as the bull took out his grievance against the trunk of the tallest tree.

Brandt turned off the ignition, furious with himself. This entire area was populated with Mopani that had been eaten uniformly squat by elephants—he should've been on the lookout for the giant pachyderms. Instead, his blood had been raging and his brain clouded by this fiercely intriguing—and damn sexy—princess he was supposed be saving, not getting stomped to death by a sexually frustrated bull in musth.

Like the goddamn situation with Carla—he'd let himself get sucked in, and it could have gotten Dalilah killed.

They sat for a while, dust settling around them, on them. Heat pressed down, the sounds and scents of the bush filtering back into their consciousness as they watched the dusty gray giant in the distance.

"Jesus, that's one mean-ass, sexually frustrated bastard." Brandt turned to Dalilah. Her black eyes were huge, her face bloodless and streaked with dust. "You all right?"

She nodded, her gaze flicking nervously to where the beast was uprooting his tree as she reached up to wipe sweat from her brow with a trembling hand. The gesture smudged a gray streak of dirt across her face.

Brandt stared at the streak, adrenaline still slamming through his body.

"How did you know it was going to charge?" she whispered. "Usually it's a mock charge."

"Usually?"

"I…I've been on a safari before. Sometimes the game-viewing vehicles get too close, and the elephant does a little run, but it never ends in a full-blown charge."

"Did you see the moisture down the sides of his face?"

"The tears?"

"Not tears. Temporin from glands behind his eyes. And the urine dribbling down the insides of his leg—" Brandt nodded toward the shuddering tree. "That young bull is in full musth—high as a kite on sex hormones. That sharp, bitter odor was a dead giveaway. Humans can usually pick up that scent from a few hundred meters away." He paused. "I should've noticed before we even got into that situation."

"I didn't notice anything."

"Not your job to." He dragged his hand over hair thick with dust, then he swore softly. "You could see he meant business the instant he tucked his trunk under and his ears back out of harm's way. Musth bulls, especially the young ones, can be extremely aggressive and unpredictable. You need to give them a wide berth."

"Like someone else I know."

He looked at her in surprise, then threw his head back and laughed. The release felt damn good. Talk about sexual frustration—this woman could read him like a book and had the nerve to say so.

"I get the impression you only smile or laugh when everything around you is going to hell in a handbasket," she said, a glimmer of amusement twitching at the corners of her own gorgeous mouth.

"Damn," he said softly as the laughter eased and tears of mirth leaked into the dust around his own eyes. "You take the cake, woman." He gave another snort of laughter, then, as he sobered, he said more quietly, "I could really get to like you, you know."

She went silent. They sat like that for a while, hearts racing, adrenaline pounding, a kinetic energy arcing between them, pulling them together even as they both fought against the sexual impulse. Slowly, very slowly, Brandt reached up, even as his brain screamed *don't,* and he touched her, wiping the dirt from her brow with the pad of his thumb.

Her gaze held his, dark, loaded. His groin went hard and he couldn't breathe.

"You're getting dirty, Princess."

She broke the gaze, looking down at the diamond ring on her hand in the sling.

Before he could say anything, she'd turned away from him, hair falling in a curtain across her cheek, hiding her expression.

"Dalilah?"

"It's nothing." But her voice was thick.

Brandt frowned as empathy squeezed his chest. He was feeling all sorts of emotions he didn't want, but in spite of his best efforts, Princess was winning, and he was powerless around her. Brandt didn't like the feeling.

Irritably he grabbed the rifle and climbed out of the jeep. He dropped to his knees and peered under the chassis. Oil pooled heavy and dark in the sand, confirming his worst fears—a ruptured sump. He reached under the vehicle to dip a finger into the liquid to be certain.

"Brandt!"

"Just a sec. I need to—"

"Brandt!"

He bumped his head as he jerked back out from under the jeep and peered up over the hood. His heart stalled at the terror on her face. She pointed.

"He's coming back!"

Brandt spun round. *Holy crap.* The bull was not content with his tree—the big bad pachyderm was heading their way in another cloud of boiling dust.

He braced a hand on top of the door, hurtling clean into the driver's seat and dumping the rifle on her lap. Firing the ignition, he hit the gas and slammed the gears into Reverse, wheeling hard and spinning the jeep around a hundred and eighty degrees. He floored the accelerator, bombing forward through scrub, bashing against rocks. The elephant loomed in the rearview mirror and the trail of black blood leaking from the jeep's innards grew thinner and thinner. Panic clawed at Brandt's throat—the engine was going to seize any second now, but the bull was closing the gap. He began planning how to get Dalilah out of the vehicle should they stall.

"He's falling back!" Dalilah yelled suddenly. She was twisted round, rifle balanced on the back of her seat, aiming and ready to fire with one hand.

Brandt glanced up into the rearview mirror. The elephant was dropping back into a trot.

He slowed the jeep, but kept going until the animal turned and started retreating, this time heading toward a faint wisp of gold spindrift rising above the Mopani scrub. Relief gushed through Brandt's chest—the bull was rejoining his herd, finally. But the jeep's engine coughed, choked and stalled.

He sat back, breathing hard.

Dalilah was, too.

Brandt pounded his fist on the dash, angry. This was a good vehicle—it could have gotten them far. He might have been able to mend the oil pan, but now that he'd run the engine without oil until it died, it was toast. Their jeep was dead, done, gone.

She watched him, then glanced nervously into the cloud

of dust settling in their wake, silence suddenly loud, not even the call of a bird, or the sound of insects.

"You really can't fix it?"

"No," he said. "I can't goddamn fix it."

He raked his hand through his dark blond hair again, dust making it stand up in front. He swore again, softly.

"I'm sorry, Dalilah."

"Brandt, you saved my life a couple of times over already. You have *nothing* to be sorry about." She reached for his thigh. A touch, just fingertips against skin. A quiver ran through his muscles, like a small electrical shock chasing over his skin.

"And now that I'm still alive," she said softly, voice thick, "I have to say, that was truly incredible to witness. Honest."

He looked slowly into her eyes.

"You mean it," he said. It wasn't a question. She really did get off on the thrill. Everything about this woman was exciting, unanticipated. There was nothing safe about her at all.

"I keep forgetting," he said quietly, devouring her with his eyes. "You're no newcomer to Africa. How many safaris have you been on?"

The guttural sound of his voice curled into her chest, the intensity in his ice-blue eyes cutting her to the quick. But something in Dalilah hardened as she saw where he was going with this—he was aiming for his switch again, seeking something to dislike in her, a way to shut her out.

"A few," she said guardedly.

"And before you arrive at the safari destination of your choice, you fill in one of those forms, check off what animals you want to see? A lion kill. An elephant charge. Like going to Disneyland. Big tip to the guide at the end of the trip if he delivers?"

She removed her hand from his thigh.

"I thought," she said quietly, "that you might be trying to irritate me, get under my skin in order to keep me angry. Or that maybe you were being a jerk because you had issues over something in your past. But I was wrong." She paused, looked up and directly into his eyes. "You're just a prick. An arrogant, self-absorbed, pigheaded bastard."

He said nothing.

Tension simmered between them. Sexual. Fierce. She could see it in his face. She could feel it in herself. And in the distant sky dark forms circled. Vultures.

She turned away. "Fine. You've got your assignment from my brother, you've got a package to deliver so you can get paid. Where do we go now, and how?"

Abruptly he reached for the rifle in her lap. He yanked open the glove compartment, removed a pouch with maps. Unhooking the GPS from the dash, he swung open his door and jumped out.

Brandt spread the map out on the hood and bent over to study it, sun beating down on his back, his skin gleaming with sweat. Dalilah watched the lion tattoo on his biceps as his muscle flexed when he moved. *Tautona.* They were right—he was a gnarly scarred lion of a man without a pride or the social skills required to belong to one. No wonder he prowled and hunted alone, lived in his own territory.

Sweat pearled and dribbled down between her breasts, the sling and splint making her feel irritably hot. She glanced up as a massive bird flew low overhead, its wings beating with a soft *whoosh whoosh whoosh* through the air. A snake writhed in its beak. There was a scent of hay, or sage, coming from the grass and in the distance she saw dark shapes moving slowly. Buffalo? Nerves whispered and Dalilah's attention shifted to the rifle lying on the hood near Brandt's hand. She just wanted this over now.

"We need to go on foot," he said, fiddling with the GPS.

"Obviously."

He shot her a sharp glance.

Dalilah recoiled at the look in his icy eyes. More softly she said, "Which way?"

He jerked his head to the map. "You want to see, come look."

She muttered a curse, got out, went round the hood to stand beside him. The sun baked down on them like a furnace and Dalilah realized just how much she was going to miss the shade provided by the jeep's cover.

"This is where we were headed via vehicle—" He pointed to the topographical map, the hairs on his bronzed arm gleaming gold in the sun, his skin glistening. "Along the plain, toward this rift." He jerked his chin up to the horizon. "The rift is that way—it's a big cliff that runs for several kilometers. The idea was to drive north where the terrain levels out a bit, and then drive up onto the plateau here." He jabbed his finger on the map. "From this point the plan was to head to the paved road here."

He pointed to a thin line bisecting the eastern part of Botswana from the South African to the Zambian border. Dalilah squinted against the glare of the sun and shaded her eyes, studying the map, conscious of the scent of him. And the smell of oil and dust.

"That road serves as a main thoroughfare for occasional truck convoys carrying oranges from Zambia, copper from the Congo, laborers, cattle. It bisects a game conservation area here, where I wanted to cut off the road and head through bush to the west, there." He jabbed his finger at a space of nothing.

"What's there?"

He rubbed the dark blond stubble appearing on his jaw, not looking at her, thinking. "My farm," he said quietly.

"Your *farm?*"

He didn't answer. He was busy plotting a route into the GPS. He glanced up, squinting into the distance. "Now we'll have to walk directly west to the rift wall, and climb up. On one hand it'll be slow. But it will also save us having to drive a full day north in order to access the plateau via jeep. You up to a hike?"

"Do I have an option?"

"Nope." He hooked the GPS onto his belt. "Amal will have found my plane by now and be looking for a way over the Tsholo. Like I said, they'll come fast—our tracks will have baked like clay into the mud. If we climb up the cliff, they won't be able to follow us up the face with horses or jeeps. They'll still have to drive the full day north to get up onto the plateau and then they'll have to cut back again for our tracks. It'll buy us a small advantage."

Fear coiled cold and tight in Dalilah's gut as she thought of Da'ud, his throat slit in his bed, of her dead parents. Of all the terrible things the Ghaffar clan had done to her family and country. Amal would spare her no mercy— she knew that. Her death would be violent. He'd make her suffer, and he'd make her brothers suffer, too.

Shading her eyes, Dalilah squinted into the distant glare. Heat shimmered off the veldt in waves. It would be just her and Brandt out there, crossing these Botswana plains. She wasn't sure that they'd make it, but it was better than waiting for Amal.

"Can we take the two-way radio from the jeep dashboard?" she asked quietly.

"No one to communicate with." He went around to the back of the jeep and opened the rear compartment. Dalilah watched as he took out a blackened kettle and a small camp stove, which he balanced on a flat rock. Filling the kettle from the water container on the backseat, he lit the stove and set water to boil.

"Keep an eye on the kettle," Brandt said as he began emptying the backpack he'd stolen, laying the contents out on the backseat, deciding what to take, what to leave. Out of the pack came a small cosmetics bag, a wallet and a camera with zoom lens.

"Arm all right?" he said, opening the first-aid kit, selecting supplies.

"Fine."

He shot her a quick glance. "It doesn't hurt?"

"Not much."

"Good."

She felt like a spare part waiting for water to boil as he busied himself selecting items and stuffing them into the pack.

"Here." He tossed her a khaki hat. It came spinning through the air and dropped into the dirt just short of her reach. She picked it up, dusted it off and was about to put it on her head of thick, dust-caked tangle of hair when she stopped.

"Do you have a spare piece of string, or a shoelace, or something?"

He glanced up, crooked a brow.

"To tie up my hair."

For an instant he looked dumfounded. "I…uh, ya." Using his pocketknife, Brandt severed a strip off a finely woven triangle bandage from the first-aid kit. He held the strip out to her.

"Could you help me? I can't do it with one hand."

A flicker chased through his cool eyes. He didn't want to touch her again.

"Sure," he said, coming over.

Dalilah lifted her hair off the nape of her neck. It was hot and thick, and she was relieved to have it off her skin.

"I'd love to braid it, but that's probably beyond your expertise, so could you just tie a ponytail?"

She felt him hesitate, then grasp her hair. His fingers brushed against the sensitive skin on the back of her neck and goose bumps chased down her spine. Dalilah swallowed. It was like this man was permanently charged with electricity and each time he connected with her body, she grounded the charge.

He pulled and yanked at her dust-caked curls and she realized he *was* actually trying to braid it. Emotion, sharp and sudden, pricked her eyes, even as a wry smile crossed her lips.

"There," he said, stepping back, examining his handiwork.

Dalilah reached behind her head and fingered the braid. "Not bad," she said, turning around. "You surprise me."

They were close again, face-to-face. His gaze held hers for several beats, then flickered to her mouth, and heat pooled low in her belly.

He grunted, quickly averting his face as he bent down to take the kettle off the gas as it came to a rolling boil. "If a man can tie flies, I don't see why he can't braid hair." He turned off the gas and poured water into a pale yellow enamel mug containing a tea bag.

Another little revelation about him, thought Dalilah—he farmed and he liked to fly-fish. She found the idea of those rough, strong hands working with tiny colorful threads and feathers and beads as he sought to imitate insects by creating the small lures oddly endearing. Maybe it was because she'd seen her own father do this—fly-fishing had been one of the king's pleasures, and her dad had taken her on several fishing trips to remote and exotic lodges in Norway and Canada. A deep sadness sank through her chest at the thought of her father, his assassination. And it brought sharply to mind the marriage contract with Haroun, the impending wedding, and Dalilah suddenly felt exhausted. She seated herself on a rock and put the hat on her head, shading herself from the climbing sun.

"Powdered milk? Sugar?" he asked without looking at her.

"Black. Three sugars."

That made him look up. "Sweet tooth?"

She gave a shrug. "Why else would anyone call me 'sweetness'?"

That made the corner of his lip quiver as he repressed a smile.

"Careful. Enamel is hot, stays hot," he said as he handed her the mug.

The tea was dark and sweet and tasted like nectar.

He opened a plastic baggie and offered it out to her. "Biltong?

She regarded the dark twists of dried meat in the bag.

"Kudu," he said. "It's like jerky, except better. Spiced and salty—salt will help with the sweat loss."

"I know what it is. Thanks, but no."

"Dalilah—"

"I'm not hungry."

"Suit yourself." He repackaged the biltong, not taking anything for himself.

"It's not because it's meat," she said. "I'm just not hungry."

He shrugged. He was busy fiddling with the camera, inspecting the zoom.

"Looks expensive," she said as she sipped her tea.

"Poor tourists from Germany had their bags all packed

for a morning game drive." He stuffed the camera into the pack. "They wouldn't have gone anywhere in that rain, though."

"Is that an attempt to assuage your guilt for stealing their stuff?"

"I was just doing my job."

"Even if it means robbing others in order to collect your paycheck at the end of the day?" She took another sip of tea. "I guess that's the definition of *mercenary*."

He resecured the sleeping bag to the bottom of the pack, which was looking rather big and heavy now. "You can't push my buttons, Dalilah."

"I'm sure I can."

He shot her a challenging glance. "You sure you want to risk it?"

She laughed.

"Glad the tea is making you feel perkier. Save that energy—you're going to need it."

Dalilah finished her tea and watched him move. She loved the powerful shape of his legs, the way his back muscles rolled under his damp shirt, his efficiency of movement despite his bulk. Dalilah thought of his words again.

When I do choose to make a promise, that's everything in my book.

Again the urge rose in her to explain herself to him, but she tamped it down this time.

Just survive this, survive him, and all will go back to feeling normal. You have to do this for your father, your country, your family...

Brandt poured the rest of the whiskey from the large bottle into a silver hip flask that he'd taken from the side pocket of his safari shorts. She thought of his drinking, his issues with his past. Her brother.

"Why'd you quit the Force du Sable?" she said suddenly.

He paused, then continued pouring.

"I didn't say I worked for the FDS."

"You said you were an ex-merc and that you worked with my brother. He was with the FDS until he took over the military in Al Na'Jar, and he's still allied with the private army."

He grunted.

"So, why did you quit?"

"The thing about being a merc," he said, screwing the cap onto the flask, "for me, anyway, is you've got to believe in the jobs you take. You have to know why you're prepared to kill someone for cash. When you're a soldier fighting for your country, you still get paid, but you get orders that technically you can't refuse. It kind of absolves a soldier from the personal responsibility of murder. I didn't have that absolution, and there came a day when the monetary reward no longer justified the act of killing. What used to be easy no longer was."

She stared at him.

"So you stopped believing, and you quit."

"Something like that."

"Was it a particular incident that provoked this?" *A woman.*

He cut free the rest of the rope that laced the jeep canopy to the bull bars and began coiling it.

"There's always one job that does you in," he said, tying the coil of rope to the bottom of the pack with the kettle. "You think cops, soldiers, become inured to violence? They don't. That's for fiction and TV. What really happens is they keep pushing it all down until something snaps." He held out his hand out for the mug. "You ready to roll?"

She flicked the dregs of her tea into the bush, got to her feet, came up to him.

"What was it, Brandt—what happened? Was it that woman you mentioned, the one you said died because of you? The one who burned you with a broken promise?"

"Like I said, Dalilah, my past is not your business. And your future is not mine."

Her lips tightened. He took the cup from her and stuffed it into the pack, closing the flap and buckling it tight.

"Yet you believe in *this* mission?"

He held her eyes a long, simmering moment. And she could feel his conflict, feel a lot of things.

"Like I said, I owe your brother. And I *never* renege on a promise." He turned and hefted the pack onto his shoulders. "Even if it's a bitter pill to swallow. Next time, the sheik owes me."

He snagged his rifle.

"And what pound of flesh would you want to exact from Omair?"

His eyes dipped over her body, almost as if involuntarily, and he opened his mouth as if to say something, then changed his mind, ignoring her question instead.

"Remember, single file, behind me. Do everything, and I mean everything, I say. This is lion country. If you run, you're lunch. Like I said, there's nothing here you can outrun anyway. Best to stand your ground."

He started out ahead, rifle propped against his shoulder, muzzle aimed into the air. Dalilah sucked in a deep breath, and she followed.

The sun climbed to its zenith in the empty vault of a sky, turning white-hot. There was barely any shade or shadow with the low scrawny scrub, and not even a wisp of cloud now. The heat was furnacelike. Insects buzzed and the grass rustled as they walked.

Dalilah focused on the rhythmic sound of their footfalls. They were moving along a game track—the internet of the bushveldt, Brandt called it, where animals read the stories of who was going where and doing what. She could make out the heart-shaped prints of cloven-hoof ruminants, large and small. The pattern of a snake in red sand.

Sweat began drying on her skin now, even as it formed. She saw a lion print to the side of the track, big as her splayed hand. She knew it was a lion from a previous safari—rounded pad prints like a giant kitty, no nail marks because of feline retractable claws. Dalilah glanced up and scanned the plain. The grass around them was longer, taller now, and tawny. The sense of being watched, hunted, prickled over her skin once more.

Dalilah sped up a little to be closer to Brandt and the gun. To keep herself focused in spite of the heat and fatigue, she forced herself to concentrate on Brandt's powerful legs, the slide of his calf muscles under deeply tanned skin, the happy little sway of the black kettle at the bottom of his pack. Brandt Stryker, her only safety net out here. Her source of protection, food, water.

But as they moved toward the hazy red cliffs now visible in the shimmering distance, Dalilah got a sense that the deeper he led her into this hot, wild terrain, the more she was going to be forced up against a wall within herself.

And when she got there, what would she do?

Would her future survive this epic journey? Would it survive *him*?

Chapter 9

Brandt studied the sky, wishing for another storm that might hide their tracks. Instead, the sun hammered down relentlessly, baking their tracks into the earth. Best he could do for now was keep moving fast toward the rift wall and get up onto the plateau before nightfall.

He'd chosen this route on the map because there was an abandoned airstrip atop the plateau with a tiny old customs building. He'd landed there years ago, and even though the building was in ruins now, it would provide shelter from predators during the night. There was also a tiny village about a day's trek from the airstrip. He might find a vehicle there.

Several hours later the sun had changed its angle and Dalilah began to lag farther and farther behind. Frustration bit into Brandt as he checked his watch—almost 1:00 p.m.

"Keep up, Dalilah! We need to get up the cliff before dark!"

"I'm trying—these boots are too big."

He paused, waiting for her to catch up. But she was tiring, her gait shortening, and she was stumbling repeatedly in the oversize men's boots. It was wasting her energy. The wool socks he'd given her were good, but she was going to get blisters. Still, she'd have to live with some pain if she wanted to get out of this alive.

Again he berated himself for losing the jeep, losing focus. For letting her get under his skin and pry into his life. As he waited for her to catch up, tension torqued tighter—this was not a good place to linger. The grass was long and tight here, and he worried about lions. He touched the hilt of his panga, then his knife, then his pouch with the bullets, mentally keeping track where everything was as he scanned the long grasses, watching for the slight twitch of a flattened ear, the flick of a dark tail, Brandt concentrated on the ambient sounds of the bush, listening for the sound of a gray lorie, the warning cough of an impala or the alarm whistle of a zebra.

Stay aware, Stryker. Don't lose it again.

When Dalilah reached him she was sweating and breathing hard, and she bent over, bracing her hand on her knee.

Brandt uncapped the water pouch, held it out.

"Drink."

"There are nicer ways to order people about," she snapped, snatching the water and drinking thirstily before he stopped her, taking it back.

"Got to ration it," he said, recapping the pouch.

"You're not having any?"

"Not until we find a new source. Maybe up there. See?" He pointed to a dark line bisecting the looming cliff face. "That could be a small waterfall, especially after the rains last night."

She squinted up, trying to catch her breath. "I need to sit for a minute."

His jaw tightened.

"Please."

Brandt relented. "Just for a second, okay? It's not a good place."

She lowered herself onto a rock, taking her hat off and dragging her hand over her hair. Despite the dust, it still gleamed rich blue-black in the sunlight. Her skin was glowing from exertion. Brandt felt he was going mad— she was more beautiful to him by the second. It was driving him to distraction—bewitched by the exotic princess.

She looked up with those big liquid black eyes fringed by long lashes.

"What are you thinking?"

He shook himself. "Nothing," he said, unhooking the GPS from his belt, and rechecking their route, waypoints.

"If you've got satellite coverage for that—" she jerked her chin at his GPS "—a satellite phone could have worked out here."

"Too bad I lost mine while saving your ass at the lodge, huh?"

Her mouth flattened. She glanced away, watched a row of red ants carrying pieces of some dead animal.

He hooked the GPS back. "Ready?"

She said nothing, but got to her feet, clearly spent.

Brandt set a slightly slower pace so she could keep up, but losing time ate at him. The sun was moving in its arc over the sky, and shadows were growing longer already— they needed to get up that cliff before darkness fell.

"What do you farm, Brandt?" Dalilah called from behind after a while. "How much land do you have?"

The question startled him. He'd hoped she'd given up poking into his personal life.

"Big enough."

"For what? Game? Cattle? Maize?"

Brandt wanted to remain silent, keep to himself, but on another level he knew talking would keep her mind off things. "My land forms part of a privately held game conservation area," he called over his shoulder. "It's a block of about ten kilometers by twenty."

"So…" She jogged a little to keep up, her voice breathless. "You offer game viewing?"

"Not in my segment."

"But your neighbors do?"

"I never see them."

"I mean, do your neighbors run safaris?"

Irritation sliced through him. "Yeah."

"Do you ever plan to?"

He stopped, spun round. "No, because I don't like people, Dalilah. Running camps for idiot tourists who ask too many stupid questions would drive me mad."

She had the audacity to smile. "You're already mad."

Brandt glared at her. "I'm thinking postal."

She met his glare. "I bet you weren't always like this."

"Like what?"

"Bitter and twisted."

He wiped sweat from his brow. "And what makes you so sure?"

"I also bet that you're trying to grow things on your land."

"So now you're psychic?"

"You called it a *farm*."

He moistened his lips.

"So, what are you trying to farm?"

"Have you forgotten we've got killers on our ass? Come on, we need to move." He resumed marching, faster now, hotter under the collar, part of him trying to escape her, even as he needed to keep her close. He thought of the whiskey in his pocket. *What are you seeking alcoholic relief from, Brandt, me?*

Yeah, he thought. *You got that right.*

But relief would not come, not even from the bottom of his whiskey flask until this was over. What unsettled him more was that he actually wanted to answer her last question, tell her what he was trying to do with his land. He never had a need to share, not this stuff. Yeah, maybe he might shoot the breeze and bounce ideas off the blokes in the pub in Gaborone, or around the safari bar while the guests slept before he flew home.

But this woman?

Maybe it was because she knew water-delivery systems, understood the complexities of farming in drought-ridden soil, understood how to deliver solar power. She came from the Sahara herself. She wasn't just an ordinary woman.

"I put a new tank up last week."

"What?"

"A water tank," he said over his shoulder. "And I installed an enhanced solar system for heating the water, with extra panels for the house, and an enlarged security fence to keep wildlife out of my growing area. The solar system will be connected to provide power for lights, radio communications, battery charging, computers, VSAT, cell-phone charging. The works. Got a borehole and windmill system, too. For the fields, I tried pumping water from the river."

She caught up again. "And what are you trying to grow in the fields?" she said, right behind him now, a fresh energy and curiosity in her voice. Brandt realized the conversation really was helpful to her. And she was truly interested, from an academic point of view.

"Maize," he said. "I started with maize. Mangoes. Macadamia nuts. Avocados. But then I lost the irrigation from the river."

"Why?"

"Some elephant destroyed the concrete delivery troughs. She must have enjoyed the feel of sinking her feet through the concrete because she walked along the troughs for kilometers, just punching through the trough. Wrecked the whole system."

"Like some people enjoy popping Bubble Wrap—will pop until an entire sheet is done."

"Bubble Wrap?" He stopped, turned around.

She tried to smile, but he could see she was beyond tired now. "You know, like that puffy plastic sheeting used to package delicate things for transport. Some people like the sensation and sound of popping the bubbles."

Something softened in Brandt, and this time he smiled. "Perhaps it's futile," he said quietly, "but my goal with the farm is really just self-sufficiency. I want to hunt only for meat, and pretty much grow everything else that I need. And then trade my produce and meat for labor and other things."

"Ah, you mean your goal is to interact with as few people as possible." In spite of her exhaustion, a wicked, teasing light twinkled in her black eyes, and suddenly Brandt saw a glimmer of her older brother in Dalilah. He was reminded of how Omair used to joke with him, how the sheik had used his wry wit to soldier through some of the toughest situations, and Brandt felt a sudden kinship—in some strange way he felt he knew this woman better than she realized. He smiled.

"Yeah," he said. "But until I am self-sufficient I still need to fly those irritating tourists across Botswana to safari lodges all the way from the Okavango to Tuli and the Makgadikgadi in between."

"Or take missions like this one."

"This is different." He handed her the water pouch as he spoke, and when she was done, he recapped the pouch. "You sure you don't want that biltong?"

"I'm sure."

Several more klicks into their trek, Dalilah spoke again.

"That plane that was stripped in Zimbabwe—it was your livelihood, then?"

Brandt grunted in affirmation as he crouched to examine prints he saw in the dust. He touched the soil gently with the pads of his fingers, then glanced up, squinting into the distance. A pack of wild dogs had just come through here. Uneasiness crept over him.

"Omair will pay," she said, "for your plane."

"Damn right he'll pay—I'm billing him for expenses." He turned in a slow circle, looking for movement in the grass.

"Right," she said quietly. "I keep forgetting—I'm just a package."

Brandt told himself not to answer. He led the way, even more watchful now. Wild dogs were not nice killers. At least a lion kill was quick, clean, quiet. But the dogs went for the stomach, ripping out intestines while the quarry was still alive. Noisy. Which tended to draw other predators to the scene fast.

But as they neared the red rift wall of rocks, she said, "When did you come to live in Botswana? How long have you actually been here?"

He blew out a breath of irritation.

"Ten years."

"The length of your vow not to kill."

His stomach tightened and a warning buzz started in his brain.

"Whereabouts in South Africa were you born?"

"Nelspruit," he said crisply. "Small Afrikaans town founded by Boers along the Crocodile River. Or it was then. It was renamed Mbombela after apartheid."

"So you grew up there?"

He grunted and bent down. More tracks. He looked up, watching the sky, birds. Listening.

"So why did you become a mercenary in the first place?" She was circling back to how he knew Omair, and how, exactly, Omair had saved him ten years ago. His head started to throb and his chest went tight. Carla was not her business. His failed marriage, his son, his farm, his old life in South Africa—not her damn business, either. Brandt had blocked that part of his history right out of his consciousness. He just didn't go there—no point. He was no longer that man.

"Dalilah, please, do me a favor, just stop talking. Just for a while."

Her jaw firmed and her cheeks pinked, a flare of hurt darting bright through her eyes. Then those almond eyes narrowed.

"I don't usually have to work this hard to get people to be civil to me."

Frustration flared across his chest.

"Then don't. Save your breath." *And mine.*

Her jaw dropped. "Look," she snapped, "if I'm going to spend the amount of time with you that it takes to get up that cliff—" she jabbed her good arm at the red-rock wall ahead of them "—and over the plateau on top, then across another half of Botswana, we might as well be civil, get to know each other."

"I know all I need to know about you, Dalilah," he

said quietly. "You're Omair's kid sister. And you're a princess—a precious commodity to your kingdom, and you're about to become queen of almighty Sa'ud. People want you back. A desperate man wants you dead. I'm the lackey in the middle."

"You know *nothing* about me!" She spat the words at him in exasperation. "I'm more than someone else's princess, someone's fiancée. Someone's commodity. I'm my own damn person, too!" She fisted her hand, and beat it against her chest. "I worked hard to get where I am, and I pay my own way, I'm a foreign investment consultant with a solid legal background. In my spare time I volunteer for ClearWater, and if I do spend my family fortune, it's always for my volunteer work. If I do use my family name, it's to raise funds for impoverished villages so that they can get access points to clear water. And yes, I attend a ton of glitzy charity events, but it's to raise funds so I can come here, to Africa, to places like Zimbabwe, and do good work. Work that makes a difference in people's lives, Brandt! And I might live in a plush Manhattan penthouse, but *I* paid for it, and I have friends there who *like* me for who I am...." Her voice hitched, and she swore, turning away, her eyes bright with tears.

She was cracking, thought Brandt. He had to go easier on her.

She spun back, calming her voice, but when she spoke it was shaky. "The only reason I'm in this position now is because my brothers weren't open with me, and I couldn't take adequate safety precautions because of it." She took off her hat, shoved back her hair, damp, tendrils stiff with mud. "How do you think *that* makes me feel? My controlling brothers taking over my life again, and then lump me in with someone like you." She rammed the hat back onto her head.

Surprise rippled through Brandt.

Then he said, very quietly, "Are you going to keep doing this charity work, keep your nice Manhattan apartment when you marry in nineteen months?"

She stared at him, the pulse at her neck racing, color in her cheeks high, maybe too high. Grasses rustled softly in a sudden hot breeze.

"Well, will you?"

Her hand went to her stomach, pressed, as if she suddenly felt sick. And he could see her searching for an answer.

"No," she said after several beats of silence, her voice not sounding quite her own. "I will work, though, for the Kingdom of Sa'ud, Haroun's diplomatic functions. I'm sure I'll find some charities—I...I'd have to live there, of course."

He took a step closer.

"And that makes you happy—that's what you want?"

She met his gaze. "Why are you asking me this?"

"Because you sound pretty damn passionate about the other stuff you were just yelling at me about. And you were so darn motivated to get me to take you to Harare to ink that water deal that you weren't even thinking about the attackers on your tail."

She swallowed, glanced away. "It's because this was my last opportunity to do something with my ClearWater work." She inhaled deeply. "I wanted to leave some kind of legacy, show that my freedom was worth something. Apart from..." She faded, her eyes gleaming with emotion.

"Freedom?" he said. "Versus marriage—is that how you see it?"

She moistened her lips.

"Yeah," he said, his eyes going to her ring. "Give it all up for some dude who owns most of the world's oil. For a moment back there in Zimbabwe, I was really impressed. But I read you wrong."

"You'd respect me more—be impressed if I *wasn't* going to marry? Marriage takes compromise."

"And what's Haroun giving up—what's his compromise?"

Her eyes flickered.

He snorted. "You're talking to the wrong man about marriage, Princess. Been there, done that, failed miserably. Sometimes compromise is not what it's cracked up to be."

"So you were married once?"

"That's none of your damn business."

She blinked, then gave him a measuring look. Brandt swallowed, his gaze locked with hers.

"What does impress you, Stryker?"

"If you're following your passion, Dalilah," he said quietly, "I'm impressed, whether you marry or not. And ClearWater, your job, your independence, is very obviously your passion." He shrugged dismissively. "Trade it all off for a life behind palace walls? I'm not seeing a clear picture here."

When she didn't reply, he said, "It must make you happy. Or you wouldn't do it."

"Yeah…it makes me happy," she snapped, though she looked anything but.

He regarded her intently, nodded his head, then turned and began to march on.

Dalilah felt sick. She couldn't move. He'd laid it all out right there. She couldn't do it—she couldn't marry Haroun. Tension coiled in her gut. But she couldn't call it off now, either. It was a binding contract, a treaty between countries. Her brother, King Zakir, was relying on it, so was his King's Council—her whole family. Her nation.

"You coming or what?" he yelled over his shoulder.

"I didn't ask for your approval," she called after him. "I don't care what you think!"

He spun around again. "So why'd you just tell me all this? Why'd you kiss me like that, Dalilah, huh? What are you not getting with Haroun Hassan?"

She swallowed. She'd fallen right into it. She'd set herself up.

She turned her back to him, looked out over the gold grass, the big sky, the route they'd traveled. Immobilized. Trapped.

"Dalilah?"

She *couldn't* move. Tears filled her eyes and she wouldn't let him see.

"Dalilah?" She felt his touch, gentle on her shoulder.

Her heart began slamming against her ribs. She felt dizzy. Confused. It was fatigue, she told herself. Critical incident stress. She waited until her vision came fully back into focus.

Then she turned. Spine stiffening, she lifted her chin, met his eyes and forced a dry laugh. "Don't flatter yourself about that kiss. Like you said, an itch to scratch."

He moistened his lips, nodded slowly, eyes narrowing.

A bird flew overhead, big wings whooshing, a momentary shadow.

He swung his rifle back onto his shoulder, muzzle aimed into the air, and resumed his stride into the veldt.

"Damn you," she muttered softly in Arabic. Then she cursed herself—why should she even care about explaining herself to this broad-chested mutt? Why did she want his approval so desperately?

But she knew why. She liked Brandt—there was something about him she respected, and there was a profoundness buried in him.

Most of all, she was trying to explain it to herself, and he was the punching bag in the way. And a catalyst.

They neared the bottom of the cliff and it loomed even higher than Dalilah had anticipated. The red rocks trapped the heat of the sun, radiating it back like an oven.

Dust devils swirled near the base, fine sand sticking to perspiration on Dalilah's skin. The game trail to the approach petered out, and grass grew shoulder-high, scrub dense.

Brandt stopped, shaded his eyes, searching for a route up.

She heard a sneeze in the grass to her left and froze. Brandt spun around, lowered his rifle and clicked off the safety, attention trained on the grass.

"What is it?" she whispered.

He put his finger to his mouth.

Another sneeze.

"Impala," he whispered. "Warning."

A group of antelope suddenly flew at them from the grass. Dalilah shrieked and ducked as the buck leaped high and over her, violently kicking backward with his rear legs.

Brandt ignored the impala, aiming his gun at the vacated grass.

Her gaze shot to him in fear.

"Wild dogs," he whispered. "That rocking-horse jump makes it harder for the dogs to grab their stomachs and disembowel them."

The dog pack was only seconds behind the impala—small mottled black-and-tan predators with huge ears, white tail tips, snarling teeth as they gave full chase.

Dalilah heard a terrible gurgling death rasp as somewhere in the long grass the pack sank their teeth into an unlucky antelope and began ripping it apart alive. She grabbed Brandt's arm, blood draining from her head and bile rising in her throat as she listened to the wet tearing, ripping grunts and growls.

"Nasty way to go," he whispered. "That sound will attract bigger predators. We need to move fast." Taking her hand, Brandt led her at a fast trot to the steaming base of the cliff, not letting her go for a minute. Dalilah was grateful because she felt she'd just hit rock bottom in every way, and was crashing hard.

At the cliff base, she slumped onto a rock, put her face in her hand. She wanted to cry, just release everything inside, but she also wanted to hold it all in. She began to shake. Brandt placed his hand, large, firm, calming, on her shoulder.

The tears welled.

He looked up at the sky, and she knew he was at a loss to know how to handle her. And he had to be tired, too.

Then, as if making a decision, he lowered himself onto the hot rock next to her and tentatively put his arm around her. Then he committed, pulling her tightly against his body.

Dalilah leaned into him, drawing comfort from his solid strength, his confidence, the steady beat of his heart, and she let the tears come.

"Hey," he whispered. "It's going to be okay—I'm not going to let anything happen to you."

She sniffed, met his eyes. "No, she said, very quietly. "I'm sure you'll do your best. Or Omair will probably kill you."

He smiled, a soft light entering his pale eyes, and he took her hat off, moving hair away from her dust-streaked face.

"Yeah. And if Omair doesn't kill me," he said softly, "Haroun will."

She held his gaze.

"Brandt, thank you. I know I'm just a job, a package—"

"No," he said softly. "Not just a package, not anymore." He smiled, sadly this time, a worry entering his eyes. "You're too stubborn for that."

Chapter 10

"It feels as if it has a presence," Dalilah said, looking up at the wall. "Like it's got eyes."

"The Batswana call it Solomon's Wall," Brandt said. "Sangomas—the local witch doctors—claim it's a place where old spirits live and watch over the plains to the Tsholo."

"Must be about seventy yards high," she whispered.

"Around sixty meters of columnar basalt straight up, higher in other places. The wall runs for maybe forty or fifty kilometers—a rift caused by volcanic upheaval thousands of years ago."

She studied the big blocks of rock—cubes of various sizes stacked one atop the other almost as if by a giant human hand, an ancient ruined city wall now being pried and twisted apart by the gnarled roots of crooked trees and sparse shrubs that had found sustenance in crevices.

Again the hot breeze, an almost imperceptible sensation, rustled over her skin, as if the wall itself was softly exhaling. A prickle ran over her skin.

"It feels like it doesn't want to let us through, or over."

"This land has a way of doing that, like something primitive whispering just beneath the veil of the surface, reflecting back your own emotions."

She looked at him oddly, something shifting in her. Brandt handed her water. She met his eyes as she drank. He still didn't take any, but he felt thirsty now.

"You going to be okay?" he said.

She forced a wry smile and cast another glance up the cliff face. "I'm scared of heights."

"Because you're afraid of falling and dying?"

She bit the corner of her lip. "I suppose that's what it boils down to."

"You could look at this two ways—if we stay down here, you probably will die at Amal's hands. Or you could let me help you climb, and only stand a faint chance of dying at your own hand."

"Oh, great. You sure have a way of making someone feel like they have some nice options—stay down here and get my head cut off, or go up there and get smashed."

He crouched in front of her and looked up into her face, examining her, weighing how much mettle she had left, how far he could push her. "Dalilah, you *can* do this. You've shown me that you've got more grit than most men. You're a survivor. You have everything it takes and then some."

She turned her face away.

"No, *look* at me." He took her hand in his. "I'm going to help you over this. Once step, one rock at a time. We'll take it at an angle instead of straight up. It'll be easier that way. And near the top, there's water." He pointed. "That dark stain on the rock? Waterfall. We'll rest on that ledge up there by the water, then go the last short haul. We can be up on the plateau and in shelter before dark. I'll build you a fire, we'll eat. You can sleep. Then tomorrow, we start fresh. We're a team, okay—got that? No man left behind. Ever."

She gave a half laugh and her eyes flicked briefly to her finger with the ring. "After everything I've been through so far, this suddenly feels like the biggest, insurmountable hurdle of all."

Brandt had a sense she wasn't talking just about the wall, but about the argument they'd had over her marriage versus independence. He felt there was something much deeper and darker at play there, but he was not going to judge, or dig further. Right now he had to keep her focused on moving forward and up, on the positive.

"Listen here, Dalilah, I'll make you a harness, and you'll be tied to me with rope. I *won't* let you fall. You've just got to keep looking up, never down, never backward." He got to his feet, his body casting her in shadow. "Tomorrow we'll make for a small village where we might even find transport. From there, smooth sailing and we're home."

"Home," she said softly as she studied the wall. She rubbed her brow. "I'm not sure I know where that is anymore," she muttered.

She was talking about moving to Sa'ud, the upcoming marriage, Brandt was certain of it. But he didn't want to go there, not now. He removed the coil of rope from his pack that he'd cut from the jeep canopy. "I'm going to use this to fashion a harness around your chest, and I'm going to remove your sling for now, just in case you need balance from that other hand, but go easy on it."

He began to loop knots as he spoke. "The idea is for me to climb up a boulder or two, find a secure perch, then haul you up. You'll help by using your good arm to pull and your legs to climb and leverage against my resistance. We go this way rock by rock, step by step. When you're tired, tell me, and we rest. Then when your mind is clear and focused again, then—and only then—we take another step." He paused, assessing the rock face. "And from the top, we'll see right across this plain. We'll see if Amal is coming."

He removed her sling and looped the rope around her back, and under her arms above her breasts, securing it with knots. But when the side of his hand brushed against her breast, her eyes ticked up to his, and the memory of their kiss suddenly hung briefly in the heat between them.

"There." He cleared his throat and stepped back, smiling as encouragingly as he could. "Ready?"

She inhaled deeply, nodded.

But exactly what she was ready for, Dalilah wasn't sure. All she knew was that she had to take the first step, get up over that first rock—and she was going to have to place her full trust in Brandt.

She believed he would not let her fall, that he'd help her up over this hurdle. But the other hurdles that would come after?

Once she got "home" she was on her own. And for a brief insane instant, she didn't want to scale this cliff. She wasn't ready to go home.

Amal stared over the wide, roiling Tsholo at the Botswana bank on the other side. Rage as violent as the floodwaters seethed inside him.

It was already afternoon, and jeep tracks showed his quarry had crossed the river right here. Before the waters had come down. Who was this bastard that had taken the

princess? How had this person known that he was coming for her?

When Amal found him, he was going to disembowel
the bastard, hang him from a tree for the jackals to tear at
his innards while he was still alive. He'd make him watch
what he was going to do to the Al Arif woman.

"There's a bridge," the old tracker was saying quietly
at his side.

Amal spun to glare at him. "How far?"

"North, maybe half a day or more in the jeeps. But
sometimes the first flood of the wet season washes parts
of the bridge out. And there's border control there, on the
Botswana side."

Amal glowered at the old man. He hated Jacob's eyes,
the way they seemed to harbour a quiet, secret knowledge.
Amal didn't trust him, but he needed him. Once he sighted
his quarry, he'd kill the old man and that dog in a flash.

"Screw border patrol," he snapped. "It'll be sundown
soon. We drive through the night, fast." He marched over
to Mbogo.

"Mark that spot over the river on the GPS," he said,
pointing to the high bank on the Botswana side. "If we
make good speed we can be there by dawn tomorrow.
We'll pick up their tracks there. They won't get away."

Halfway up, Dalilah looked down. Mistake. Far below,
the plain stretched—brown and gold, grasses, acacia
scrub, stunted Mopani. Dizziness swirled, heat and dehydration taking their toll. Her muscles began to shake
and sweat dripped from under her hat.

She slipped, rope digging into her skin as she jerked
out and crashed back into rock, breath slamming out of
her chest. Above her, Brandt braced, taking the brunt of
her drop with the rope. He held still for a moment as she

hung there, small stones skittering out from under his boot heel as it began to slip. A shower of stones clattered down on top of her.

"Grab that branch near your face!" he yelled. "Dig your toes into that crevice above your knees—just feel your way. And don't look down!"

She groped for a piece of twisted old root. Grasping it, she found purchase with her boots, dug her toes in, and took some of the weight off Brandt. He hauled her up as she helped by pulling on bits of bush and roots. Once over the ledge of the rock, Brandt grabbed her and held her body tightly against his. Dalilah's heart jackhammered. She could feel his heart, too, pounding against his ribs. Their bodies were drenched with perspiration.

"I got you," he whispered, his breath hot in her ear. "Take it easy, okay? Calm down. Just relax. If anything kills a person out here it's panic, got that? You're in control of your own mind."

She nodded, mouth tight, trying to tamp down the wild fear rampaging through her, blinding her focus, narrowing her vision. She didn't know how much more of this she could take.

"Did I mention," she whispered against his neck, "that I really do hate heights?"

"And did I mention," he whispered in return, his breath feathering her cheek, "that you never cease to surprise me, Princess?"

"I hope you mean that in a good way."

She felt him smile. It made her feel better. Calmer. As if she had a partner.

"We're a team, remember? No man left behind."

She nodded, and it felt good to know that this guy had her back—the kind of guy who could be hard on her when she needed to push herself, but tender when she needed a soft touch. A man who'd push her to follow her passion and be the best woman she could be.

And as Dalilah held on to this scarred lion of a man, she realized that's what she wanted out of a marriage. And it sunk like a cold knife deep into her chest—she'd never get that with Haroun.

I'm not seeing a clear picture here...

Neither was she. Not anymore.

He held her steady until her heart rate lowered, until she could focus and think properly again. Then he cupped the side of her face and made her look up into his eyes.

"Remember," he said firmly, "looking backward serves zero purpose, understand? Only think of the future."

"Is that what you do, Brandt?" she whispered. "Never look back?"

Surprise flickered through his eyes. Then his lips twisted into a slow, wry smile. "Touché, Princess. But let's keep this about the cliff, all right? We'll save my past for later."

She held his gaze, his lips so close, his arms so strong. A team suspended between sky and earth, and for an upside-down moment Dalilah was oddly grateful to be here right now, with him, to have been afforded this tiny window of reprieve, even under these circumstances. A chance to rethink her future before she made a terrible mistake from which she could never turn back.

An hour later, wet through and caked with red clay, muscles screaming with exertion, Brandt reached down his hand and hauled Dalilah over a big slab and onto a wide ledge of rock that ran almost fifty yards along the cliff face. Dalilah caught her breath as she heard water and felt a waft of cooler air kissing her cheeks. They were almost at the top of the cliff, and through a crevice above, cascading into a pool carved by time and pressure into rock, was a fall of gloriously clear water. Thirst rose fierce and sharp. She shot a look at Brandt. A grin split his rugged face, his teeth stark white against skin that had turned an even darker bronze from a full day under the baking sun. The dancing light in his eyes reminded her of a summer swimming pool with its surface recently broken by a swimmer—sunlight refracting off the surface. Cool, welcoming.

And she'd never seen anything more beautiful.

"You should do it more often," she said.

"Climb cliffs with you?"

She laughed as she pushed past him and dropped to her knees, dipping her hand in the clear, coppery-colored water.

"No, silly. Smile. I like your smile."

His smile faded, his gaze darkening, becoming unreadable.

She cupped water in her hands—it was the color of clear Ceylon tea. "It's cool, Brandt!" Dalilah took off her hat and bent forward, splashing it over her face, feeling like a child. Laughing.

"God, this is heaven." She shot him a look over her shoulder. "Is it okay to drink, do you think?"

He was staring at her, and she felt suddenly aware, self-conscious, then that gorgeous broad grin crept over his face again, splitting it into facets and crinkles, making his blue-sky eyes dance again like a summer pool in sunlight. Then he braced his hands on his hips and laughed. "And what's so funny?"

"You! You look like a female warrior with war paint out to do battle—and you're still all trussed up in the harness and trailing rope."

She peered into the surface of the water. In the rippling reflection she could see her face was now streaked with dark mud. She grinned. "I really must look a prize."

"A hell of a lot cuter than you did in that cocktail outfit when—" He caught himself.

"When what?"

"It's nothing." Brandt came forward, untied the rope around her and swung off his pack. He dropped it to the slab with a thud, kettle clunking against rock. Crouching, he moved the rifle strapped across his torso to one side, then cupped his hands, tasted the water. "No cleaner in the world—just colored by minerals."

"Still could have parasites, bacteria—"

"I'll take that chance. This rock pool has been baked dry and clean by the sun all winter—it's only flowing again now since the fresh rains."

"Animal feces could be upstream."

"Spoken like someone who understands water risks in Africa," he said, pooling more water in his hands and drinking deeply, regardless. It was the first time Dalilah had seen him drink anything since the whiskey this morning. He'd saved their supply for her, and now he was slaking what was clearly a deep and desperate thirst.

He filled the water canteen, capped it, then stuck his whole head into the cool pool, rinsing his face. He got up, flicked his head back and raked his hands through his short hair, biceps flexing, and Dalilah was struck by a thought—she could love this man.

It turned her mood suddenly dark and heavy.

"Drink, Dalilah. And wash off—we'll rest here a bit. We have enough light to get to the top before sunset. He dropped to his haunches again and opened his pack, removing two small airplane-size bottles. "Shampoo and lotion," he said with a flourish of his hand. "You could take a full shower under this waterfall. Nature's spa."

Dalilah stared at the bottles. Her eyes flashed to his. "You brought *those?*"

A wicked tilt lifted one side of his mouth. "Traveling with royalty, aren't I? Gotta keep a princess in the style to which she's accustomed."

"And there I was thinking you were going out of your way to make me feel *un*comfortable."

"Well, just enough to keep you focused."

"See, I was right."

"The princess is intuitive."

She touched his hand. "Brandt."

His body went stone-still.

"Call me Princess one more time," she whispered, close to his mouth, "and I swear I will use that panga of yours to kill you."

Energy shimmered between them for a beat, then abruptly Brandt averted his eyes and unsmilingly yanked the sarong out of the pack.

"Get undressed, take a full bath. I'll go over there, behind that jutting-out rock. Out of sight, but within earshot. You'll be safe. Use this to dry off." He thrust the sarong at her. "If you want to wash any clothes, lay them out on those hot rocks once you're done. Stuff will dry in minutes. You can get that splint wet—I have more bandages and another splint if we need one."

He hooked up his backpack, made for the jut of rock, went round it and disappeared from sight.

Dalilah stood there, sarong in hand, staring after him.

A few yards away, screened by the rock, Brandt settled back onto the hot ledge.

From his backpack he dug out the high-tech digital camera with zoom lens. One thing he hadn't found in the jeep, or in the pack, was a pair of binoculars, so the camera zoom lens would have to suffice.

Using the powerful lens, he scanned the landscape
below, but he was unable to cut thoughts of Dalilah from
his mind. Somehow—he wasn't exactly sure how or
when—she'd gone from being a principal to someone he
actually cared about, so help him God. Yeah, it was shades
of Carla all over again, but Brandt couldn't undo what had
changed within him, so he was just going to have to soldier through this now.

He panned over to an area of thorny trees. A small
herd of zebra rested in shade. Not far from them buffalo
moved slowly in a group. He swept the camera slowly to
the east, saw dust rising. His heart kicked. Zooming in
closer, he realized the dust was being raised by elephants,
not Amal's jeeps.

In the sky, above the bushy area near the elephants, five
vultures wheeled. One dropped suddenly, like a bomb into
the long grass, then another. Probably after the remains
of the dog kill, he thought. If it was a fresh lion kill the
birds would drop only as far as the trees, fearing retaliation from the lions.

There was nothing else that caught his eye. No glint of
metal or flash of glass, no other telltale line of dust rising
into the air. Most of the animals were resting in the heat,
waiting for the cool of night, when the real cycle of violence and activity would begin.

Brandt leaned back, rifle on his knee, camera in his
hand, and rested his head against the rock, listening to
sounds of the place—the clicking of insects, birdcall, rustling feathers as smaller raptors rode the cliff thermals
above him in search of mice and other small prey, water
splashing into the pool.

The sound of the waterfall changed as Dalilah presumably moved under it. Brandt's pulse worked a little faster,
his chest tightening as he thought of her buck naked in the

pool. He heard another splash, and before he could stop himself, Brandt eased forward, copped a peek.

Everything in his body stilled.

Apart from her blue SAM splint, the princess was naked, standing under the waterfall, head back as she rinsed shampoo out of her hair, her eyes closed in pure, unaffected pleasure at the sensation of the cool water drumming over her body.

Her skin was dusky, nipples dark rose-brown, pointing straight out from the coldness of the water.

She turned, and Brandt caught sight of the dark delta of hair between her thighs, the glint of a green jewel in her belly button. She was exotic even unclothed—the princess of an oil-rich Saharan kingdom, as far removed from his lifestyle as a woman could get. And she was set to marry an Arabian prince who might well be one of the wealthiest men in the world when he became king.

Unattainable. Wrong side of the tracks.

Brandt told himself to look away, but he couldn't. He was utterly mesmerized—she was the most beautiful thing he'd ever seen out in this dry, scrubby, hard country. Like a bird of paradise that didn't belong. That he couldn't have.

Yet…somehow, naked, stripped, out of her element, she did fit, at least for this moment standing under that water. Just him and her, the water, rocks, sky, bushveldt stretching out for miles below—it seemed the most natural and beautiful thing on this earth. And in this moment, Brandt wanted to possess her with every molecule in his body, with a deep, raw hunger that went beyond the physical. It was a longing, a craving that made him feel suddenly lonely in his life. And he realized Dalilah was awakening in him powerful things he'd long buried.

A desperation swelled fierce and hot in his chest, and almost involuntarily, Brandt slowly put the camera to his

eye, adjusted the lens, focusing on how the sleek curves of
her body echoed the smooth contours in the red rock. He
clicked almost before he registered the action, capturing
wet hair slicked over her shoulders, the aristocratic slant
of her nose. The pleasure in her features as she closed
her eyes.

On one level he knew he was stealing these images,
that he shouldn't be doing this. But Brandt also knew
Dalilah's presence in his life was rare and fleeting, that
he could never have her in the way he suddenly wanted
her, and he was desperate to hold on to a part of her, a
memory he could return to once she was gone from his
life. A touchstone.

Photography had saved Brandt before. Capturing images of things that moved him deeply in war zones had
become an outlet for his conscience. Returning to those
images taken over the years had kept him grounded, reminded him why he'd made the choices he had. Photography had become, in part, the reason he could no longer
fight, or kill.

Right now, though, he wanted to capture this moment
in its purity and beauty—to remember this bittersweet,
poignant, painful sensation Dalilah was reawakening in
him—for reasons he couldn't begin to articulate to himself yet.

He zoomed in closer, focusing on the winking of the
emerald jewel at her navel, the hollow at her throat, the
valley between her rounded breasts as he clicked.

She flicked her wet hair back suddenly and droplets
of water sparkled in a graceful arc like diamonds in the
sunlight—natural jewels, flickering to life one second,
then falling and melting into the pool the next. Yet he'd
caught them. That was rarity, pure wealth. Not an osten-
tatious Argyle pink stone bought by dirty oil money.

Brandt lowered the camera, blood racing.

Dalilah reached for her bra and G-string on the rocks, and began washing her underwear in the pool using the shampoo, affording him a vision of her rounded buttocks.

Heat sliced through his brain, blinding him a moment, throbbing low in his belly. She came to the edge of the pool and bent over, breasts swinging forward as she laid out her clean underwear on the hot rock, steam rising instantly. Through the valley of her breasts, a gap of sunlight was visible between her thighs to the apex where her hair was wet and dark. Something dark and carnal overtook his thoughts and his mouth turned dry. He raised the camera again, but this time he couldn't click the shutter. As desperate as he was to feed the hunger within him, to make love to her with his lens, something had shifted, and it suddenly felt wrong. His breathing grew lighter, faster, tension, conflict whipping through him.

She reached for the sarong, started wrapping it around her torso.

Brandt leaned back, barely able to breathe, heart thudding in his chest, his groin hot, hard, his brain thick as molasses. He willed himself to calm, willed the desire pulsing between his thighs to abate.

But she edged around the outcropping of rock, wrapped in the sarong, damp spots on her breasts, and his pulse spiked back into overdrive. Brandt quickly scrubbed his hands over his face, avoiding meeting her eyes. "Done?"

"Just waiting for my things to dry so I can change." She hesitated. "You okay?

No.

"Yeah," he said, voice clipped. He stood, his erection making him feel like that frustrated bull elephant—this was insane, the level of lust coursing like molten lead through his system. This woman was like a drug he'd tasted and couldn't get enough of, messing with his body and mind.

"You going to have a go? It's like heaven."

Hell, yeah.

He grunted and stuffed the camera back into his pack. He needed more than a shower—he needed a bucket of bloody ice. Brandt handed her the gun, still not meeting her eyes. "Wait here. Keep an eye on the plain."

Brandt edged past her, trying his damnedest not to make contact.

Dalilah fingered the weapon in her lap, her hair drying quickly into a mass of thick curls around her shoulders. She jumped as something touched her bare foot. Looking down, she was startled to see an oddly shaped mouse with a long nose like a trunk. She smiled—elephant mouse. More of the strange little creatures peeped out, scurrying suddenly over the ledge on which she sat. One started to drink from a tiny puddle of water that had dripped from her hair.

As she watched the mice, she noticed red ants attacking a writhing insect struggling to escape, while along a deep crevice in the rock more ants bustled back and forth in a straight line ferrying gelatinous white eggs.

It struck Dalilah that the bushveldt on the micro level was as violent and intense as on the macro level. Life. Sex. Birth. Death. A constant fight for survival.

Looking up, she saw vultures dropping from the sky in the distance, and she thought of the wild dogs ripping apart the impala, the baby elephant being dragged to muddy depths by the crocodile. The crazy bull elephant. The dead leopard and motherless cub. She was a part of it all, living in the moment.

Alive.

Vital.

More so than she'd ever felt in her entire life. More than she'd felt in New York.

She thought of Haroun and immediately her head began to hurt.

Dalilah leaned forward around the rock, checking to see if Brandt was almost finished. Her breath caught in her throat.

He was still under the waterfall, naked. And clearly physically aroused.

Her pulse began to race. Unable to tear her gaze away, Dalilah watched Brandt reaching for the shampoo. He squeezed some into his hand and worked up a soapy mass of bubbles with which he washed his hair, his biceps flexing his lion tattoo as he washed his hair and lathered the soap down his arms. Then his hands worked over his washboard abs, going lower to soap the dark blond hair between his legs. The size of his arousal was startling, his bare thighs deeply tanned, rock-solid.

A wild white heat seared into her belly and a desperate desire rose in Dalilah to straddle him, fill herself with him, press her breasts and belly against that solid, lean torso.

He stilled suddenly, as if he sensed he was being watched.

Slowly, his head turned, and he caught her eyes. Panic sliced through Dalilah. She couldn't swallow, breathe. Couldn't hear, could barely see as her vision narrowed onto him.

He held dead still, his eyes pale slits as he met her gaze for several long, slow beats. Then slowly he turned, continued washing.

She let out a whoosh of air and sat back against the rock, her cheeks flame-hot, her hands shaking. What had just happened here?

Embarrassment shot through her.

When he returned he was dressed. He held out his hand for the gun and said, "Your stuff is dry. Go change back there. Call me when you're done and I'll give you a dry splint." His voice was hard, ice-cold. Emotionless.

She opened her mouth to speak, mortified by what had transpired between them. By the raw need awakened in her own body.

"Brandt, I…" Her voice came out hoarse, then caught in her own throat.

He turned away, hefting the pack up onto his shoulders before she could manage to finish her words.

"Sun goes off like a light switch around six-thirty— we're running out of time." He shrugged the pack onto his back, buckled it up tight. "We need to get up onto that plateau and find a place to hole up for the night before dark, or we won't live till dawn." Then he met her gaze, paused. "And you won't live to see that wedding of yours."

Dalilah swallowed. It was a harsh reminder, a snipe at her—or himself. She wasn't sure, but it made her feel small and humiliated. And angry. She wasn't the only one turned on here. And he had no idea what it felt to feel that kind of sexual attraction and to have never been able to act on it.

Chapter 11

The sky was a riot of violent pinks and the evening sun was sinking fast in a giant orange ball to the horizon. Already Brandt could feel the cool fingers of the coming night in the air as they traveled along the rim of the cliff. He began to move faster over the scrubby, rocky ground hoping he hadn't made a mistake, praying the old airstrip was here somewhere.

Relief washed through him when he caught sight of what used to be a wooden arch that marked the entrance to the airfield. The old customs building—essentially a one-room square—stood in ruins in the middle of empty scrubland not far from the old archway. As they neared, Brandt saw that burned and blackened rafters were all that remained of the thatched roof. Coppery-orange streaks from mud and rain stained the sides of the once-whitewashed walls. Windows and doors were long gone. But it had been built from brick and the four walls stood solid. It would keep them safe from night predators.

As they reached the ruins, the sun slipped below the horizon and the sky turned a soft pearly gray. They'd made it just in time. The paving around the building had crumbled into chunks as tough roots pushed through. Alongside the building were parts of an old bench where people had once waited for bush planes, supplies and guests arriving for safari.

Brandt could still read part of a sign that had been painted onto one wall—*Welcome to…* The rest of the phrase had fallen off in a chunk of plaster.

"Welcome to the airport hotel," he said wryly.

"What is this place?" Dalilah asked, turning in a slow circle.

"Abandoned airstrip. This building was once a customs office." He jerked his chin to the surrounding bush. "Lots of dead wood out there—we'll be able to keep a fire going all night, keep predators at bay."

"Customs? Out here?"

He dumped his pack inside the doorway. Dirt had blown into the building and small rocks, crumbling brick and plaster, dead leaves, insect husks littered the pocked concrete floor. "They put customs posts in places that saw a lot of tourists flying in," Brandt said, unsheathing his panga. He made sure his voice remained cool and distant.

"There's a safari outfit not far from here called Masholo, but mostly this airstrip was used to service guests coming from Zimbabwe, until that market dried up. Masholo also built their own private airstrip."

He left Dalilah standing next to the hut while he strode off into the scrub, and with his panga he lopped off a branch with leaves. He used the branch to start sweeping out the interior of the building, checking for spiders and scorpions while there was still enough light. "We'll clean this up, build a fire there, and there." He pointed to each doorway. "Smoke will be vented straight out the top, and we can get some good rest until dawn. I could see no sign of Amal coming over the plain, not tonight. Our only worry should be wildlife, and there's enough wood out here to keep the curious at bay."

"Here, I can do that," she reached to take the branch from him.

But he moved away. "It's fine—relax."

"Brandt!" She snatched it from him, skin connecting. Both stilled. Their eyes met—the knowledge of what had happened on the cliff, still unarticulated, simmered intimately between them. Both had an edge of anger to them.

Anger suited Brandt. Anger was the only emotion he knew how to handle right now.

He let go of the branch and let her have at it.

He went to collect wood while the princess swept out the interior with a stick broom—ironic in some fairy-tale way to be sure, but Brandt was not in the mood to be sardonic.

After stacking wood into small pyres inside the crumbling doorways, he went to gather more logs and branches, which he piled within reach just outside the window.

"Here's the rifle," he said, propping the gun against the interior wall. "It's loaded and good to go if you need it."

She stopped sweeping. "Why, where are you going?"

Avoiding her eyes, ignoring the concern that had entered her voice, Brandt said, "To get some hay for insulation. With these clear skies temps could drop below freezing tonight. You'll feel it through the concrete."

Hiking out to an area of long, dried grass, Brandt lopped off enough thatch to make a giant bushel which he hefted back to the ruined building. He laid the straw on the floor in a corner of the room, sealing in the warmth of the sun trapped inside by the concrete. He laid out the sleeping bag on top.

"Take a load off." He nodded to the bag.

Dalilah hesitated, then lowered herself slowly to the bed in the corner. She sat with her back against the wall, knees propped up, watching him.

When the sky turned charcoal-gray—too dark to see telltale smoke from afar, Brandt lit the fires.

Orange flames crackled to life, instantly throwing out warmth and casting a dancing glow on the walls. It made the room feel safe, comforting. A little too intimate. Up through the rafters the Milky Way flickered slowly to life and the occasional bat fluttered overhead.

The chirrup of settling birds grew to a cacophonous crescendo, backed by whistles and rustles, the beat of wings in the dark and the stirring *whooop yeee whooops* of hyenas beginning to move for the night hunt.

Brandt placed two old bricks and some stones at the edge of the fire, and he raked some of the coals between them. Filling the kettle with enough for one cup, he set it atop the rocks.

He opened the bag of biltong, offered it to Dalilah without meeting her eyes.

"Brandt."

He glanced up. Her eyes were inky bright and there was a look of need in her features. She wanted to explain, talk. He didn't. He just wanted this over.

"What is it?"

"I need to go to the bathroom."

"What? *Now?*"

"I'm sorry."

"You should have told me before I lit the fires."

Her cheeks flushed.

"Look, you can't afford to be all ladylike and coy out

here, Dalilah. If you need to take care of business you take care of it." Irritated, he jumped back to his feet and put the headlamp on. He handed her the other lamp. "Put it on."

While she adjusted the Petzl, he swung himself easily out through the old window, clicked on his light, then helped her through. The scent of her freshly shampooed hair washed over him before he could put her to the ground and the image of her naked in the mountain pool sliced back into his head and firmly imprinted itself in his mind.

"Go behind those trees," he said as he walked her down to a clump of acacia, their twin beams flickering over grass. "I'll stand guard and wait right here."

Dalilah went alone behind the clump. Shadows lunged and darted as she moved, as if dark hands of night were clawing at her, hungry. She hesitated as she heard a scurry of nails over rock, then a rustle through the grass. Heart thumping, she turned in a slow circle, and tiny green pairs of eyes glinted back at her.

"Brandt—there's something out there!"

"Just duikers. Hurry up. Watch for snakes and scorpions."

Dalilah struggled with one hand to undo her pants and balance as she squatted. She'd barely had to go all day—dehydration seemed to be taking care of that. She scrunched her eyes, forcing herself to relax enough to relieve herself, but having trouble, knowing he was listening, the lack of privacy.

This man was getting to know her more intimately than she'd dared allow any other man. Once she was done, Dalilah did up her pants and inhaled deeply, pressing her hand to her stomach as she gathered herself.

She came out from behind the tree.

"See?" Was that a glint of his teeth, a grin in the dark? "It gets easier each time."

"I'm not so sure about that," Dalilah retorted, cutting slightly ahead of him, reasserting some personal space and dignity as she aimed for the warm, flickering light of their little ruined building. But he was right. It was a little easier each time.

This man was pushing her into new spaces, bit by bit, minute by minute, tilting her paradigm of the world, forcing her to let go of the reins she seemed to have been holding too tight over too many years.

Did that constitute true freedom—not caring what others thought? Doing things you wanted, not what others expected of you? Or was that just selfish?

The kettle was boiling by the time they were settled back into the building. Brandt poured water over a tea bag and handed her the sack of dried meat.

"It's all we have right now."

She declined, but accepted the mug gratefully.

The stars turned bright and a moon started to rise. But a bitter cold also began to press down.

"You need some protein, Dalilah," he said, poking at the flames. "We could be out here for days."

Silence.

He glanced at her. "I'm serious. My job is to ensure your survival—and you need proper fuel. The only way to get it out here right now is to eat that biltong."

She snatched angrily at the bag, took out a dried twisted cord of meat encrusted with spices. She ripped at it with her teeth, chewed.

He was watching her intently.

"Don't worry—I'm going to swallow it. I'm hungry, not stupid."

Brandt snorted and turned to stare into the flames as she chewed.

"Ethical choice?" he said after a while.

"You mean vegetarianism?"

He grunted.

She nodded. "Pretty much. I used to hunt once—my father *made* all us kids learn to shoot, kill. Live off the desert the old way," she said. "He wanted a royal family who was still in touch with our Bedouin roots, with the citizens of Al Na'Jar."

"Omair told me he'd learned to hunt and shoot with his father."

She glanced up sharply. "He did?"

"Never told me his sister did, too."

"You were close to Omair?"

"Close enough."

"Did he also tell you we used sight hounds to hunt—salukis? My brother Zakir uses the salukis now because he's blind." A sad, wistful softness entered her voice, which made Brandt look up again.

"Those dogs are his eyes," she said. "So is his wife."

Brandt threw another log on the fire. Sparks shot up to the blackened rafters.

"The lessons with your dad clearly paid off with that leopard. You're a fine shot. Especially with one hand, under that kind of pressure."

She was silent for a long while, cradling the mug of tea with her good hand as she sipped. "That cat was so beautiful. Probably as afraid as I was—just protecting her cub and herself. I made myself her enemy by sitting in that tree."

Every minute more he spent with Dalilah, the deeper Brandt was being drawn in, and she was doing it again now, burrowing under his skin, into his chest, probing a way to his heart. He really needed this to be over.

He jabbed irritably at the fire. "It's an acknowledged survival trait, Dalilah, being able to see beauty even when your own life is under threat—it stops you from giving up, despairing."

"I didn't like the killing as a kid," she countered crisply. "I don't like the idea of killing animals for consumption now. And I don't like handing it off to big agribusiness that denudes the environment, either. So if I can help it, I don't foster it."

"Is that how you got involved with ClearWater, solar power, sustainable farming?"

She puffed out a lungful of air. "I suppose. I'm from the Sahara—I understand how precious a commodity water is to most of Africa." Her eyes went distant. "I guess my father taught us well on some level. There were some real values that came out of the desert forays he forced us on."

Respect for Dalilah deepened, but at the same time Brandt couldn't understand why, if this ethic was so ingrained in her, she wanted to give it all up for a restrained life trapped behind palace walls with Sheik Hassan of Sa'ud. And this dichotomy in her personality niggled at him because he'd glimpsed sadness, resignation, in her eyes when he'd confronted her on her choices. And in spite of her engagement to another man, she was clearly attracted to him—there was something developing between them, even against both their wills. That told Brandt she wasn't fully committed on some level. Because when you truly loved someone, in that first heady blush when you decide to marry and spend a life together, you have eyes for only that person. At least, that's the way it had been for him.

But it wasn't his concern, he thought, turning to poke at the flames.

"I'm impressed you maintained your shooting skill," he said. "For someone who hasn't used a gun since you were what, five, six?"

"I shoot for relaxation."

His brow crooked up. *"Relaxation?"*

"At a range, clay-pigeon shoots. That part of shooting—the sporting aspect—I did enjoy as a kid. I liked the focus, controlling my breathing, getting into the zone." She gave a soft laugh. "I was better than my brothers at it. They were after the kill and got too pumped up. I had far more control." She paused. "I always wanted to do better than my brothers."

He grinned in spite of himself, then laughed. "Your brothers are not an easy act to follow, let alone trump."

She smiled, a little rueful, and stared into the flames for a while, mug in hand. "My whole life has been a struggle to get out from under their shadow, to prove myself, to carve my own niche in the world…" Her voice faded. Brandt could see that look of sadness entering her features again, of resignation. It puzzled him.

He shook himself, grabbed a stick of biltong, ripped off a shred with his teeth, chewed in silence. Flames crackled and popped.

She broke the silence. "In winter I do biathlons and practice my shooting that way. I travel to a ski resort in Norway, usually. Sometimes Canada."

"Does Haroun travel with you?"

Her eyes shot to him, the sudden tension in her body unmistakable. Brandt's curiosity deepened in spite of himself.

"Well, does he go with you? Does he ski?"

"No."

"He doesn't ski? Or doesn't travel with you?"

She fiddled with her bootlace, her complexion looking drained. "You know, I'm really exhausted. I…I need to sleep, if you don't mind. I can keep watch for you later if you like."

"Go ahead. Get in the bag. It's high-tech stuff—will keep you warm."

She hesitated. "Would you mind helping me with my laces?"

Brandt put his mental walls back up and quickly untied her boots. She snuggled down into the sleeping bag and closed her eyes, resting her head on the rolled-up sarong.

Brandt fed the fire, listening to the hoot of owls. And when her breathing changed, he watched her sleep— freshly washed hair fanning around her exotic face, glimmering ebony in the coppery firelight, her skin smooth, lips slightly parted.

Quietly, Brandt lifted the camera, stealing something small for himself as he clicked.

Her eyes flared open.

"What are you doing?" she said, edging up.

"Do you mind?" he said, gesturing to the camera.

She sat up sharply "What—*why?*"

He held the camera to his eye again, adjusted the lens. "The image is perfect."

"Brandt, no!"

He lowered the camera.

"I… Please, don't."

He said nothing.

"I can't have that kind of photo of myself out there, Brandt." Her voice was crisp, her eyes hard.

Coolness settled in his gut. "You think I'm actually going to sell these to some cheap tabloid?"

Something crossed her face, and the cold in his stomach hardened. He snorted harshly when she didn't reply, and he put the camera down. "Even out here, you're managing your image." Brandt couldn't keep something out of his voice. Bitterness—jealousy. He didn't even know himself what was suddenly biting, eating at him right this instant. Maybe it was the fact she'd chastised him.

"Brandt—"

He jabbed a stick into the flames. The fire exploded a flurry of hot orange sparks that shot up into the night.

"Brandt! Look at me."

He turned his head. Those eyes—God, those smoky, sensual eyes, lambent in the firelight—were boring into him. And those lips.

He knew what those lips tasted like.

The memory of her naked rose in his mind, luminous skin shimmering with water. The dark wet delta between her thighs. His groin went hot at the thought. Good thing she didn't know what photos he'd already stolen like a thief in the night.

"What?" he said when she didn't speak.

"Tell me why you wanted to take photos. Tell me what you were planning to do with them."

"Keep them," he said simply. "It's what I do, Dalilah. These days I shoot with a camera, not a gun, if I can help it. I shoot rare and beautiful things, things with meaning to me. Images I return to so that I can be reminded of what I value in life. Or what stands to be lost."

Her eyes shimmered, nose pinking slightly.

"And for God's sake," he snapped, "give me *some* credit. The last thing I'd want is His Royal Highness of Sa'ud, or his lackeys, finding these and hurting you because he thinks you've tainted your image by being out here with me or something. What in hell do you think I am? I don't want anything to goddamn do with the world and all its tabloid crap out there!" He flung his arm out wide gesturing toward the window, the night, anger rising irrationally in him as he lost the battle to tamp it down.

Like that bloody bull elephant, he needed to go take it all out on a tree or something.

He sucked in air, deep, and attempting to moderate his tone, he spoke more quietly. "And you know what, that's why Omair trusts me with you. He knows I'm not going to blab my mouth about saving your ass from Amal."

Brandt realized the irony as soon as the words came out of his mouth. Yeah, maybe Omair trusted him to save Dalilah and keep quiet about it, but no doubt Sheik Al Arif also trusted his old merc buddy Brandt Stryker to keep his big grubby hands off his engaged little sister.

"Because, believe me, Dalilah, Omair is going to want to keep this whole damn mission quiet. When he comes to pick you up, he's going to ship you somewhere safe while he goes after Amal himself, now that he has a lead on him, and he doesn't want international authorities stopping him while he metes out his own kind of desert justice. That's my bet. You're the bait that has finally lured Amal Ghaffar out of the African woodpile." Brandt reached over, took her empty mug, and tossed the dregs onto the fire with a sizzle.

A strange look crossed Dalilah's face, as if he'd hit something raw and close to the bone.

"Is that what you think—that, my brothers are using me as a lure? And that's why they never told me about Amal? Because that's bull."

He shrugged. "Maybe they didn't plan it that way, but it works now that Amal has been flushed out. Omair can end this war once and for all."

She stared at him, eyes big, shining, then she swallowed, looking vulnerable, overwhelmed.

And suddenly Brandt felt bad. He wanted to hold her, protect her. But an image of Carla curled into his mind. It was a night like this. Just Carla and him. Her big dark eyes searching his—that same look of smoky allure and vulnerability. So feminine. So sexy. It pressed all his male buttons. Heat prickled over Brandt's skin.

He winced suddenly as the memory of Carla's screams sliced through his brain. The memory of her naked body, being tortured as he was forced to watch. He swallowed, his pulse beginning to race, claustrophobia biting at him.

And for a nanosecond, Dalilah's face was Carla's. Past and present began to collide—walls seemed to be closing in. Amal and his men coming, just like those men had come for Carla. Sweat began to pearl on his brow.

Dalilah was watching him oddly. Brandt lurched to his feet, grabbed his gun and the headlamp.

"Get some sleep," he snapped, desperate to fight the PTSD nipping at the corners of his brain. He didn't want her to see him like this. He didn't know how far he was going to be pulled back this time. "Where are you going?"

"To get more wood. I'll be right outside if you need me."

Outside, in the endless, cold dark, Brandt relieved himself then went looking for more wood. He dumped a fresh bundle outside the window, and peered inside.

She was bundled up in the sleeping bag, face turned into the corner, fast asleep. Good. She needed it.

He slid his back down the outside wall, knees propped up, gun at his side. Switching off his headlamp, he dug into the pocket of his cargo shorts for his flask. He took a shot, then another, then a third, his eyes watering as he put his head back against the wall and stared up at the velvet sky spattered with stars.

He knew why he was getting these flashbacks again. He was falling for Dalilah, and it scared the crap out of him. It was also pathetic—the princess and the pauper? He gave a soft snort and took another drink.

Even though she was obviously physically attracted to him, too, so what? They had sexual chemistry. That's all it was. She might as well be attracted to the palace man-servant. He was simply the wrong side of the proverbial tracks.

After another swig from his flask Brandt cared a little less, and a nice soft buzz blurred the edges of his mind. He allowed himself to slip into the comfort of the whis-key's warm embrace.

Then suddenly he heard her voice again in his mind.

What are you seeking alcoholic relief from, Brandt... why do you take pictures, Brandt...?

He hated the hypocrisy in himself. Yes, he sought relief from his memories, from the flashbacks. Through mind-less sex. Plenty of drink. Death-defying adrenaline highs. But still, he'd been compelled to shoot photographs in war zones—needing to keep touchstones, to remind himself why he'd done what he had in the past. And why he had to stop killing. The photos still hung on the walls of the house he'd built on his farm.

It was his private hell—this dichotomy inside him.

But the images that truly haunted him were not cap-tured on film. Those he would never escape.

They rose now from the dark depths—Carla's beaten, abused body. The pierce of her screams, like knives in his heart. The image of men raping her as the buildings around them burned. The pain, the impotence, of being shackled to a pole, bleeding, forced to watch, to hear, to smell. *That* was *the* thing he'd tried to kill with whiskey. But it didn't work like that—you couldn't just go in like a surgeon and blot out one part of a whole.

And there were other images, going further back, also burned onto his retinal memory, but deeper, as if he'd shot them on film himself. His ex-wife, caught naked with his own brother in their marriage bed.

Their mauled son lying in the grass. His brother shooting Brandt's dog.

This part of Brandt's past had been buried very, very deep, and he didn't like to let it surface. Ever. But Dalilah had opened a fissure, and slowly it had been oozing to the surface.

Brandt drank some more, watching the sickle moon rise higher, the stars move over the heavens like a giant celestial timer. He emptied the flask and allowed bush sounds to embrace him, like a familiar and safe lover—crickets, frogs, the rustle of a porcupine not far from him. The distant cackle of a hyena. The *whoosh* of an owl hunting overhead in the darkness.

Then suddenly, a soft, guttural huff.

Brandt went from drunk to stone-cold sober so fast it felt like an electric shock zapped his body. Quietly, he clicked the safety off his rifle, chambered a round, reached slowly up for the Petzl lamp on his forehead, clicked it on. Shadows leaped and shimmered as he scanned the darkness.

A pair of eyes glowed green, looking right at him maybe twelve feet away. The wide-spaced eyes of a big predator. *Jesus.* A chill washed over him and Brandt pushed himself slowly to his feet, his light and gun trained on the animal. It moved across the beam and he saw a ghostly pale pelt. Dark mane. Lion. Male. *Huge.* Every nerve inside him screamed to flee. Brandt swallowed, holding dead still— facing the animal square, his brain racing. The lion's tail swished and the beast gave another soft warning cough. He was unafraid. Alone, which was unusual. Dangerous.

Slowly Brandt reached for the windowsill behind him.

The animal came closer, jaws slack. It was breathing him in, testing the air around him, getting his scent.

Brandt eased up onto the sill.

The lion's tail swished again.

Ever so carefully, Brandt dropped back into the room.

He paused, keeping the beam of his light on the male's face.

It edged a little closer. Too curious. Brandt saw scars on side of its face, across the top of an eye. It was an older male, with no pride. Exiled. Hunting alone. This was trouble.

Brandt's gaze flicked to the fires inside. He eyed a glowing log. Should the lion leap and his first shot not hit true, he'd grab that log as a next resort. Finger curling around trigger, he hissed softly.

"Yaaa."

The lion moved its head, flicking its tail.

"Yaaa!" Brandt yelled louder, waving his arm. Then he released a huge imitation roar.

The lion's tail swished as the beast licked its jowls. Then it broke its gaze with Brandt, and like a ghost, slid back into the night, ceding territory.

Goose bumps chased over his skin as Brandt tried to swallow. His heart was hammering, mouth bone-dry.

The bush night sounds filtered back into his consciousness but he continued to glare into the blackness where the lion had vanished.

Had he even seen it? A solitary old male lion, doomed to prowl the veldt alone. Never mate again. Never be part of a pride. Never watch over a territory for his own family of felines. Destined to live out the rest of his life around the fringes of others' existence.

Tautona.

The hair on the nape of his neck prickled. The animal

had chased him back inside where he should've been all along, close to his principal. The weird feeling down his neck intensified and Brandt's gaze slid over to the dying embers in the fire. He became conscious of how bitter the cold weighing down from the night sky had become. His attention flicked to Dalilah.

She was curled in the sleeping bag, hair a thick soft fall over her cheek. Brandt inched over to look at her face.

Her skin was bloodless. Lips the wrong color. She was shivering. He dropped quickly to his knees, setting the gun beside him.

"Dalilah!" He shook her shoulder.

She was unresponsive.

Brandt felt her skin with the back of his fingers. She was ice-cold, and her pulse was weak. *Hypothermia.* Brought on by the sudden freezing temperatures. Compounded by injury, shock, dehydration, exhaustion—it had all been creeping up on her, a perfect storm of triggers that he'd missed. His fault.

"Dalilah!" Brandt slapped her face lightly.

Nothing.

Panic licked through his gut.

Hypothermia could kill in a situation like this. He shouldn't have left her! He hadn't noticed how cold it had become—he'd allowed the fires to burn too low, been too absorbed in the resurfacing of his own nightmares.

For an instant he was paralyzed, hurtling down, down, down, back into the black tunnel of his Carla nightmare... caring for his principal so much that he'd been blind to the danger signals that had led to the loss of her life. Then in his mind's eye, suddenly, the green eyes of *Tautona* gleamed back. Predatory. Powerful.

Yes. Power. Focus. *Do* this.

Brandt's mind turned razor-sharp. Just because something terrible had happened once before, it didn't mean he was doomed to repeat it. He could *not* allow the past to stop him from securing this woman a future.

"Dalilah!" Brandt slapped her face again and he began urgently rubbing her arms. "Come on, girl, stay with me. I am *not* going to let you do this! I will not let you die!"

Chapter 12

Her thick lashes fluttered and her eyes opened slowly.

"Brandt?" she murmured, confused. "Where…are we?" Her words were slurred. But she was lucid—that was the main thing. Brandt's heart almost bottomed out of his chest with relief.

But she was not in the clear, not by far. Even moderate hypothermia could kill if left untreated. He needed to warm her core temperature *stat*.

Quickly he built up the fire, but the crackling flames weren't radiating as much warmth through the building as earlier—the heat was being sucked up into the clear sky.

He pulled the hot bricks and small rocks away from the edge of the fire. Allowing them to cool partially, he filled the kettle with water. While he waited for the water to boil, Brandt rubbed her arms gently. Rough handling in this situation, he knew, could spark deadly heart rhythms.

"I'm making you some hot, sweet tea, okay? You want some tea, Dalilah?"

She murmured something, turned her head away.

"Dalilah, *look* at me, talk to me!"

"Cold," she murmured. "So cold."

The water was starting to boil. There was slightly more warmth in the room as flames continued to grow and steam rose. Brandt tossed more logs onto the fire. Moving as fast as he could, he ripped off his shirt. Bracing against the chill, he quickly wrapped one of the warm bricks in the fabric. Unlacing his boots, he removed them and took off his socks. Into each sock he stuffed a heated rock, then he emptied his pockets and unhooked his knife, GPS and other paraphernalia from his belt. Undoing his belt, he dropped his pants, cursing his habit of not wearing underwear. It wasn't unusual—many safari guides went commando, a practice born of convenience, and comfort. It kept one cool and dry in often-terrible humid heat. But there was no time to even think about that. He wrapped another warm brick in his shorts. Needing more insulation, Brandt scanned their supplies. The sarong! The kettle started to boil as he removed the sarong from under her head and rolled it around the other warm brick.

Brandt unzipped Dalilah's sleeping bag, untied the sling he'd replaced after their shower, then quickly opened her shirt and placed the heated stones in high heat-loss areas—under her armpits, groin, next to her neck. He wrapped her up, zipped the bag closed, made sweet tea, then knelt beside her and held her head up.

"Drink," he urged.

She started sipping, but still no color returned to her skin, no warmth. Tongues of panic licked deeper. Brandt set the mug down and took her face in his hands, looking directly into her eyes. "Dalilah, listen to me. You've got moderate hypothermia. If it gets any worse, we're in serious trouble, and we have no way of getting medical help out here. I'm getting into that sleeping bag with you." He unzipped the bag again as he spoke, moving fast to snuggle in beside her so as not to allow any more heat to escape.

Ensuring the hot rocks and bricks were in position, he zipped them both up inside the bag and slid his arms into her shirt, pulling her body close against his naked one, wrapping himself around her.

"I know it's not comfortable," he whispered. "But it's a hell of a lot better than freezing to death." He wriggled in closer, hooking his leg over her, drawing her tightly against him as he found the best and snuggest fit against the curves and dips of her body. He drew part of the sleeping bag up over her head.

Brandt had always had a high metabolism, had always given off tons of heat. Unfettered by clothes, it came off him in waves now. Insulated in this high-end, and thankfully large sleeping bag, along with the heat radiating from the hot rocks, he started to cook. And finally he could feel her body warming.

Emotion burned into his eyes. He held her tighter, rubbing her arms gently, wrapping himself around her, enveloping, protecting. And as he lay there with Dalilah in his arms, as the fear began to slowly abate inside him, something raw and powerful and long dead awakened in its place. Protective instinct. It stirred now inside Brandt with the quiet ferocity of a sleeping dragon being roused from hibernation. And it came with a powerful desire to nurture, to hold. And to be held in return. It was raw, and it made him vulnerable.

It made him want something he hadn't wanted in years. A partner. A lover. Commitment. A sense of future shared.

Brandt closed his eyes, aching with the pain of the sensation, and with remorse—for almost failing Dalilah. For failing Carla. For having lost his faith in love all those years ago because of his ex-wife, Yolanda, and his brother.

He kept rubbing her arms gently, and when he felt the shivering stop, her body softening against his, sweet emotion blossomed through his chest.

Brandt placed his fingers against her neck, feeling for her carotid. Her pulse was strong again, steady.

"Warmer?" he whispered against her ear.

"Hmm," she murmured. "Tired. Very tired."

"Sleep, Princess," he whispered tenderly against her ear.

She fell into a deep sleep, her curves pressed into his, her breathing going deep and rhythmic. Brandt felt tears pooling in his eyes, and he let them wet his cheeks as he breathed in deep, snuggling closer, breathing in her scent—a fragrance of flowers from the shampoo she had used under the waterfall.

And for a moment he was suddenly vaulted way back to his youth, when he met the first woman he'd ever loved. A woman he knew he would marry from the instant he laid eyes on her. When she did accept his proposal he was king of the world. Everything was possible, right was right and wrong was wrong and the future was as open and infinite as the Botswana sky above him.

Dalilah stirred in his arms, moving closer, and the firm, soft, rounded warmth of her breasts pressed against his chest. Her lips were so close to his, parted.

Brandt glanced down at her mouth, imagined kissing her again. Heat pooled, low and dangerous, in his groin, and arousal stirred.

Here he was, naked and holding in his arms a woman he wanted, physically, but couldn't have. A woman he dared believe he could actually come to love, but one he had to deliver safely for marriage to another man. He moved his hand down her splint to touch the ice-hard stone on her finger. The diamond that bound her to another.

He needed to remember this.

She'd made her choice. She was a princess, he a washed-up merc scarred by too many battles.

But deep down in his gut, Brandt now knew that saving Dalilah—someone he now cared about—could actually be his salvation. If he could protect Dalilah, where he hadn't been able to protect Carla, maybe it would free him from the loop of his past.

If he could feel love for this woman, yet keep focus and his hands off her, Brandt knew suddenly, instinctively, this would be the gift she gave him. Freedom from his crime of the past. But in order to get there, he did have to give himself permission to *feel* again. He had to be vulnerable.

And it scared him.

Brandt chose to embrace this. In the dark night, with Dalilah soft in his arms, his finger on her ring, he promised himself he wouldn't stop caring, and he'd see her through. Saving her would save him.

This conscious decision, this sudden sharp conviction, cracked something free in Brandt's heart. He felt the night breeze on his face, and his muscles relaxed.

For the first time in ten years—and more—Brandt was finally seeking a way to mend, to heal. He was ready to face the pain of his past head-on, instead of seeking relief in the bottom of that damn bottle.

Brandt checked his watch—4:00 a.m. He eased out of the sleeping bag and stoked the fire, flames warm against his naked body. Making sure his gun, panga and knife were all within reach, he eased back into the sleeping bag and zipped himself in. She turned around, murmuring as he embraced her.

High above in the indigo vault of sky, stars moved. Dew began to settle and temperatures dropped a little further. But in his arms Dalilah was warm. Brandt eased himself into a new position, not wanting to wake her, and he closed his eyes, allowing himself to drift down to a light level of rest, something for which he'd been trained, a state where he'd remain conscious of ambient sound, movement. He'd wake in an instant should anything shift in the atmosphere, even in the most subtle way.

Brandt woke sharply, pulse quickening, senses acute. He listened to the night, trying to discern what had changed. He realized it was a difference in the rhythm of Dalilah's breathing. Fear laced through him. He looked at her face. She was flushed and she moaned softly.

Brandt checked her pulse. It had quickened. She moaned again, suddenly stirring restlessly in his arms. Then with a sharp start he felt the tightness of aroused nipples against his chest. She murmured again, moving her hips. His heart began to slam so hard he thought it would burst out of his chest. She arched her lower back, pressing her pelvis against his naked groin, as she hooked her leg over his. The warm rock between her thighs slid to the side.

Brandt lay dead still. But she moved again, her shirt opening, the other rocks sliding out from the crooks of her arms. He felt the sharp angles of the jewel in her navel pressing against his abdomen.

Sweet heaven, he couldn't breathe. She rubbed her pelvis against his, her leg caressing his, and he felt her pulse fluttering fast as her breathing quickened. She was coming on to him in her sleep, dreaming of sex.

His vision narrowed. His groin heated, his body hardening, quivering with need.

Her arm draped over his bare torso, and she stirred again, edging even closer. Brandt glared at the stars, willing himself to hold still. It was just a dream.

Her leg moved higher, the inside of her thigh chafing him to the sharp, painful exquisite peak of arousal. His erection began to throb. Brandt tried to breathe—he should get out of the bag, *now.* While he still could.

Yet he couldn't. His need was growing so fierce, Brandt feared that if he moved so much as a millimeter in any direction right now, he might just come.

Her hand, soft, warm, moved up his waist, and she murmured words in Arabic—smooth, guttural, impossibly seductive. He groaned. She'd stop any minute, he told himself. *Just hold on for another minute.*

But she turned her face to his and pressed her lips against his mouth. She began to kiss him, suddenly aggressive, hungry, predatory. And Brandt snapped. He yanked her hard against his body, kissing her back, sliding his tongue into her mouth as he moved his hand down her body, cupping her buttocks.

Dalilah groaned, moving her leg higher. Brandt was blind now, incapable of thought, conscious only of delirious sexual contact. Her tongue twisted with his and he moved his hand around, slipping it into the front of her pants, cupping her groin.

She made a soft noise, opening her legs as his fingers met smooth, damp, hot flesh. She widened access, her body going hot, her pelvis suddenly thrusting. Brandt slid his finger up inside her and his vision swirled into a kaleidoscope of scarlet and red. She was tight—impossibly tight. It made him wild. He slipped another finger inside.

She went dead still.

Her eyes flared open.

Breathing fast, she stared at him, eyes widening in what looked like sheer horror. Brandt pulled back.

"Oh, no," she whispered. Then she exploded up from the sleeping bag, frantically trying to free herself from its confines. "Oh, no, no, no!"

Confusion raced through Brandt. "Dalilah?"

She scrambled to pull her shirt closed over her chest, to get out of the sleeping bag, panic in her features, her hair a wild tangle.

"Dalilah, stop! Wait." She must be delirious, he thought, not thinking right. He placed his hand firmly on her shoulders. "Steady. Stay in the bag, stay warm, wait while I stoke up the fire, make you some tea."

He extracted himself from the bag and her eyes slid down his naked body, his arousal a testament to what had been going on in the sleeping bag. Her hand went to her mouth, a look of utter confusion and fear on her face.

"Dalilah, I'm sorry. You were… You had hypothermia. I was warming you up."

Her gaze lowered to his erection.

"Brandt—" She sounded mortified.

He felt just as stunned.

"Dalilah, look, I don't wear underwear, okay? I stripped down to keep you warm. And…" How could he say this? *You came on to me in your sleep?*

Omair would kill him if he found out.

Haroun might kill *her.*

He spun away, grabbed his shorts, pulled them on, fed logs onto the fire. He stared at the flames, brain racing. Dawn was already bleeding pale light into the sky, the sound of birds rising as the bushveldt woke. They had to move. Now. There wasn't time for all this.

"I'm so sorry, Brandt." Her voice came out, soft, rough. Shock rustled through him. He turned slowly.

And his heart squeezed at the look on her face. She pushed a thick tangle of hair back from her face. "I…" She was as lost for words as he was. "I didn't mean it. I was dreaming…I…" Emotion choked her voice and tears spilled from her eyes.

He crouched beside her, took her shoulders in his hands. "Dalilah, it's okay—that was not supposed to happen. I should not have let it ha—"

"It was my fault. I was with you in my dream. I…" Another tear leaked down her cheek. She brushed it away, blushing.

His chest squeezed so tight he couldn't breathe—Dalilah had been making love to *him*.

"Hey," he said softly, "it happens to everyone. I should have stepped away. I'm so sorry, so very sorry. I—" He inhaled deeply, hesitated, struggling for words. "Look, Princess. It's no secret. I want you. You saw in that waterfall what you're doing to me—you're *killing* me—but let's just leave it all right here, okay? No one—not Omair, not Haroun—*nobody* needs to know this. It's between you and me, our secret."

Another tear fell. She looked away.

Anxiety, self-recrimination twisted through Brandt. "Dalilah, please, look at me."

She wouldn't. "You think I'm breaking a promise, Brandt. You think I'm being unfaithful, but I'm—"

"Hey—" he cupped her chin, turned her face back to his "—it's in the past. Like I said, no looking back—keep moving forward. In a few days, this will all be history."

She sat silent. Watching him. Something powerful was going on inside her head. "It won't be over," she said softly.

"What do you mean?"

"It won't be history. Not for me." Then a sharp brightness flashed through her eyes—the old Dalilah was back, the passionate one. She shoved the sleeping bag off her body, grabbed her boots, thrust her foot into one.

"I don't feel like I've broken any damn promise," she snapped, grabbing the other boot, yanking it on, too.

"It wasn't even mine—I never made it." She seemed to catch herself. Then she grew quiet.

Brandt sat back. "I don't understand."

She struggled with the laces of one boot, unable to tie them with one hand, frustration biting at her movements. "It's a political contract, between my deceased father and Haroun's dying father."

He stared. "What is?

"My marriage was arranged when I was five."

He was speechless.

Seconds ticked by. "An arranged marriage?" he said, trying to wrap his head around it. "When you were five years old?"

"Yes. A political alliance between the two kingdoms."

He dragged his hand over his hair. "But...you do love him, right?"

She swallowed, looked up and met his eyes. "Brandt, I barely know him."

"What do you mean?"

"Five times—I've been with Haroun only five times in my entire life."

"You've *slept* with him five times?"

"No! I've been in his company five times. Each time with a chaperone. I haven't even kissed him. I feel nothing physical at all for him, so there you have it now. Happy?"

Brandt's mind reeled, his entire paradigm tilting drunkenly on edge. And pieces of the puzzle that had been niggling at him suddenly began clicking into place—her sad look when he pressed her on her engagement. The quiet desperation in her eyes when he'd asked her if giving up her job and charity work was worth marriage to a king. Her attraction to him.

A mad excitement, anticipation, hope, rushed through him all at once, as if floodgates had been abruptly flung open in his brain. Birds grew loud outside and baboons screeched. Out of the corner of his eye he noticed the sky growing lighter. But he was riveted to the floor by this news, unable to move.

"I know that doesn't excuse what happened here," she said quietly, "but I wanted you to know because—" Her voice hitched and moisture pooled in her dark eyes. "I care that you think well of me, Brandt."

"Do you want to marry him?" Blunt. Simple. Top question on his mind.

"I must."

"Must?"

"It's a binding contract. Two kings, two kingdoms. A political accord. Everyone expects it. My brother, King Zakir, needs it. His ruling King's Council needs it. It will bring a lucrative oil partnership, defense contracts, an economic alliance—"

"And you're the pawn on the chessboard? The chattel to be exchanged. Whatever happened to women's emancipation?"

Her mouth tightened, eyes narrowing, a flicker of defiance shooting through her features. "Haroun is as much 'chattel' as I, if that's what you want to call it—this is not a female thing. He has to uphold his end, too."

"And you're going to do it, uphold this contract?" He waved his hand between them.

"It's my *duty* to uphold it, Brandt. It's been my obligation as a royal since I was five years old. I've grown up with the knowledge. I've accepted I was born a royal, and with that comes obligations other people don't have."

She hesitated, holding his gaze. "Or sometimes can't understand."

He spun around, dragged both hands over his hair, then ricocheted back to face her.

"Jesus, Dalilah, how can you marry a guy you don't even know, let alone *love?* Do feel *anything* for him? Like…"

"Like I feel for you?"

He went dead still. Swallowed. Throat dry, muscles shaking. She'd said it. Out loud. She felt for him. And he'd told her what she was doing to him. What was patently obvious to both had now been made vocal, and that admission cracked Brandt's world open like the shell of an egg, and he didn't know what to do with the mess spilling out.

Rays of light bled into sky, savage slashes of pink, orange, yellow. Amal would be on the move and a voice in the back of Brandt's mind was saying, *Hurry, hurry. Move—now!* Yet a different voice was urging him to deal with the moment properly, not to let something—someone—so precious slip through his fingers forever.

"No, Brandt," she said softly. "I don't feel anything for Haroun other than civility. He's is a nice-looking, smart man, and he seems kind, and—" She looked as if she was going to cry suddenly, then steeled, her chin rising in defiance. And in that brief second Brandt could see the two women inside Dalilah doing battle. One the exotic, determined, flamboyant powerhouse, a proud princess committed to her country and diplomatic function. The other a gorgeous, vulnerable and compassionate woman who needed love in her life.

Dalilah Al Arif had one stiletto planted in an ancient desert world, the other firmly in a new one.

Her cheeks heated and she cursed suddenly, softly, in Arabic. "I wish you'd put some more clothes on."

Brandt jolted back, grabbed his shirt. "You're sacrificing your freedom, that's what you're doing," he said coolly as he pulled on his shirt and cinched his belt buckle. "You're giving up everything you are, who you've fought to become, for your kingdom, for your brothers?"

Anger was creeping into his voice now, and he couldn't help it. "You can't do this, Dalilah." He rammed the GPS back into his belt, grabbed his sheathed knife.

"Why not?"

"It makes you unhappy. You don't have to be a shrink to see that." He waved his hand at the crumpled sleeping bag. "Your kiss, your body, your eyes, everything tells me you want more than a cold marriage, that you don't want to give up the niche you've carved for yourself in the world. You just told me that your whole life you've been fighting to get out from under your brothers' shadows. Now this?"

"You're just saying this because you want to sleep with me."

He reeled, then looked carefully into her features. She was testing, pushing him, he could see that. Maybe to test her own resolve, hell knew.

"No," he said quietly. "I have no right to even try to fight for a woman like you, Dalilah. I could never win, anyway. Besides—" his gaze went to her ring "—if I slept with you, it could get you killed. Trust me—I know."

He resheathed his panga, grabbed his gun. He slung the rifle across his chest and pulled the camera out of the pack.

"I need to go see if there's any sign of Amal. It's getting late." His tone was brusque. But as he was about to step over the coals, he paused as something hit him like a mallet—she'd been engaged all her adult life.

I've never even kissed him...

He spun round. "Dalilah, have you ever dated anyone else?"

Her face flushed. She got slowly to her feet. "No," she said. "The contract stipulates I come to the marriage… pure."

Something akin to violent protectiveness surged through his chest. Brandt felt his neck go wire taut.

"You're a virgin," he said very softly.

She swallowed, the color in her cheeks going high.

His jaw dropped. Princess Dalilah Al Arif, foreign-investment consultant, global activist, one of the most stunning women he'd ever met in his life…

"You've *never* been with a man? Never even kissed anyone?"

Her eyes began to water.

He stared at her, his brain spinning like a top. He'd kissed her, caressed her—this woman who'd been a mere girl when her father had signed a document stipulating she go to another man's bed untouched. To live in a gilded cage of a castle, fenced behind tradition and diplomatic protocol.

And suddenly it sliced him—a hot, vehement rage. This was not supposed to be his business, but by hell it now was. He'd crossed a line. His actions alone in that sleeping bag could cost her life if anyone ever found out. And on the back of the rage rode a raw and basic urge to protect her—from herself, from a future decided by someone else. From her brothers and her own kingdom.

Yet here he was being paid to deliver her to that very fate.

His hands started to shake.

"Dalilah," he said, his voice coming out low, dark, dangerous. "Tell me one thing, and tell me honestly. Do you want to do this? Is it your choice?"

"Yes," she whispered. "It's my choice to uphold my duty."

Brandt spun around and hurdled out the window. He stalked over the veldt toward the cliff edge, conflict torquing inside him. Thrown into the bloody mess was guilt, for touching her like that, for kissing her.

A *virgin.*

Bloody hell.

Way to go, Stryker, you imbecile.

At the cliff edge, he climbed a rock and put the camera to his eye. Zooming in, he panned the landscape. Already sunlight was rippling gold over the grasses. Carefully, he studied the distant line of trees fringing the Tsholo, then he moved the camera to the north.

He stilled. A fine line of rising dust was catching the first full rays of sun. He zoomed in as close as he could. He could make out what looked like two jeeps, four horses, moving south. And fast.

Adrenaline slammed through his body. He leaped down from his rock and ran back to the building.

"Dalilah!" he called as he neared. "They're coming! Get the stuff together!"

He reached the door, began kicking out the coals, throwing sand over the remains of the fire.

She was on her knees struggling to roll up the sleeping bag with one hand. He grabbed it from her.

"They're over the river," he said, breathing hard as he rolled the bag. He stuffed the rest of their gear into the pack. "Give me your feet."

Quickly he trussed up her laces, then he tied the sleeping-bag roll to the pack. "They're heading south, cutting back along the river. When they hit our camp, they'll track back to our jeep. Once they find that, they'll come fast toward the cliff following our prints. Looks like they have two vehicles and horses."

He hefted the pack onto his shoulders.

"Our only consolation is that when they do hit the cliff wall they'll be forced to drive about forty kilometers farther north through some tricky terrain if they want to get up on the plateau. If we move away directly perpendicular to the rift, they won't cut across our tracks, which means they'll have to drive that forty kilometers all the way back to this point before they find our sign again."

He started out the door.

"Brandt."

He stopped, met her gaze.

"I'm scared."

He hesitated. "I know." He grasped her hand. "Come, I've got you." He paused. "And know this, I will die before I let anyone touch a hair on your head."

Her eyes filled with tears "Brandt—I could love you."

Emotion sucker punched him so hard his eyes pricked with tears. He swallowed, controlling himself. He wanted to say so much, and couldn't. "We need to go," he whispered. "You ready?"

She nodded.

They left the small customs building at a fast trot, fueled by the knowledge Amal was right on their tracks. The sun burst suddenly over the plateau—fierce and fiery orange—rays of heat instant. The air was dry.

It was going to be a killer day.

Chapter 13

Brandt moved faster and faster as the sun climbed higher and burned down hotter. Dalilah half ran, half stumbled behind him. She was already desperately thirsty, and blisters from yesterday were rubbing raw in her over-size boots.

Humiliation, desperation, burned through her chest. She'd opened up, made herself so vulnerable, told him she was falling in love with him, while confirming at the same that she was going to marry Haroun. How stupid could she possibly be? What on earth had she hoped to achieve?

Had she thought he'd miraculously rescue her from having to make her own decisions? From her own desires? From her obligations?

All she'd done was make it tougher on him, and on herself, and she'd made herself a wanton fool in his eyes.

"Faster, Dalilah!" he yelled from ahead of her.

"Dammit, I'm going as fast as I can!"

He marched harder, his stride wider. She had to start running full tilt to keep up.

She stumbled, hitting the ground with such a hard thud that it forced him to spin round. The look on his face was ferocious, eyes icy cold. He unsheathed his panga, grabbed a nearby branch and hacked it from the tree. He lopped off the pieces of frayed wood on the end, then he thrust the stick at her.

"Use it to keep balance." He was breathing hard, body glistening with sweat, the sun shining gold on his hair.

"You have to stay focused and *move*. We need to find a vehicle now, before those guys get over the cliff, or we're both as good as dead, because we'll be outgunned and outmanned."

About another mile out and Dalilah could no longer breathe. She bent over, bracing her good hand on her knees, hyperventilating as she strained to catch her breath, drenched in sweat.

"I said keep up, stay right behind me!"

"I'm trying," she snapped.

He stopped, wiped sweat from his brow, frustration burning in his features.

"My boots are too big. You have a longer stride. You're fitter, trained." Emotion filled her eyes, her fear of Amal, her desperation over what was happening between them, her physical inability to match his pace—it was all overwhelming her.

He opened his mouth to say something, but before he could, she said, "And don't think I'm whining. I'm *not*—I'm just saying it like it is. Those are the facts in front of you—so deal with it!"

"*Deal* with it?"

She lifted her head, met his eyes. "Yeah—deal with it."

"The fact you've signed your life away to a man you

have no desire to sleep with? Deal with the fact I'm try-ing to save you—that you've saved yourself—for *that?* So your brothers can benefit?"

Slowly, angrily, she pushed herself back to an upright position, dizziness swirling. "You really are an ass."

He snorted. "I'm a simple guy. I boil things down to the basics, and those are the basics." He paused. "Aren't they? I'm saving you from Amal's murderous animals for what? So you can marry some other tyrant?"

"Haroun is not like that! I don't have to justify my-self to you."

"Then why did you tell me?"

Dalilah's pulse pounded.

He muttered a curse and thrust the water pouch at her. She swigged, wiped her mouth with the back of her hand, shoved it back at him.

"I don't expect you to understand!"

"You're right, I don't."

"And why the hell not?"

"I thought you said—" He stared at her. "Look, drop it. Now is not the time."

She looked daggers at him, her cheeks hot.

He glanced at the sun, then his watch, irritability and tension rolling off his body. "You ready?"

"I need to rest another minute. I can't go on like this." She began to sit down on a rock, but his hand shot out and he grabbed her good arm, yanking her away from the rock. Shock, rage, sliced through Dalilah and she shook him off. "What the—"

He jerked his chin to where she'd been about to sit. A scorpion, translucent brown, scuttled, sideways, tail curved high in warning. She stared at it, then started to tremble, her head pounding in pain as she fought the emo-tion threatening to suddenly overwhelm her.

He was watching her intently.

"Okay," he said. "Sit. Five minutes—that's it." His tone was softer, but underlying it she heard the frustration, the urgency. Amal was gaining. Her life was unraveling.

He fiddled with his GPS while she rested on the rock. Sun pressed down relentlessly, no shade anywhere for respite.

Brandt hooked the GPS back onto his belt, then as if he couldn't hold it in, "It's just—" He stopped himself.

"Just what?"

"Nothing."

"Say it, Brandt. You owe it to me."

He glanced away, struggling with something. Then he said, "You just don't seem the type to go through with an arranged marriage, Dalilah."

"Oh, and what *type* might that be?"

He rubbed his brow. He seemed to be fighting the need to go there, but it was eating at him nevertheless.

"You're liberated, strong, independent…Jesus, Dalilah, you have more assets than…" He swallowed. "All those things you forced on me about yourself—your job, being an investment consultant, buying your own penthouse, having good friends, doing volunteer work that satisfies you. You shoot like an ace. You're strong…and goddamn beautiful." His voice hitched, going thick. "You're desirable enough to make a man weep."

Her eyes gleamed.

"And no matter how you package it to me, or to yourself, you're throwing it away because some man signed you over to an Arabian prince when you were five."

"Not some man, Brandt. My *father*. A king."

"Doesn't change what it is."

"It *does*. I'm a royal. I have obligations. This is bigger than just who I want to sleep with."

His eyes darkened, a muscle working on his brow.

"You know what," she said suddenly. "I lied—I *did* expect you to understand, because of the importance you said you placed in a promise. Because of the way you spoke about loyalty and honor." She held her arm up. "And that is what my ring is about—loyalty, honor, duty."

He stared at her, then the ring.

A vulture circled up high, casting a shadow. Brandt rubbed the back of his neck.

"It's the double standard," he said quietly. "That's what irks the hell out of me. Your brothers got to marry whoever they wanted. Omair was the king of one-night stands before he took a bride. Yet you—you can't enjoy those same freedoms and choices. You're sold like a pawn for their benefit."

"And what about my benefit?"

"Really?"

She glared at him, her pulse racing. Then she said, very quietly. "You know, I wavered once, several years ago. I had met a guy that I liked. A lot. And one night… it led to a kiss, and I wondered if I could go through with this. Then, the very next morning, I got news of the coup in Al Na'Jar—my mother and father had just been murdered in their own beds—their throats slit by their own guards. And on that same night, my oldest brother, Da'ud, was murdered on his yacht off Barcelona. Assassins also went to Zakir's penthouse in Paris and the only reason he escaped was because he was out that night." She inhaled deeply.

"Da'ud had been next in line to take the throne and he'd been ready for it. But Zakir wasn't prepared to lead—he never wanted to. He was a playboy and an entrepreneur, yet he was compelled to return to Al Na'Jar, where he took the throne in a very troubled and violent time of rebellion. Zakir did his duty, Brandt. He gave up his life for our kingdom. And he didn't tell anyone he was going blind as he did this." Her voice grew thick, emotional. Caught.

"Dalilah, this is not the time to—"

"No! I want you to hear it. I *need* you to hear this. Omair didn't shy from committing to relationships because he didn't want one. He *had* to. He couldn't have a normal life. He couldn't involve a woman in what he was doing. He was driven to hunt the globe to bring those assassins to justice, desert style. A blood honor. Only through that process did he find Faith, his wife—and he was able to bring her into his life because she was like him, a soldier. An assassin. She understood him, and his life."

Brandt opened his mouth, but Dalilah raised her hand. "No, hear me out, Brandt, please. Tariq was a neurosurgeon and he was engaged to a woman he loved more than life itself. But Amal's father had a bomb planted on our royal jet and Tariq's fiancée died in his arms as he tried to save her. Tariq was badly scarred in more ways than one, and he lost the use of his arm in that blast. His career was over. In some ways he died himself that day. And it took a long time, and the help of a special woman to bring him back to life."

She paused, looking into his eyes, emotion ballooning in her chest. "And me? I went to school in the United States. I got to pursue my career, my interests. Sure, I built something, but I never suffered like they did." She inhaled deeply. "My brothers did their duty, *are* doing it. And now, this is my cross to bear, my way to give. It was my dead father's wish."

He stared at her. "You're doing it out of guilt," he whispered.

"I'm doing it for family and kingdom."

Something changed in his face. "It's not right, Dalilah," he said quietly. "It's not you."

"You barely even know me, Brandt."

"Oh, I know what you're made of. You put someone into a life-and-death situation and you get to see pretty damn quick what's at the core of that person. You've got what it takes—you've got so much. I hate to see you throw your life away."

"I'm not throwing it away—I'm gaining a political advantage."

"Yeah, well, apparently you've made up your mind about that one. So, don't come looking to me for endorsement, because I don't think your brothers deserve what you're doing for them. How well do you know this Haroun anyway—apart from meeting him five times?"

"Well enough."

"Will you be safe? Are you certain he won't hurt you?"

"What are you saying, Brandt?"

He hesitated, turned away, stared out over the bush. Then he turned back, as if having made up his mind about something. "I'm saying I know things. I did covert intelligence work in Libya. Those two Egyptian men who killed that Sa'ud sheik's fiancée in Dubai were known assassins—the Libyan authorities were looking for them."

Tension thrummed.

"Doesn't prove anything," she whispered.

"Those men had done contract work for the Kingdom of Sa'ud before, Dalilah, paid for by Hassan royalty."

"Work?"

"Murder for hire."

Blood drained from her head. "And you know this because of your covert work?"

"It wasn't a robbery gone wrong in Dubai, Dalilah. That

woman was killed by the Hassans because she'd tainted the royal family by sleeping with another man."

"Does Omair know this, too?"

"I don't know what Omair knows. He wasn't with me on the job in Libya."

She stared at him, her brain reeling.

"Haroun had nothing to do with that incident. He wasn't part of it."

"Are you so sure—a Sa'ud sheik about to become king? Do you think, in the eyes of his kingdom, he'd be allowed to be seen tolerating any indiscretion on your part? I just don't trust the House of Sa'ud."

Silence quivered between them. She could hear bees buzzing somewhere, the shriek of a raptor. Her head hurt.

"He's probably slept with a thousand women himself, and expects *you* to come to his bed a virgin."

Heat flushed her cheeks. "That's unfair," she said quietly.

"That, Dalilah, is the way the cookie crumbles with men like Sheik Haroun Hassan. Trust me, I know. He can have whatever—or whoever—the hell he wants, when he wants, but you can't."

"You don't even know him."

"Yeah," he said softly. "Well, apparently, neither do you."

Tension simmered between them.

"Why—" her voice came out in a hoarse whisper "—are you so bitter? Is it because your own marriage didn't work?"

He came close. She could feel his heat, a kinetic energy rolling off him. He bent down, abruptly cupped the back of her head, and kissed her. Hard. Angry, fierce. She stiffened under him, then instantly melted under her own fire, opening her mouth, reaching up behind his neck, pulling him into herself, kissing him so wildly she could taste blood. Tears came from her eyes, her tongue twisting with his, tasting the salt of him, feeling the rough stubble of his jaw against her cheek.

He pulled back suddenly, breathing hard, his eyes wild.

"That's why," he whispered.

She was shaking, her eyes burning.

"Because I care. Because I've fallen for you, Princess. And because I can't have you, and Sheik Hassan can."

Moisture pooled in her eyes.

"And believe me, Dalilah, I tried not to care—I'm *trying* not to care. But…" His eyes glittered. "I *do* respect your honor, your decision to marry for politics, for your kingdom. But what I can't swallow is that you'll be sacrificing your identity when I can see it makes you so unhappy."

The tears in her eyes slid down her cheeks. He appraised her silently for a moment, struggling with something himself. Then he checked his watch. "Five minutes are up, Princess." He spun away sharply and began to march over the dry, baking earth.

"We've wasted enough bloody time!" he muttered over his shoulder. "Amal will be right on our asses at this rate."

It was almost 11:00 a.m. when Brandt stopped suddenly and held up his hand. Dalilah, zoned out from heat and almost five hours of continuous walking, bumped right into his back.

"What is it?" she whispered.

Then she heard it, a lowing, the distant clang of a bell.

"Livestock. We must be close to the village."

They came over a ridge and Brandt quickly motioned for her to get down.

He lowered himself beside her, just under the lip of a sandy ridge baking under the noon sun.

"Lie flat," he said softly.

They studied the village from their hiding spot. It was fenced and contained several small square houses, painted brightly, with corrugated tin roofs. Papaya trees grew in barren red ground. A few dogs lay in shade and chickens scratched in soil. Goats bleated behind an enclosure while barefoot children played in what looked like a schoolyard—dusty brown legs. A burst of bright laughter reached them.

Dalilah's heart twisted.

It felt so strange to hear children laughing, see them playing, to think of a weekday and school hours while they'd been on the run, hunted by violent killers still on their tracks. And now she was lying here with this man she was beginning to love, and couldn't have—it made it all seem so surreal.

There was a small fenced-off vegetable garden beside the school building and a tower with a water tank nearby. A windmill creaked in the hot breeze. No phone lines. No electricity. A little oasis of life separate from the rest of the world. Dalilah watched as two women with yellow plastic containers in a cart bent over a tap with a hose attached, filling the vessels. A toddler played in the sand at their feet.

It drove home suddenly the reason she was here in southern Africa. The deal in Harare.

The dead delegates. Her brother sending Brandt.

She looked at him.

Because I care. Because I've fallen for you, Princess. And because I can't have you, and Sheik Hassan can...

Did her brothers care? She'd never spoken to them about her marriage doubts. Apart from that one instance of hesitation right before her parents were killed, Dalilah hadn't even articulated her fears to herself. Until now— until the Zimbabwe trip, until she'd met Brandt, and kissed him. Until he'd abducted her—physically ripping her out from the very fabric of her life, affording her a reprieve.

How *could* she expect her brothers to understand or care if she hadn't spoken to them? Dalilah wondered what her father might say if he were alive today, and she told him she wanted to marry a man for love.

Brandt felt her watching him and turned to look at her.

"What are you thinking?" he said.

"About their water. About my volunteer work and what it means to me."

Brandt held her gaze, something softening in his eyes, then he turned back to the village. "One jeep," he said. "Over there, parked behind what looks like some kind of communal building."

"Can we bargain with them for the jeep, do you think?"

"I don't want them to see us. If Amal gets wind these villagers have any information on us, he'll slaughter them all—like he did everyone at the lodge."

"You want to steal it?"

"Liberate it, temporarily."

She smiled. "I'll pay them back for it once we're safe."

"Your brother will."

"No. He won't."

He shot her a fast glance, brow raised.

"This is not his mission. Not anymore."

Brandt opened his mouth, but she spoke first.

"I don't care what you say about paying him back, or owing him. That's between you and him. This is about *me*. My life. My mission. I'm taking it back, taking control. My brothers don't run my life." Then she muttered, "As much as they might try."

He laughed, softly, darkly. "They do control it if you marry for them and not for yourself," he said.

She held his gaze. "If I marry, it'll be my choice."

His features tightened, eyes narrowing.

"If?"

Dalilah's heart beat faster. She hadn't intended phrasing it that way. She averted her eyes.

A woman came out of the school building and rang a handbell. The noise of the children rose as they pushed and jostled and raced to line up in front of her. The woman waited until the line fell silent, then she led the kids single file into the building. In the shade of a tree two men were talking.

"How can we get that jeep with all these people about?"

Brandt took the camera from his pack and panned the village using the telephoto lens. "We could wait until dark," he said. "But that could cost us valuable time. The foot-and-mouth fencing makes it more difficult," he said, adjusting the lens and focusing on the jeep. "There's only one way in and out and that's through the cattle gate and disinfectant troughs over there."

"Is that fencing and trough to control the spread of hoof and mouth, then?" she asked.

He nodded. "The disease devastated Botswana some years back," he said. "See, next to the cattle gate is a smaller trough for people to walk through so they don't carry the disease on their shoes."

They lay a while longer in the sun, watching for opportunity.

Brandt cursed softly. "I hate the very idea of bringing Amal close to this place. This village," he said, "is what Botswana is about for me. This peace. This lack of outside distraction, just people living in the present with what they've got."

"Is that why you came to Botswana, Brandt?"

He grunted, moved the camera, focusing in on the jeep again. "The longer we wait, the closer Amal gets. It's becoming a toss-up between keeping this village safe, and you alive." He swore again, set the camera down, fingered his gun, watching, thinking. She could see he was conflicted.

He turned and looked toward the western horizon. She could see him calculating alternatives.

"That road you mentioned—how far is it from here?"

He rubbed the back of his neck—it was being burned by the sun. She could feel her own skin burning and was grateful for the hat. He had none.

"It's not just the distance to the road. Once we hit that road we need to go south, then veer off into bush again. It would take us days on foot."

"Maybe we could flag down a vehicle on the road."

"The traffic is sporadic at best. We could be sitting ducks waiting out there." Tension was tightening his voice. He was being eaten up with this immobility, the waiting. She swatted a fly. Another hour ticked by, but life continued to move in the village.

"I made your brother a promise," he said quietly, as if thinking out loud. "No matter what you say about this mission being yours or his, I'm going to get you home alive. And I need that jeep to do it."

The sun hit its zenith, small and white-hot in the hazy sky. Dalilah took off her hat and smoothed back her hair, wiped her brow. Brandt handed her a stick of biltong. They chewed in silence.

"So, what did happen ten years ago, Brandt, that has you paying Omair back like this now?"

His mood darkened. Then after a few beats he said, "I think you already have it figured out, Dalilah."

She hooked her brow up. "How so?"

"You've been digging information out of me in bits, storing them like puzzle pieces in that pretty head of yours—I figure you've put most of the puzzle together."

A dung beetle tried to roll a ball of dung up the sandbank. It got almost to the lip, then the dung rolled back down. Like a small black crepuscular tank the beetle scurried after it, started again. Almost at the lip, the ball escaped the beetle's grasp, rolled back down, and the beetle once again began the upward push—a Sisyphean task. Beetle needed a damn break. She picked up a stalk of dry grass and pushed the dung ball over the lip for the beetle, then dusted her hand off on her pants.

"You want me to tell you what I've got, then?" she said finally.

"Not really."

She poked holes in the dirt with her stick, thinking. "I'm going to tell you anyway."

A wry smile twisted his mouth. "Why does this not surprise me?"

"I got that ten years ago something happened while you were with the FDS. Maybe on a job. It involved a woman, and it involved betrayal. And you blame yourself for her death—it cracked something inside you." She glanced at him. "It made you bitter, leery of any level of commitment, afraid to fall in love again."

His eyes bored into her, intense. A muscle began to tick at his jaw.

"Omair intervened and saved your life somehow." She paused, thinking. "It had to be something big, or you wouldn't be here with me now, paying him back like this."

She doodled her stick, then slid her gaze back to meet his. He wasn't smiling. He looked dangerous—a look she'd glimpsed in him before. She swallowed, throat dry, feeling nervous suddenly. "But the part I haven't figured out," she said, "is that you mentioned you were betrayed twice. Promises broken twice."

He remained silent, regarding her intently.

"So—what happened? Does it have something to do with marriage?" she said after a while.

"Why do you ask that?"

"Because you said you were not the one to talk about marriage, that you'd failed at that."

"Dalilah." His voice was low, cool. "Why are you pressing me like this—what difference does it make to you?"

Her face heated. She glanced away, watched a row of little red ants trying to attack a dragonfly—iridescent green and turquoise. She thought of her jewels, her wealth. Her ring.

Slowly she glanced up and met his eyes again. "Because you're not the only one who cares, Brandt."

"And that's where it ends."

"Does it?"

His eyes narrowed sharply. "What are you saying, Dalilah?"

"I don't know what I'm saying." But she did know— she was thinking beyond caring for him. She was thinking about the possibilities of acting on her affection. Of being with him beyond this mission.

He moistened his lips, a pain gleaming in his eyes, brief, then gone. He wiped his brow, fingered his gun.

"When I was twenty-one," he said slowly, "just after I got out of the army—they had conscription back then in South Africa—I married the woman I loved. We had a son."

Shock whispered through Dalilah—this she had *not* expected.

"What's his name, Brandt? How old is he?"

"He's dead."

Double shock. Dalilah's brain raced, a reticence to push further fighting with her now-intense curiosity.

"What happened?"

He checked his watch as if the time would miraculously give him a way out. He shifted his body on the sand, features tight. He was like a caged lion who couldn't handle immobility, trapped with her questions in this cauldron of dust and heat.

She touched his hand. "It's okay, I don't need to know."

He inhaled deeply. "His name was Stefaan, Stefaan after my father. A beautiful blond little boy, hair like white fluff—blue eyes." His voice thickened, catching. His eyes were raw.

Emotion gripped Dalilah's throat.

"He was two years old when he was mauled and killed by our dog." Brandt looked away, getting a grip on himself. "It was my fault. I left the two of them alone in the garden for one second—went in the house to get lemonade for Stefaan." His voice was flat now, empty. "Yolanda, my wife, blamed me for it. We ended up in different rooms, different beds. She wouldn't—couldn't—look me in the eyes. Sometimes I'd feel her watching me, though, and I'd turn, and recognize pure hatred on her face." He inhaled, blew out a long, slow breath, wiping sweat from his brow again.

"She was in pain. We both were. Yolanda looked to my older brother for comfort. Pieter." His jaw tightened around the name. "Pieter had always had a thing for Yolanda, and he stepped in and took on the role of comforting her. And sleeping with her." He paused, a long while. "He shot the dog."

Words defied Dalilah. But she suddenly understood

Brandt wholly, the bitterness. The issues with promise and commitment.

"It was my damn dog," he said very quietly. "A Staffie cross, russet coat. I found him living wild in the bush when I was stationed up at Caprivi. I sneaked him home, named him Jock." He made a wry smile. "Like the old story we all read as kids, *Jock of the Bushveld.* Do you know it?"

She shook her head.

"Written by Sir James Percy Fitzpatrick in the 1800s, a true story about his travels across the veldt with his dog. Jock's become part of South African culture. My Jock was a good dog—I thought he was fine with kids. Until that day. I still don't know what set him off. Maybe Stefaan just got in his space."

She touched his arm, gently. His skin was hot. He stared at her hand.

"Brandt, I'm so sorry. You should have been able to grieve together—"

"Damn right." He ground out the words. "I figure she'd have eventually cuckolded me with that brother of mine. Losing our son was a catalyst—gave him opportunity."

The wind rose, dust picking up in small dervishes.

"Is that when you joined the FDS, after your marriage fell apart?"

"Yeah. Buried my boy. Buried the dog. Sold the farm. Got as far away as possible. I worked with men who understood loyalty. And I earned good money, played too hard, didn't think too much."

"Except for the photos."

His eyes shot to hers. But he said nothing.

"And then you met someone else?"

He snorted softly. "Carla. Daughter of a Nicaraguan police chief. He had a big drug crackdown looming, a battle with a cartel leader whose son his daughter had started seeing. He wanted me to get her away and keep her away—he expected bloodshed and retaliation, and he figured the cartel would use his daughter to get to him. My job was to abduct her and hide her, protect her. It was a mission that took months. She was beautiful—dark hair, smoky eyes, dusky skin, body to die for. She pushed all my buttons." He glanced her way. "You remind me of her."

Dalilah swallowed, another puzzle piece clicking into place—his conflict over her, his brusqueness when they'd first met.

"You fell for her."

Brandt was silent a long while. "I crossed a line, Dalilah. A line I had no bloody right to cross. She came on to me. And I fell for it."

"What do you mean, fell for it?"

"She was using me, and I didn't see it coming. We were in a remote mountain area. Just our camp, me and her. We started sleeping together. I lost focus enough to think I didn't have to watch her every second. I began to trust her, and one night she used my communications equipment to tell Alejandro—the drug lord's son—where she was. His father sent Alejandro and some men. They attacked two nights later. He killed her."

"Alejandro *killed* her?"

Brandt closed his eyes and his voice went strange. "He was never into Carla. They were using her all along—her father was right. They surprised me, beat me, tied me up where I was forced to watch and hear them rape her. Then Alejandro slit her throat." He swallowed. "They let me live—to deliver the message to her father."

Horror washed up her throat. "Oh, God, Brandt."

How did someone come back from that?

"People do make mistakes in life," he said quietly. "You

learn from them and move on. But my mistakes—they re-
sulted in death. I tried to run from the images in my head,
the sights, sounds, smells…her screams. But they would
wake me in the night. That's when I hit the whiskey—
looking for relief. I was blind drunk for months, living in
a slum. That's when your brother came to Nicaragua, to
find me, haul me out. He took me back to the FDS base
on São Diogo, sobered me up, slapped me around and
forced me back into some sort of functional shape. And
that, Dalilah, is why I'm going to hand you back to Omair
in one piece, or die trying."

No man left behind.

The final puzzle pieces locked into place. Emotions
rushed through her chest.

"So that's when you quit military life—you vowed to
get out, to stop killing."

"I used to think of violence as a harsh but justifiable
means to an end—most soldiers do, or they couldn't keep
doing the job. But violence has consequences—it always,
always comes with collateral damage. You think soldiers,
cops, become inured—that's a myth. Most perpetrators
of violence just keep pushing their reactions down deep,
until there's too much buried, and you wonder why they
snapped."

A profound and powerful affection for this man swelled
so fast and hard in Dalilah's chest it was painful. This
powerful body of Brandt Stryker's housed a man with
depth and compassion. He'd been hurt inside and out, and
was badly scarred because of it.

Dalilah understood that kind of scarring—her family
had been through it with her brother Tariq. And she was
filled now with the need to nurture, hold him, love him,
heal him and it made her eyes burn because it scared her.

His gaze flicked to her engagement ring.

"That's also why I know marriage is not what it's cracked up to be," he said quietly.

Without thinking, Dalilah leaned forward, took his roughly stubbled cheek in her hand, drew his face toward her and kissed him. Softly, tenderly.

Brandt melted into the sensation of her lips over his, the touch of her hand against his skin. His eyes burned with a sweet kind of pain as he kissed her back gently, so gently it hurt every aching, burning nerve in his body. And he wanted her—all of her—for himself.

He wanted to take her home. Make her his.

Brandt had never taken a woman back to his farm.

His world narrowed as he threaded his fingers into her hair, soft and thick in his hand, and he drew her closer to him.

Then a slow prickle started up Brandt's neck—a hunter's instinct. A sense of being watched, preyed on. He froze. Her body stilled under his.

"Don't move," he murmured against her lips, his hand going for his gun, finger curling into the trigger. He breathed in slowly, very slowly, then whipped onto his back, spinning the rifle round.

Chapter 14

A little black face peered at them from between the scraggly branches of dry scrub. Brandt's heart slammed against his chest, fury lacing through him as he released his finger from the trigger—he should have been aware, heard this kid approaching.

Now they'd been spotted. This small child, and possibly his whole village, had just been put in jeopardy.

Brandt raised his finger slowly to his lips, telling the kid to stay quiet. But the boy exploded from behind the bush and bolted on skinny little dusty legs and bare feet toward the village, calling out in a high-pitched voice.

Brandt swore, lurching to his feet as he took chase. He dived for the boy, tackling him to the ground. The child squealed in terror, squirming like a snake in his arms. Brandt held the kid steady until he stilled. Eyes huge and white with fear looked up into his face. Again Brandt cursed—the boy was only about eight years old.

"Take it easy," he said in Setswana. "It's okay. We mean no harm. We just want to buy that old jeep parked inside the fence. What's your name, boy?"

"Wusani."

"Who does the jeep belong to, Wusani? Can you bring him out here to me?"

The boy remained motionless, transfixed by Brandt's eyes. Brandt was used to this—the color of his eyes was likely unusual to this child, and possibly frightening.

Slowly releasing his grip on the boy, Brandt repeated his question. "Wusani, who owns the jeep?" But the kid dashed off.

Brandt dived, caught him again, got him in a hold.

"Listen," he said, urgency biting into him, "I need your help, son. There are some bad men searching for us. They want to hurt that lady over there." He pointed to the rise, Dalilah's head just visible.

The child looked where he was pointing.

"I need to take her somewhere safe. Fast. And I need the jeep because my airplane doesn't work."

Brandt could see the wheels turning behind Wusani's dark brown eyes, bright with a mix of fear, intelligence and curiosity. He looked Brandt up and down.

"I'm a pilot," Brandt said. "I fly planes." He pointed to the sky. "You ever been in a plane, Wusani?"

He shook his head.

Out of the corner of his eye Brandt saw a man coming out the village gate, calling for the boy.

Crap. This was going downhill fast—he'd hoped to limit potential damage by keeping this between as few people as possible.

"Who's that man, Wusani?" Brandt said with a jerk of his chin toward the man.

"He's my grandfather."

An old man, wiry, approached with a stick in his hand. It had a shiny knob on the end. He stalled when he caught sight of Brandt and Wusani. Brandt released the child, and the boy raced to his grandfather.

"It's okay," Brandt called out in Setswana, putting down his rifle and showing his hands. Another man, younger, was now exiting the village gate. A group of women near the fence stopped to stare.

Brandt inhaled, approaching them, preparing for a lengthy Botswana greeting—anything less would be an insult.

He introduced himself to the wiry old man with salt-and-pepper curls. The young man joined the group, and Brandt introduced himself to him, too. The young man said he was Wusani's father.

Brandt asked who the village headman was, and whether they had cattle. He congratulated them when they said they did—livestock was money and status. They in turn asked about his own cows, and congratulated him when he said he had a few head. He felt the clock ticking, time dribbling away like sand between his fingers.

The old man told Brandt the chief's name was Baikego Khama.

"Everyone calls him B.K." His wizened face cracked into a gap-toothed grin, gums pink. More villagers were gathering near the fence, curious. Brandt's heart sunk— there was no way out of this now.

From his pocket he took the wad of greenbacks he'd liberated from the Germans. All eyes went to the money.

"U.S. dollars," he said. "I'm interested in buying that jeep under the tree over there. Who owns it?"

"It belongs to the village," explained the old man. "But B.K. controls who can use it."

"Can I speak to B.K.?"

They nodded and made a gesture for Brandt to follow them. Brandt motioned for Dalilah to come over. She scrambled down the bank, and picked up his rifle, bringing it to him.

Wusani skipped on his skinny little legs beside them as they entered the village and made their way to the headman's hut. They passed the jeep. It was old, and on the side of the door were faded letters that read: *Masholo Safari Lodge.* The vehicle had likely been sold to this village when the camp offloaded it, thought Brandt.

Wusani's dad went up to the chief's door and knocked.

"Your grandson doesn't go to class with the other kids?" Brandt asked the old man as they waited a respectful distance away.

A shadow crossed the man's face. "Wusani runs away from school." He shook his head. "He's a smart boy, like his uncle who works for the mine. But Wusani muddles his letters—he can't learn to read and so he runs away."

Dalilah glanced at Brandt, curiosity raising her brow.

He took her hand, squeezed. "Just small talk," he explained in English.

The chief came out of his hut.

Brandt greeted the headman with deference and began the whole greeting routine all over again. The chief had a Zionist badge on his shirt—a common southern African practice, claiming allegiance to the African Zionist church. He was likely a good man, a principled man. And Brandt's head hurt as he thought of Amal coming closer and closer, what he might do if he thought these good people had helped him and Dalilah in any way.

"My name is Brandt Stryker, from over that way," he told B.K. as he pointed west. "They call me Tautona where I come from."

B.K.'s eyes went to the lion tattoo on Brandt's arm.

"I have a plane, and I fly tourists to lodges all over Botswana. I've flown guests to Masholo Lodge, too. Do you have villagers who work at Masholo?"

B.K. said there were.

"They will know of my plane," he said, drawing Dalilah closer. "And this is my friend."

There was no point in hiding his identity—his tag was emblazoned across the tail of his Cessna, and Amal wouldn't have to dig too hard to find out who the plane was registered to.

"We want to buy, or borrow, your jeep—my plane is not working, and we have far to go." Brandt took out the wad of greenbacks again, fanning them out so the chief could see the amount. "We're also in a hurry."

Suspicion crossed B.K.'s face. He looked up from the money into Brandt's eyes.

"It's not enough money to buy the jeep," B.K. said.

Brandt inhaled slowly, tempering his mounting sense of urgency. "I will bring more money when my plane is fixed."

B.K. shook his head.

"What is he saying?" Dalilah whispered.

"He's saying it's not enough."

A group of five women, one with a baby wrapped onto her back, another with a toddler at her feet, had gathered nearby. Brandt felt the fire of panic burning through his gut. This was just going from bad to worse—they had to get out of here.

The toddler waddled over to Dalilah and she smiled, dropping into a crouch. The baby touched her face and she laughed, a husky, warm sound. Anger braided through Brandt.

"Leave that kid alone," he whispered harshly in English.

Surprise widened her eyes. "Why?"

"Don't touch them—just leave these people. We shouldn't even be here, talking to them. We're putting them in danger by being here!"

She swallowed and stood up, a strange expression crossing her face.

He turned back to B.K. "Look, I know it's not enough," he said in Setswana. "But I have cattle. I have a farm. I *will* return with a new jeep for you. A much better one, and more money."

B.K. turned to Wusani's grandfather, and they moved off to the side where they were joined by three other men including Wusani's father. They argued in low tones.

"What is it?" Dalilah asked.

"It's not enough cash for the jeep, and they don't trust that I will return with more." Sweat beaded on Brandt's brow—he felt as if he was going to implode. He spun round, paced. "We should have just walked."

"We've waited this long already."

"We're not getting that jeep now. And they've seen us and know we're desperate for a vehicle. Do you think they're going to let us creep back in here to steal it as soon as it gets dark? They'll try to stop us, and I'm not hurting these people. Not taking it by force."

Dalilah stared at him, that odd look still on her face.

"Do they speak English?" she said suddenly.

"Hell knows. Some of them, probably. The teacher for one."

She spun around, pointedly taking it all in, her gaze touching on the school building, the water tower, the creaking windmill, the goats, the straggling vegetable garden, the colorful houses with their tin roofs, then alighting on the toddler.

"This is what I wanted," she whispered.

"What?"

"This. My goal. My work. The mission in Zimbabwe." Her eyes shimmered with sudden, fierce emotion. Her mouth went tight, her hand fisting. She turned suddenly and marched toward the group of men arguing quietly under the thorn tree near the chief's house.

"Dalilah!"

She didn't heed him.

"Dalilah!" He ran after her, took her arm, whirled her around to face him. "What are you doing?"

She shook him off and went up to the men. "I can pay for the jeep," she said to them.

They all looked at her.

"Do you speak English? Do you understand me?"

"Yes," said Wusani's father.

"I can buy the jeep." She was wiggling the ring on her hand, desperately tugging it off her swollen finger as she spoke, and it struck Brandt suddenly what she was doing.

"Dalilah—no!"

"And gas. I want spare gas—petrol, for the jeep?"

She yanked the ring off and held it up to them. Sunlight caught sparks of grapefruit pink. The platinum setting gleamed white.

"I will pay with this."

The men stared.

Brandt took her arm. "Dalilah," he said into her ear, "they have no idea what that's wor—"

She angrily shrugged him off again.

"Does anyone here know anything about diamonds? Do you know what you can buy if you sell this stone?"

A murmur went through the group as energy shifted.

"Go get Teep," the headman barked at one of the younger men, suddenly all clipped business. He shot a glance at Brandt, then at Dalilah, then the huge rock—an apple of temptation.

"Teep," he said quietly, while staring fixedly at the rock, "is my son. He works at the Botswana diamond mine. He has come back to the village to see his family."

A tall and devastatingly handsome man who looked as though he'd been carved from ebony came striding toward them, Wusani scampering excitedly at his heels. He wore perfectly pressed khaki pants and a crisp white shirt. His black leather shoes had been polished to a high gloss.

His greeting, thankfully, was less traditional and brief. He took the ring from Dalilah, held it up to the light. His body went dead still, but Brandt could see the subtle shift in his muscles, the quickening of his pulse at his carotid. He swallowed and looked slowly at Dalilah, as if in disbelief.

"They don't even have pink ones like this in South Africa." His English was impeccable, British accented.

"Ten carats." Dalilah said. "Cut and polished from a rough 21.35-carat gem mined from the Argyle mine in the East Kimberley region of Western Australia. It's set in platinum. If you give us the jeep, spare gas, camping supplies and water, you can keep the diamond."

"What in hell do you think you're doing?" Brandt whispered, pulling her aside.

"I'm doing what I want to. I want the jeep and I want to get out of here."

Teep drew his father aside, and they conversed in low tones.

"Jesus Christ, Dalilah," Brandt whispered. "You can't give away a sultan's ring like that—"

"Haroun can afford it, Brandt. Look at it this way, it's buying my life. He'll have to understand that. If he doesn't, he has a problem. Besides, I'll reimburse him."

"What's that thing worth anyway?"

"Two point five."

"Million?"

She said nothing.

He stared at her, his brain reeling. "Dalilah, what decision, exactly, are you making here?

"Just leave me, okay!" she snapped, reading the deeper questions in his eyes. "It's my decision, not yours."

"That's more money than these people will know what to do with."

She raised her arm and swept it in a wide arc, taking in their surrounding village. "They need a new school. Those kids could do with shoes. That water tower needs to be replaced. They could install solar power, get hot water and electricity into their homes, increase their crops with better irrigation. More cows, another windmill, a new jeep, maybe even a secondary-education fund."

He just stared at her. The group of men, including B.K., were now looking at her, too. More women were gathering nearby and the school kids were coming out. The whole damn village was coming to witness this event now.

Urgency exploded in him.

"It's what I've always wanted, Brandt," she said quietly, urgently. "I have wealth and I want to help." Her eyes glittered with passion. "This continent is my home, and this is my dream."

"This is more than just about the jeep and helping African villages, isn't it?"

"This is about my life, Brandt," she said quietly, "and what I want to do with it."

A quiet rustling wildfire of hope ignited suddenly in Brandt—hope for something he didn't even dare want to think about. Chief B.K. was approaching them, but

Brandt's brain had suddenly stalled and all he could do was stare at the princess.

"Teep says this is a good diamond," B.K. announced.

"It's a damn fine diamond," Dalilah said.

"Why do you want to give us this stone? Is it stolen?"

She moistened her lips. "No, it's not stolen. I want to give it to you because we need that jeep very badly, and because I can see your village needs new water tanks, and a new school, and a proper vegetable garden."

He regarded her intently for several long beats.

"Well—is it a deal?" she said.

B.K. bowed, softly clapping his hands together in a sign of thanks. He followed this by making a sign of the cross for good measure.

"Thank you," he said. "Thank the Lord for this gift. You may take jeep, and all our petrol, and any supplies we can give. Teep will help you. Tell him what you need, and he will get the villagers to bring everything."

"We're in a hurry," she said.

"Yes—we will be quick."

Dalilah smiled triumphantly at Brandt, an expectant look in her face.

"I'm not saying thank-you," he growled. "If Amal comes here, finds that ring…" He pointed after B.K., then swore and stalked off toward the jeep. She ran after him.

"I'm not asking for your thanks, you…brute."

He huffed, walked around the jeep, evaluating her purchase. Afternoon shadows were already lengthening. Doves sounded in the trees.

On the rear of the jeep someone had scratched the word *Skorokoro*.

"You see that?" He jerked his chin to the scrawled inscription. "It means too old to work. You paid two-point-five million for a lemon that might not even get us to the road."

"If you have issues, I'll drive. It's my jeep now."

He grunted.

"You just don't like a woman taking over, do you, Brandt? Or is it the fact I have money?"

He stopped dead, turned to face her square. "No, Dalilah, it's Haroun. I don't like that family, and you've just given away his ring—I don't know what constitutes a violation in his goddamn tradition."

Her face sobered. "You're afraid for me."

"Hell, yeah. Nothing about this is right." He waved his hand at the jeep, the village. "We've probably brought harm right to their door. And now—" He stopped speaking as he saw Teep approaching with two women dragging a cart of boxes loaded with supplies.

Teep handed him the jeep key as the women began to load the supplies into the back.

"Food, water, spare petrol, camping stove, pot, kerosene lamp, spare tin of kerosene and a blanket." Teep hesitated, then said, "And two tins of motor oil."

"Thank you," Brandt said, irritably taking the keys. "Does it leak oil, then?"

"A bit."

He grunted irritably. "You have any spare ammunition lying around?"

Teep's eyes shot to his.

"For my rifle. Might need to hunt."

Wariness crossed the man's features, but he called out over his shoulder for someone to bring rifle bullets.

A man came running with two boxes of shells.

"Get in, Princess," Brandt said as he took the boxes. "Your chariot awaits."

She muttered something in Arabic and climbed into the passenger seat.

Brandt got in, turned the ignition.

The engine coughed, then sputtered to life with an unearthly growl.

"Skorokoro, you better have some juice in you," he said as he pressed down on the accelerator.

He gave a wave of thanks and they trundled toward the gate, someone running ahead to open it. The children ran behind in their dust, squealing and waving. One of the women began to sing, and others joined in, waving them goodbye.

But as they reached the gate, Brandt stopped the vehicle just before the cattle grid and disinfectant trough.

"I'll be right back," he said, throwing open the door.

Dalilah shot him a look—he was edgy, she thought, like bottled fuel ready to blow. "Where are you going?"

But he was gone already, engine still running, door open. Dalilah spun around in the passenger seat. He'd taken the chief aside, his head bent down, urgency in the set of his body as he discussed something. A whisper of trepidation ran through Dalilah. The shadows were growing longer, the colors of the bush turning gold.

Brandt got back into the driver's seat and shifted gears. They bumped over the cattle bars, and he laid on the gas. Dust boiled out behind them, catching the sun's yellow rays. The jeep had some power in it, even if it sounded cranky. Dalilah took off her hat before the wind could snatch it from her head, holding her hair in her fist to keep it from whipping her face.

She glanced at his profile. His hands were tight on the wheel, his features pulled into a frown.

"What did you say to the chief when we left?"

"Told him if men come to his village asking about us,

to say that we stole the jeep—then to show Amal our tracks to the road."

"Why?"

"I don't want Amal to think they helped us or that they're hiding anything. I don't want to give him any reason to hurt them."

She swallowed, thinking of the villagers' faces, the children, the bright, white smiles, the happy school. The babies.

They came to the road. It was narrow and the paving was pocked with potholes and being eaten away by thick grass along the edges. A rickety wooden arrow declared the Limpopo River border with South Africa was to the left, and another arrow pointed right to Bulawayo.

Brandt wheeled onto the rugged road and headed south toward the Limpopo.

"We'll travel about twenty klicks down this paved section, then cut off into a tract of controlled conservation area. We'll do some countertracking at the junction, and hopefully Amal will lose our vehicle tracks for good along here."

"Countertracking?"

"Hide our tracks so it's not obvious that someone recently veered off this road into sand."

In the opposite lane, a vehicle came toward them, shimmering in the distance. It blew past—a blue-and-white Botswana police van heading north. She shot Brandt a fast look.

"They can't do anything, Dalilah—the police here generally don't even carry guns. It's why I like this country. It's a good place." She heard the bite of self-recrimination in his voice. He felt he was bringing bad things into a haven that he'd chosen to come to and try to heal all those years ago.

He drove faster, the combination of potholes and bad suspension sending jarring shocks right through her teeth. Dalilah gripped the side of the door for purchase as Brandt swerved wide into the oncoming "lane" to avoid a particularly large hole.

Just as he veered back into their own lane, he suddenly swerved again, this time to avoid a warthog that burst out of the tight grass on the side of the road and scampered across, followed by babies, tails held erect.

The sun was sinking toward the horizon and the wind was warm against her face. The plains rolled away in endless browns and golds. Dalilah touched her naked ring finger, a crazy sense of freedom overcoming her as they barreled down this road, through empty land as far as the eye could see. The more she thought about it, the wilder the excitement racing through her heart—she wasn't going to marry Haroun.

She'd decided that when she took off the ring. But coupled with a delirious sense of liberation, Dalilah was also deeply anxious about how to break the news to Haroun, to her brothers and to the world, especially after their official engagement had been reported by media around the globe. The guest list was already being prepared. And Brandt was right—one invitation was being sent to the White House, too.

She glanced at him. Strong, protective, sensitive, caring. He had no idea what he'd done for her, and at this moment Dalilah just wanted to stay out here, travel this road with him, with the warm wind in her hair. But she couldn't outrun the inevitable looming consequences of her decision not to uphold the treaty.

There *would* be an end to this road, and she still had to face it. Brandt slapped the dash suddenly, and made her jump.

"What is it?"

His hands fisted tight on the wheel. "We shouldn't have interacted with them. You shouldn't have touched the kid. They're going to get hurt."

"My touching that toddler isn't—"

"We shouldn't have been there, Dalilah! We should've split the instant that Wusani kid saw us." He gritted his jaw, face going darker, shoulders tighter.

"Brandt, we can't change what happened now."

"Our tracks lead right up to that village. Amal is going to go in there and start asking questions—"

"And the headman will tell him we stole the jeep, like you said."

"One of those kids, or women…someone in that village is going to let something slip if Amal and his men start scaring them. He's going to find your ring. Amal's going to find your ring and they're finished."

They passed a dead cow on the side of the road. Two women with knives bent over, skinning it to reveal a sinewy white carcass. It must have been hit by a vehicle, and they were not going to let it go to waste. She turned away, feeling suddenly sick, fear whispering through her again. They drove by a few more signs of civilization—another road sign, two women walking with large bundles on their heads. Soon there was a high game fence running alongside them for miles.

Brandt swore again, eaten up by what they'd done.

"We had no choice but to interact, Brandt, after that child saw us."

"Because I was too damn busy kissing you—that's why!"

She swallowed. His fury at himself was palpable and increasing in direct proportion to the distance they were putting between themselves and the village. It made her edgy, nervous for the villagers. Images assailed her again—that dead delegate under the table, Amal's men mowing them all down, slaughtering innocents.

Brandt swerved sharply to avoid a man standing on the side of the road, waiting, presumably, for a ride. Next to him was a garbage bag of clothes and two wooden boxes filled with old-fashioned glass pop bottles. Dalilah guessed he was going to sell them.

"This is where we leave the road," Brandt veered off the paved section and jounced over a dirt track toward a break in the game fencing. The jeep trundled over a series of cattle grids as they entered the controlled area. He stopped the vehicle, got out, grabbed a branch from the side of the path and went back to the road, sweeping over their tracks.

When he got back into the driver's seat Dalilah saw he was pale under his tan, his skin tight—he really was broken up about leaving those villagers.

Conflict torqued inside Dalilah as they entered a gorge, high rocky cliffs on either side, casting long shadows.

"Valley of Ghosts," he said.

"Is that what it's called?"

He nodded. "A superstitious place."

They traveled for a while down the gorge, cliffs narrowing in on them.

He sensed her uneasiness. "Don't worry, the path veers off before it narrows too much."

"It's not the gorge, Brandt. It's the village. I mean, if they claim we stole their jeep, surely—"

"Omair has told me things about Amal," he said coolly. "He revels in destruction, pain, hurt. He's evil, Dalilah. I saw firsthand what he did at the lodge—I can see him slaughtering every one of those villagers for pure pleasure."

"Okay, so you're right, maybe we should have just walked."

"And then? You'd be dead by sunrise. Because if we were on foot, he'd be on our asses before dawn with his horses and jeeps."

She stared at him.

"So you chose me over that village."

He drove in silence.

"I'm sorry," she said quietly. And she truly was. For being an Al Arif royal, for attracting Amal, for Omair forcing Brandt into this. For bringing possible devastation to an innocent village, for pushing this man to break his vow of peace.

"Brandt," she said suddenly, "stop the car."

"What for?"

"Just stop. Now!"

He did. Dust settled. The sound of birds rose around them.

"We need to go back."

He rolled his eyes. "We can't—I'll be signing your death warrant, Dalilah. My sole purpose out here is to keep you *alive*."

"We *have* to go back."

"And do what, exactly?"

"Kill Amal."

He stared at her, stunned by the determination—and fear—on her face.

"We need to protect that village, Brandt, and we need to head Amal off, lead him away.... I don't know, trap him or something."

"Don't be naive," he snapped. "You know what'll happen, Dalilah—we'll *all* die. Villagers, you, me...I get to see a repeat of what happened to Carla."

"Oh, so it's about you."

He swore violently. "That is not fair."

She swiveled in her seat, faced him square. "Listen to me, Brandt, I can't keep running. If we don't end this now, if Omair doesn't catch him, he's always going to be out there somewhere." She pointed into the distance. "There will always be the fear that he'll come after one of my family, anywhere, anytime, somewhere in the world. I have to end this now."

"You?"

"We do. Me and you. A team."

"Dalilah—"

"Listen, Brandt, I know you made this vow not to use violence, but please, help me do this. I can't keep running, not now that I have everything to live for. I gave away that ring because I decided I couldn't give up who I am in order to marry Haroun. You helped me reach that decision. Now I'm almost there—almost free. Help me go the rest of the way."

He stared. Something unreadable in his face. Something changing in the lines of his features, in the quality of light in his eyes—anticipation, hope. It fueled her.

But he said, "Dalilah, I cannot endanger your life. I just…can't. My job is to protect you."

She grabbed his arm. "Brandt, this is not about your job, it's not about delivering me to Omair—I'm not going anywhere. This is about *us*. About…maybe trying to make things work."

The muscle in his jaw ticked. He swallowed. "What are you really saying, Dalilah?"

She glanced away. What *was* she saying? Then she spun back to face him. "I'm saying that when this is all over, I want to come to your farm, Brandt. I'm saying I want to get to know you better—if you'll let me."

All the color drained from his face.

"But I have to tell Haroun I'm not upholding the treaty, and I have to inform my brothers. If I can also tell them Amal is gone, it's going to win me favor. That's my offer to them, my compromise. That's what I can do for my country. And I need your help."

"Christ," he breathed.

"Remember, Brandt," she whispered, "you told me yourself, whatever you do out here, don't run. Because there's nothing out here that you can outrun. I'm not running anymore. And neither are you, because if you come back with me, and we take out Amal, you'll kill those memories in your head, I swear it."

He continued to stare at her. "You're not going to marry him?"

She smiled, a little tremulous, excitement glittering in her eyes, exhilaration shining around her.

"No," she whispered. "If I marry, Brandt, it's going to be for love."

He felt as if he was on the edge of a precipice, and she was asking him to jump without a chute. He was so damn afraid that what she was promising wouldn't work out. The princess and the mercenary.

Was it even possible?

"If you help me kill Amal, Brandt, I can be free."

"No," he said. "No way am I letting you do this for your brothers. I can't allow you to have blood on your hands. It's not you, Dalilah, to kill a man. You don't even hurt animals."

"He's not a man. He's a monster. You said it yourself—he's evil."

Brandt shook his head.

"I'm not taking you back there. I'm not getting you killed." He hesitated, his brain racing through options. She was right about one thing—they couldn't run forever. If

Amal did find their tracks off the road and into this controlled game area, there was a very real chance he'd end up tracking Brandt all the way back to his farm, and Amal could reach the farm before reinforcements ever arrived from Omair. This could end in a violent confrontation either way. He cursed inwardly. He'd rather bring the confrontation to Amal, on his own terms.

"I'll go back myself," he said. "I'll hide you here, up in those cliffs."

"What?"

"You hide out here in the gorge—and if I don't return, you make your way back down to the main road and start walking south. There'll be a truck at some point. Stop the truck, get the driver to take you to the first village, find a phone and call Omair. He'll come get you. Tell him my debt is paid. Tell him I went after Amal." He opened his door, got out and leaned over into the backseat, began repacking a box.

"What are you doing?"

"Leaving you supplies."

Dalilah flung open her door, went up to him, grabbed him by the arm. "Brandt, stop. Look at me!"

He stilled, and slowly met her eyes.

"Just how are you planning on doing this alone?"

He said nothing.

Blood drained from her face. "Oh, no," she whispered. "You're going to lure him away and drive until Skorokoro runs into the ground? And then he'll kill you."

"Dalilah—"

Her face hardened. "That's rich—make me fall in love with you, make me abandon my country and my obligations, then you go on a suicide mission?"

"How," he said very quietly, "can you ever think you could want to be with me on my land in the remote Botswana wilderness, Dalilah? You're riding on an adrenaline rush. When you sober up in a few days, you'll see. I'll be history in your eyes."

She barked a harsh laugh. "Oh, and here I thought you said you knew me! You know nothing, Brandt Stryker, about my love for this continent, about who I really want to be. Who I *can* be. But you had the gumption to show me—you can't abandon me now." Her eyes glittered with emotion, and hot spots of color rode high on her cheeks. "And I'm not going to let you do this alone."

She placed her hand against his face—skin soft, warm. "Either we do this together or we let those villagers die."

"If we do it together I might be letting *you* die," he said.

"Then we go out in a blaze…we go like Thelma and Louise, like Bonnie and Clyde, like…I don't know—like Brandt and Dalilah."

He opened his mouth, but she put her fingers to her lips. "I don't want to face a future without trying to make one with you, Stryker. A team. Like you said back at the cliff, one rock at a time. And then when we're done, you take me home. Your home."

Conflict twisted so tight in Brandt he couldn't breathe.

He couldn't believe what he was hearing. She'd just given him everything…the whole world, a future, to fight for. A reason to live. To try again. Another chance.

And everything to lose.

His eyes burned as he met the fierce passion in her gaze. And he knew—he knew with every molecule in his being, that he loved this woman. This woman who never stopped surprising him, who was his match in so many ways and more. A woman who could challenge him and take him to task when he got out of hand.

She wanted him. This princess who'd never been with any other man—she wanted him to take her home.

To his bed.

Dare he do this? *Could* he ambush Amal, take him out and keep her alive at the same time? All he had was the jeep, one rifle, shells, a panga and a knife.

And his wits, he told himself. He had his smarts. He was a veteran guerrilla fighter.

A rush like thunder exploded through his chest and his brain started firing on all cylinders. It would be dark soon. Amal could have found their camp at the abandoned airstrip by now—or would soon. They were running out of time.

He thought about what he had in the jeep, in the boxes. Petrol. Motor oil. He had matches. A lighter. His brain raced. Then it hit—the man with the wooden crates of empty glass bottles at the side of the road about a klick or two back. Unless a vehicle had come down the road already and picked him up, he might still be there.

He turned to Dalilah, heart thudding a tattoo against his ribs, sweat dampening his shirt, a wild, mad exhilaration racing through his blood.

"I have an idea. Get in."

"What—"

"Get in!" He jumped back into the driver's seat and fired the ignition as Dalilah scrambled into her seat. Hitting the gas, he spun his wheels and did a one-eighty turn, heading back toward the main road. They thumped over the cattle grids and as he hit the road, he turned north.

The man with the bottles was still there. Brandt screeched to a stop beside him, leaped out of the vehicle.

Using rapid-fire Setswana, Brandt exchanged a hundred-dollar bill for the two crates of empty cola bottles.

Dumping them in the back of the jeep, he got back in

and swung onto the road. Dusk crawled over the land as the sun slid below the distant ridge. Night was almost upon the bushveldt—the violence was about to begin.

Chapter 15

Brandt pulled off the road into a low gulley. In the dark, out of sight, they worked silently with headlamps, quickly filling the cola bottles with petrol, stripping the blanket and soaking the fabric strips in gas. They used the strips to make wicks into the bottles. The Molotov cocktails—twenty-four of them—were now stocked in the two wooden boxes, safe until they were lit. Brandt then filled the cooking pot with rifle shells, and he made sure the camping stove was in working order.

About an hour later, not far from the village, Brandt reversed Skorokoro carefully up a slope, ready for a quick getaway. Leaving the keys in the ignition and Dalilah in the passenger seat, he cupped the back of her neck. In the moonlight her eyes shimmered with liquid excitement, fear. He felt the tension in her body.

Silently, he kissed her.

Then he placed his knife in her hand, took his rifle and

some spare shells, and trotted up to the lip of a ridge. If Amal was following their boot tracks from the abandoned airstrip, he and his men would pass underneath this cliff on their way to the village. It was a sheer cliff, no vehicle access up the front.

Hours ticked by. The moon and stars shifted. Night sounds filled the air.

Suddenly lights appeared in the distance. Brandt heard the purr of engines—Amal's posse. It had to be. They were moving slowly. The vehicles stopped and a shadow moved in front of the headlights. Brandt's pulse quickened—they had a tracker out front on foot. He had to time this just right.

Skorokoro had speed, but if the engine packed it in, they were dead.

The jeeps started to move again, coming closer. Brandt could make out horses in the silver moonlight.

He aimed his rifle, curling his finger around the trigger. Breathing in, he counted to three, then softly squeezed.

A gunshot cracked through the night.

Beetles fell silent, then rose in a wild crescendo again. Brandt fired again.

There was yelling. A horse reared, then jeeps started to move directly toward the cliff, veering away from their tracks that led to the village. It was definitely Amal and his crew.

Brandt scrambled down the slope, jumped over the door into the driver's seat. "They're coming."

Firing the ignition, he raced for the road, leaving clear skid marks as he swung onto the paving and barreled south. Both were tense, silent, Dalilah gripping the door.

The moon was low, big, and stars bright—all good. Brandt was thinking several steps ahead while focusing on the road. Amal would reach the ridge, realize he had to drive around it, and be delayed. They'd also come slowly along the road, looking for tracks off it. This would give Brandt and Dalilah the window of time they needed to set up, but barely.

The game fence appeared, shimmering in the moonlight as they bombed down the road.

He glanced up into the rearview mirror. No lights in sight yet. Brandt wheeled off the paved road and Skorokoro bounced and thudded over the sets of cattle grids. He made sure he left deep tire marks pointing their way. This was where Amal would have to lose his horses—they'd be unable to cross the grids and enter the game-controlled area. Either he'd have to tether the mounts near the road and pack the horsemen into his two jeeps, or he'd instruct the men on horseback to continue down the road, looking for a way into the fence, which they would not find for another fifty kilometers or so.

And leaving horses tethered was not really an option if Amal didn't want them eaten by night predators.

The rock walls of the Valley of Ghosts loomed suddenly into view once again, black shadows etched with scrub on top. He veered off the track that would have led them out of the wide part of the gorge, and entered the narrowing part instead. From this point the cliff walls began to funnel inward.

Brandt spun Skorokoro's wheels for good measure, making sure their change in direction was easily visible in the silver moonlight. Then he drove down the gorge, along the dry riverbed of sand. Cliffs started to close tightly in on either side of them, blocking the moon. In his rearview mirror he could clearly see Skorokoro's tire marks in the sand.

They arrived at the end of the gorge—barely the width of three jeeps. Here, the ground fell away into what was a thundering waterfall in the height of the rainy season. Brandt maneuvered the jeep behind an outcrop of rock. Unless Amal was checking topographical maps as he pursued them, which Brandt doubted, he would not be aware the ground fell away here in a dead end. Amal's presumption would more likely be that Brandt had continued through the gap.

He cut the ignition and turned to Dalilah.

"This is it." His eyes met hers. "Ready?"

She nodded, reached for his hand, squeezed.

"Let's do this, then," he said.

Brandt carried one of the boxes of handmade grenades, picking a fairly easy route up through the rocky gorge wall, Dalilah right behind him. Near the top of the ridge, beside a flat rock, he set the box down. Brandt balanced a bottle of petrol on the rock, checking it was level enough—it was.

"Remember, as you light the Molotovs, throw them immediately, and gravity will do the rest. You going to manage with that arm?"

She nodded. "I'll position the Molotov on the rock, light, then throw."

He handed her the lighter. "Be careful, concentrate."

She took it from him and he realized she was shaking.

"You'll be safe up here, Dalilah," he said, holding her gaze with his own. "Just stay down behind the rocks. I'll be on the opposite side of the gorge over there with the gun—I'll keep them busy. When you hear my whistle, toss the first grenade."

"I got it."

"You sure you're okay?"

"I will be."

He turned to head back down.

"Brandt—"

He stilled.

"Promise me that you'll take me home after. To your farm."

Brandt held her gaze in the moonlight and his chest hurt. "I promise," he whispered. And it solidified his intent—his plan was suddenly crystal sharp in his mind and he knew from the bottom of his soul that he was going to get her out of this alive. And once it was done, they'd both be free, in so many more ways than one.

"Good." She smiled. "Because I know you don't break a promise."

Brandt hurried down through the rocks, and this time he took two boxes from the jeep—the other container of cola bombs and a box that contained the small camp stove, a tin of kerosene and the pot filled with rifle shells.

He found a good spot that was protected by rocks and there he set down the cola bottles filled with petrol. He then trotted along the ridge about a hundred meters in the direction from which they'd come and set up the stove with the pot of bullets on top. He poured kerosene over them and steadied his breathing as he watched the darkness. It wasn't too long before he saw the flash of headlights in the distance, coming along the gorge bottom. Then came the second set—both vehicles going slowly enough so as not to lose Skorokoro's tire marks in the sand. No horses, just as he'd figured.

Brandt waited until they got a little closer. Then he turned the knob on the camp stove and lit the gas. The bullets would explode and the men would think they were being fired on from behind. He ran back to where he'd left his handmade grenades.

Taking one of the bottles out of the box, he readied his match. The headlights came closer and he could hear the purring of the engines. His heart jackhammered. Across the ridge, he caught the gleam of Dalilah's hair in the moonlight. Tension whispered through him, but he settled it—putting his mind in the zone, a place he was familiar with. And waited for his prey to arrive.

Jacob felt something was wrong as soon as the jeeps entered the dark gorge—the sixth sense of a hunter. A sense of foreboding. This was a trap—he was sure of it. But he said nothing from his seat in the back of one of the jeeps. Jock's head rested on his lap. Amal sat in front of him.

Jacob scanned the black cliff faces that were closing in on either side of them. Then suddenly a glint of reflected moonlight up on the ridge caught his eye. His heart began to pound and sweat beaded on his brow. Still, Jacob said nothing to the man in the front seat, but he quietly removed the leash from Jock's collar so the dog would be able to flee.

Suddenly gunfire sounded in the ridge behind them. All the men in the two jeeps spun around. Amal yelled for his driver to speed up.

The drivers gunned forward, but the cliff walls grew very narrow. Jacob heard a sharp whistle. Then a flare of orange fire came arcing down from the sky. The fireball hit the bonnet of their jeep and a bottle exploded into a raging burst of flame.

Another fireball came down from the other cliff wall, hit behind them. Then more bombs, followed by gunfire. The jeep engine caught fire. Amal and his men dived out of the vehicle, seeking cover in the rocks.

Jacob bailed, leaping from the backseat. Jock followed him. Mbogo was barking orders, trying to shoot up at the cliff face from behind rocks on the canyon floor.

More Molotov cocktails rained from the sky. The second jeep exploded into flames.

One of the men caught a bullet in the neck, and fell, his gun flying from his hands. Jacob scrabbled over the sand, grabbed the automatic rifle. And from the cover of a rock he aimed at five of the men now huddled in a group behind an outcropping to avoid being shot from above—they were sitting ducks the instant they moved. Jacob squeezed the trigger, his thin, old body jerking as he raked a barrage of bullets over the men. Then he shot them all again, to be sure.

Breathing hard, he stilled. Jacob quickly did the math—there'd been eleven men in total in the posse, including the one-armed Arab and his giant sidekick. But four of the men on horses had headed south when they'd been stumped by a series of cattle grids.

He'd shot five. There were two left somewhere. Jacob's heart hammered. Where were the others?

Suddenly a gleam caught his eye—the shiny bald pate of Mbogo climbing the cliff, using rocks as cover from whoever was above, and he was moving fast. Jacob's gaze shifted farther up the cliff face. His pulse kicked—*the woman.* He saw her move, moonlight on her hair, the shape of her silhouette as she darted from one rock to another.

Mbogo had almost reached her.

An explosion rent the air as one of the jeep's fuel tanks blew. Bitter smoke billowed through the gorge as flames roared and crackled. Jacob crept quickly through the shadows and smoke, wanting a clear line to Mbogo. He'd lost sight of the Arab who'd leaped from the vehicle without a gun.

Crouching, Jacob pressed the rifle stock to his shoulder, aimed and squeezed the trigger.

The big man's body jerked and spasmed under a hail of bullets. Then he tumbled, thudding down like a giant rag doll between the rocks.

But before Jacob could move, he heard Jock's low, throaty growl, and suddenly the animal was beside him, snarling. Jacob realized too late why—the Arab leaped down from a rock above him. And he felt the dagger go deep into his side.

Amal yanked the dagger out, but before he could plunge it in again, Jock lunged at the man's throat. Amal screamed, a terrible sound, followed by sick wet tearing, growling as he struggled with one hand to fight off the dog.

Jacob put his hand to his waist. Blood was soaking through his shirt, through his fingers. He pressed his hand to the wound, tried to crawl away.

Then his world went black.

Brandt stilled. Beneath the roar of flames he detected human screams that chilled him to the bone. He listened carefully, trying to separate the sounds. He thought he could hear animal snarls, like a wild dog attack. Nausea washed over him as an image of his son's body slammed through his mind.

Then suddenly there was silence. Deadly silence, apart from the crackle of fire. He wasn't sure what had happened, but someone down there had killed five men of his own party in a hail of bullets, then shot another who had been climbing up toward Dalilah, just as Brandt had been about to fire on the man himself.

He put his fingers into his mouth, issued three shrill whistles. In the moonlight on the other side he saw Dalilah wave her arm up.

Relief bottomed out of his stomach. Her orders were to stay hidden until he'd scoped out the place properly—there could still be someone down there alive.

Brandt waited another few beats. Still no sound. Heart

thudding, he made his way carefully down between the rocks, gun in hand.

Five bodies lay in a twisted mess at the bottom of the cliff.

Amal, however, was not among these five dead. Brandt crept along the gorge bottom, staying in shadows. Smoke was thick and acrid down here, the smell of fuel strong. Then out of the blackness between rocks, something came at him.

He spun around, gun leading, and then his heart stalled. An animal—a dog. Advancing toward him, blood on his mouth—like a ghost. A ghost from his past.

Jock.

For a nanosecond Brandt couldn't think as past looped into present. Then he snapped back, curling his finger around the trigger as he aimed at the animal.

But the dog lowered his head suddenly as he neared, its tail tucking in as it edged toward him sideways, wiggling, whining. That's when Brandt saw Amal's body behind the rock—throat ripped out. Arm mauled. *Dead.* This dog had killed the one-armed bandit? Another body lay in the sand a few metres away from Amal.

They were all dead, every single one of the men who had entered the ambush.

Confusion raced through Brandt's mind as he crouched down and took hold of the animal's collar. He reached for his flashlight, shone it on the tag.

Jock.

His heart began to hammer overtime, his life flashing before his eyes—images of Stefaan, mauled. His own dog, blood on its mouth. Yolanda. His brother. He was beyond exhausted—he hadn't slept for days, he told himself. He was hallucinating, here in the Valley of Ghosts—seeing a dog from his past.

Fatigue was catching up with him, that's all this was. Brandt tried to shake the ghostly sensation as he whistled for Dalilah.

While he waited for her to come down, he read the name on the dog's tag again, just to be certain he'd seen it right the first time. "Hey, buddy," Brandt said, crouching. "What happened here? Where are you from?"

The dog whimpered then slithered off to a body lying not far from Amal. He licked the man's face, then lay down beside him with another whimper.

Frowning, Brandt went over to the body.

Dalilah came scrambling down the rocks behind him. She froze.

"That's Jock!" she whispered.

"I know," he said, crouching beside the dog. Just like the animal he'd rescued from the wilds in Caprivi, the one his brother shot. It looked exactly the same—a russet Staffordshire cross, stocky and strong.

"Jock from the safari lodge," she said, still trying to wrap her own head around the animal's appearance in the Valley of Ghosts. "The lodge owner told us he was using him to track... Oh, my God." She dropped to her haunches beside Brandt. "This is Jacob. He's the lodge tracker—Amal must have forced them to trail us, Brandt."

An AK-47 lay in the sand next to him.

"It must have been Jacob," he said, looking at the gun, "who turned on them all. He killed Amal's men, and Amal must have attacked him—Jock tried to protect him."

Dalilah reached to feel for a pulse at the old man's neck.

"He's alive, Brandt! He's got a pulse!"

Quickly they rolled him over. There was blood across his abdomen, and more blood pooled dark in the sand under him. Yanking up the old man's shirt, Brandt shone his flashlight over him. "He's been stabbed."

Brandt ripped off his own shirt. Balling it up, he pressed it to the old man's wound. "Hold this! I'm going to see if I can bring our jeep round."

Dalilah pressed the balled-up shirt into Jacob's side as Brandt ran off to find the jeep. Smoke burned her throat and eyes, a fire still crackling in one of the engines.

The dog whimpered beside her, wriggling closer to Jacob. Emotion squeezed through Dalilah's chest, and her attention went to the mauled body lying a few feet from her.

Amal Ghaffar. The one-armed enemy of the Al Arif clan, dead in the moonlight, a hooked and bejewelled dagger covered with blood at his side. Killed by a dog. It seemed fitting somehow, she wasn't sure why. But however this bastard had died, a battle of decades was finally over. An era of true peace was finally possible for the Al Arif family. And it had ended in the Valley of Ghosts.

Bile rose in her throat, and she looked away.

The dog stayed with her, whimpering softly. Tears pooled and ran down her cheeks.

Two days later

Brandt and Dalilah had been in Gaborone, the Botswana capital, for over forty-eight hours now. They'd driven Jacob in Skorokoro to the nearest town, where Brandt had accessed a phone and secured a chopper. Jacob had been airlifted with them and Jock to the Princess Marina Hospital, where he'd gone straight into surgery. Luckily, he was going to survive.

When Jacob had been able to speak after the operation, he'd told Brandt he'd seen signs of the ambush as they entered the gorge, and he'd said nothing—he'd wanted Amal to die, and he'd figured Amal was going to kill him and the dog anyway. Jacob preferred going by ambush, he'd told Brandt.

They'd also learned from him that all the staff back at the Zimbabwe lodge had been systematically slaughtered, including Jacob's wife. He had no remaining family.

Brandt invited the old tracker to come stay on his farm, where the old man could heal and be with Jock for as long as he wanted. Brandt was indebted to Jacob—he'd kept the blood off both his and Dalilah's hands. He couldn't begin to say what this meant to him.

After contacting Omair, Brandt had also spent a full day with the Botswana police and military. The Botswana army had rounded up Amal's remaining four horsemen and had been in contact with Interpol and the U.S. Department of Homeland Security. A most-wanted terrorist had been killed. The hunt for Amal Ghaffar, son of the infamous Aban Ghaffar—aka the Moor—was finally over.

While Dalilah had shopped for clothes and rested in a suite at Gaborone's top hotel, Brandt had printed the photographs he'd shot of Dalilah. His favorite image of the bunch he'd had enlarged. It was now wrapped and ready to go up on his bedroom wall. He'd then deleted the files from the camera, packaged it up with the wallet and mailed it to the driver's-license address in Germany, along with a substantial check to cover any other expenses incurred for their losses. Omair could reimburse him later.

Meanwhile, a pilot colleague of Brandt's was on standby with a chopper at Madikwe Safari Lodge about thirty klicks outside Gaborone. Brandt had left Jock at the lodge with the pilot. When Jacob was ready to leave hospital, he'd have both Jacob and the dog flown up to his place together. Money was no object—Omair had wired a small fortune into Brandt's account, and he had no qualms accepting it. He'd paid his debt to the sheik. He'd done the job. And he was going to need a new plane.

The hard part—telling Omair about his feelings for Dalilah—was yet to come.

Brandt pulled up outside the hotel, a low, functional-looking building with a nice pool outside. Gaborone was a small town by city standards, and this was what passed as the top hotel.

Nerves washed through him as he gathered a bouquet of flowers off the passenger seat. He still hadn't slept and he felt a little rough around the edges, but he'd bought flowers and was dressed in new khaki shorts and a fresh white shirt. He'd shaved and had his hair cut. Brandt rubbed his smooth jaw now as he strode across the baking-hot parking lot, feeling naked without his usual stubble.

He hadn't seen Dalilah since she'd had her arm reset at the hospital, and nerves bit deeper as he entered the hotel lobby. He felt like a teen on a first date.

Another wave of anxiety washed through Brandt as he started down the long corridor to her room. He wondered suddenly if this was foolish, if she might have had a change of heart—if her words had all been in the heat of battle, and now that things were settling, she'd go back to her duty.

To Haroun.

To being the princess—the real Arabian queen—she was born to be.

What on earth made him think she'd actually want to stay at his farm in the remote bush? Would she really be that interested in what he wanted to show her on his land, on getting to know him better?

He nodded to the security detail he'd had posted outside her door, then paused, perspiration pricking over his body, his hand fisting around the bouquet of flowers. He should back out now. Call it quits. Save face, make it easier on both of them.

In spite of his anxiety, he raised his hand, rapped once on the door.

Silence.

Heart pounding, he glanced back down the corridor. Then suddenly he heard her voice inside and the door swung wide open.

Freshly showered, hair wet, wearing nothing but the hotel's white terry robe and her new fiberglass cast, Dalilah stood with a cell phone pressed to her ear. She was in the midst of conversation with someone and beckoned to him to come in, mouthing, "Omair."

"I'll come back later," Brandt said, hesitating.

She frowned, shook her head and reached for his hand, pulling him inside her room. As Brandt closed the door behind him, he caught the scent of soap and shampoo. Desire rushed through him.

She pointed to the bar as she walked over to the window, saying something in Arabic into the phone. Brandt felt tense—Omair was not going to be pleased when he learned that Brandt had not only saved Dalilah's life, but now planned on keeping his sister for the rest of his life. If she'd have him.

Was this really possible? he thought for the gazillionth time.

There was a freshly brewed pot of coffee on the counter, and a bottle of whiskey. Setting the flowers down, he poured a mug of coffee and sipped, watching her talk by the window.

She'd painted her nails—fresh red. So feminine, he thought, yet she was made of stronger stuff than many men he knew.

Dalilah pushed a lock of damp hair back from her brow,

glanced at him and smiled as she listened to her brother speaking. And he suddenly loved her wholly, so completely, it was overwhelming. It brought emotion sharply to his eyes and made him feel so incredibly vulnerable. This woman could kill him.

She was as rare as that Argyle diamond she'd so blithely given away.

His attention shifted to the double bed. On it she'd laid out her clothes for the day, and lacy underwear. Heat pooled low and hot in his groin and Brandt's mind went back to her room at the safari lodge in Zimbabwe, to how he'd touched her silky underwear in her drawer while he'd been resenting the fact he'd even answered Omair's phone call.

A lot had happened since that call. His life had changed.

Dalilah switched suddenly from Arabic to English while shooting another glance at him.

"Because he's here, yes," she said into the phone. "I do want him to hear what I'm going to say." Eyes on Brandt, she continued, "I spoke to Haroun, Omair. I told him the wedding contract is off." She closed her eyes as she waited for her brother to finish.

"Yes, I spoke to him privately first, then we had a conference call with the respective heads of state, including Zakir's representatives from the King's Council. There'll be compensation, since I was the one who broke the deal. But Zakir extended an offer to continue with other aspects of the treaty. Haroun is interested in pursuing talks in that regard."

She was silent, her eyes shining with a bright passion as she listened to her brother's response.

"It was amicable," she said. "Haroun's father might have been an old-school traditionalist, Omair, but I really get a sense Haroun wants to move Sa'ud in a new direction." She paused. "I'm not sure he wanted to marry me any more than I did. He might even be relieved."

Brandt's chest went tight as hope, possibility, began to race wild through his blood.

"No," she said quietly, holding his gaze. "I didn't break it off because of Brandt. He— This mission, my trip to Zimbabwe, the fact you all withheld knowledge of Amal from me, it all brought to a head something that has been coming for a long time, Omair."

Another pause. "I know, I should have told you about my reservations years ago. I just…" She closed her eyes. "I felt I'd done so little, that the marriage was one thing I could offer after you all had given up so much for the future of Al Na'Jar. And I wanted to honor our mother and father. But now I've done that, with Brandt's help—Amal is gone. That war is over. We owe Brandt for that, Omair."

She was silent while her brother spoke, then, meeting Brandt's gaze, she said, "I also need to tell you that while he is not the reason I broke the treaty, I have fallen in love with him."

Brandt stilled, coffee cup clutched tight in his hand.

She said her goodbyes, put the phone down, stared at him.

Brandt carefully put the cup down before his hands started shaking with the pressure building inside him.

"What did Omair say?" His voice came out hoarse.

Emotion pooled like ink in her eyes, and she swiped at a sudden tear. "He said…he understands. He never knew I felt this way, Brandt. Zakir said the same. All this time, all these years…" She brushed another tear away quickly. "I'm sorry. It's…it's just such a relief. I finally feel free, like this huge weight has been lifted off my shoulders that I didn't even realize was there."

"So he's not going to send a team of assassins after my ass?"

She smiled through her emotion, came up to him.

"No," she whispered, taking his hands in hers and leaning her head against his chest. "He said he owes you for this mission. He just didn't think I was the price you'd exact." She paused. "I think my brother likes you. I think this is going to work."

A sweet poignant ache filled his entire body. This thing between them still felt so fragile and he was so worried he'd break it under the strength of his passion for her.

Gently, he tilted her face up to his and whispered, "Are you ready to go home now?"

"Almost," she said, eyelids lowering. She opened her robe—naked and smooth underneath and rounded in all the right places. Brandt tried to swallow. She wrapped her arms around him, bare breasts pushing against his chest, her nipples tight.

His erection pressed hard and sudden against her pelvis as she drew him backward toward the bed. He bent down, kissed her, and she opened her mouth under his. Warm, the taste of mint.

But as the backs of her legs bumped up against the bed, he pulled back, breathing hard, burning up inside. This was too special. He did not want to take her virginity here in this hotel-room bed.

"Not here, Dalilah," he whispered, cupping her face. "Not in a hotel." His voice was hoarse, thick, low.

"Come back with me, to my farm." He slid his hand down her arm. "I want to make love to you there, in my bed. I want you to sleep in my arms." He paused. "I promised I'd take you home, Princess—and I never break a promise."

Chapter 16

The late-afternoon sun coated the bushveldt in yellow gold as their chopper landed on Brandt's farm.

He carried the bags off the helicopter first, then returned for Dalilah, taking her hand as they ran in a crouch under the whirling blades. He gave a thumbs-up, and the chopper lifted, banking into the sky, then growing smaller and smaller before winking out on the horizon. He placed his arm around her shoulders, drawing her close as they stood together, watching it disappear, their bags at their feet. As the sound faded, the birdsong rose around them in a raucous crescendo.

They were on a rise, and about a hundred yards out a copper-colored stream meandered into a pool of rocks. Beyond the stream was a bush runway and empty airplane hangar. In the distance, Dalilah could see giraffe and a herd of antelope moving. The air on her shoulders was rounded and warm and the sense of peace was almost palpable—no industry, no civilization, for as far as the eye could see.

Dalilah couldn't believe how exhilarated she felt, or how this had happened. She glanced up at Brandt's rugged profile and saw that he was watching her, a strange look on his face.

"What is it?" she said.

"I'm nervous."

She laughed. "You? Nervous? What on earth for?"

"Because I want you to like it."

She studied his eyes, as clear blue as the sky behind him, and she knew he was talking about both his place, and making love to her. "I love it already," she whispered, then turned to look back out over the land. "How far does your property extend, Brandt?"

"All the way to those trees on the ridge over there." He pointed to the horizon. "That's where the next farm starts. Not a soul as far as the eye can see. Come, let me show you inside."

Truth was, Dalilah was nervous, too. Brandt Stryker was a lone ranger, and she wondered how long it might take before he once again felt the need for solitude. She, on the other hand, was not a loner, nor a quiet personality, but this was also in part why she felt so drawn to this man—he balanced her. He was a rock, solid and sure and steady, and although he was yet another alpha male in her life, Brandt had made it clear he valued her passion and independence, and that this was what made him beautiful to her. But how it could all work out, she didn't know.

One step at a time, she thought as he led her up a stone path toward his house, which had been built into an outcrop of rock—lots of stone, glass, wood and a wide veranda that ran along the entire front.

She stopped to take in the architecture, the lines, the

way it all blended into the natural surroundings. It would be hardly visible by air, she thought, camouflaged into the rock.

"Designed it myself," he said, watching her. "There's a small village on my land and the locals helped me build it, one rock, one brick at a time. I flew in whatever materials I needed. Took me three years to get this far." He smiled. "And I'm still at it. Bit by bit."

"It's exquisite, Brandt," she whispered, holding his callused hand, thinking of him alone out here, under the hot African sun, putting this place together stone by stone. A home.

"It's big," she said, her gaze moving along the veranda, noting that the wooden shutters that could be drawn across the length of it. She looked up at him, right into his eyes. "Why did you build this?"

Surprise raised his brow. "That's an interesting question."

Dalilah moistened her lips. "It looks far too big for one," she said. "And you're this guy who moved out here for solitude." She shrugged. "It just…doesn't quite fit."

He shrugged, watching her eyes. "Maybe that urge to create a home—you know, the man and his castle—" he grinned "—never truly died after Yolanda. As a kid it had always been a dream of mine to have lots of land, a farm. Animals."

"The soldier-farmer," she said.

"Hey, life throws curveballs. You do what you can."

"Yeah," she said as she smiled at him. "And sometimes those balls curve right back."

"Come inside. There's something out back I think you'll like."

A warm breeze flowed through floor-to-ceiling glass sliders that had been opened along the length of the wall to expose an endless view of the bushveldt over the veranda. Old-fashioned wooden ceiling fans paddled the air slowly, and there were fresh blooms on the counter—strelitzia on long stems, like bright birds of paradise. He must have called ahead, Dalilah thought, and asked someone to open up the house, bring in flowers. Her heart squeezed in her chest.

He led her over floors crafted from rough, cool granite into the kitchen furnished with an antique Aga stove.

"This is what I want you to see." He opened the back door, and escorted her into a trellised kitchen garden enclosed by a rock wall. Herbs and vegetables grew in neat rows. Dassies—fat furry rodents with big liquid-brown eyes—sat sunning themselves atop the wall, watching them through netting that kept both them and the birds out.

Dalilah turned slowly around. "Did you plant all this?" It was a silly question, and she knew it even as it left her mouth—of course he planted it. There was no one else. It was just that she was trying to picture this burly ex-merc with his hands in this lush dark soil, which he must have brought in from somewhere, or worked up from compost himself.

He gave a sheepish grin and hooked his thumbs into his belt. Then he shrugged. "Got the lettuce, but no tofu."

She punched his arm with a laugh. "I'll live. Where does the irrigation come from?"

"Underground water table and rain tank, for the most part. I'm working on some other initiatives—I'll show you later."

She slipped her arm around him, hugged him close, huge and solid and warm against her body—she loved the feel of him, everything about him. "You surprise me, Brandt Stryker."

"Touché, Princess," he whispered. "Come," he said, leading her back into the kitchen. He opened the fridge.

"White wine all right for sundowners?" He held up a chilled bottle.

"Not whiskey?" she said.

He laughed and took two glasses down from the shelf, setting them on the counter before digging in a drawer for an opener. "Why don't you go through to the deck while I put away the bags," he said. "I'll bring this through."

She glanced at her new suitcase standing by the door. It was filled with new clothes—functional bush clothes, hiking boots, good sandals, hats, along with some sundresses and new underwear. Propped against the suitcase was a flat package he'd been carrying under his arm. It was wrapped in brown paper.

"What's in there?" she said.

He scooped it and the bag up. "Just some prints I had done in Gaborone. I'll be right back—go on through."

Dalilah kicked off her sandals and padded barefoot through the living room, wanting the feel of this place, the touch of wood beneath her feet, the sensation of the stone. Her gauzy white sundress was cool against her skin. It was a liberating feeling—Dalilah wanted to enjoy it, everything about this newfound sense of lightness and brightness and freedom, where everything in the world seemed suddenly possible. And exciting.

Old-fashioned fans stirred lazily in the living room, too. The decor in this section of the house was all dark African woods, animal skins, block-printed fabric. Large black-and-white and sepia-toned photographic prints hung on the walls—an overall retro safari look that put Dalilah in mind of Hemingway and images of great hunters.

Dalilah turned her attention to the prints. One depicted a man holding up the head of a Cape buffalo he'd shot, gun in one hand. The man had Brandt's features, but with a big beard and sideburns. A boy, maybe seven years old, stood next to him with a rifle in his own hands, white-blond hair. Both man and boy had eerily pale eyes against suntanned skin. Brandt and his father? she wondered.

There were other hunting shots, and deep-sea-fishing images. A marlin leaping with sprays of droplets sparkling in sunlight. In one image Dalilah recognized the prominent topography of Cape Town, South Africa.

Then she came to a photo of a child in a slum—this one taken in a jungle area. Another image showed a barefoot kid pushing a toy made of wire—his arm had been amputated. Yet another image showed a small girl fleeing something awful, terror wild in her face and eyes. This one looked as if it had been shot in Asia somewhere. There were more—a series with mothers with children, some poignant, some just plain heartbreaking. Devastating. Dalilah rubbed her arms, her mood shifting.

He'd told her he didn't bring people here, so these were not for show, they were for him. His touchstones. That's why he said he took pictures—to capture, remember. Brandt's words sifted back into her mind.

It's what I do, Dalilah. These days I shoot with a camera, not a gun, if I can help it. I shoot rare and beautiful things, things with meaning to me. Images I return to so that I can be reminded of what I value in life. Or what stands to be lost...

She'd thought Brandt was running from his past, seeking relief. But she was wrong. He wanted to hold on, maybe too acutely, to the memories that had changed him. No wonder he struggled with needing relief.

Over his desk of carved black wood hung a picture positioned alone in an area of prominence. She went over to it, and her hand went to her throat when she realized what it was. A toddler, pale blue eyes, white-blond hair catching sun like a halo.

Dalilah bent forward to read the inscription in italics— *Stefaan Stryker.* Along with the date of his birth, and his death. Under the photo was an old leather-bound book, *Jock of the Bushveldt,* by Sir James Percy Fitzpatrick.

She touched the old hardcover, opened it to the copyright page. *First published 1907.* There was a line drawing of a dog that looked exactly like the one from the lodge, and on the title page was an inscription written in longhand: *Vir my liefste Jacquie, baie gelukkige tye met ons eie hond, jou Pa.*

Dalilah suddenly felt him watching, glanced up.

Brandt stood in the doorway with the bottle of wine and two glasses in his hands, his features tight.

"What does it mean, Brandt?" she said, her fingers touching the Afrikaans inscription.

"For my dearest little Stefaan. May we have happy times with our own dog, your father." He hesitated, as if torn between speaking and turning away. "I'd just come across a copy of that old edition. I wanted it for him."

Dalilah's eyes prickled with emotion. "It's so uncanny," she said softly, "that the dog from the lodge looks the same, has the same name."

"Jock is a common name for a Staffordshire cross of that color. Like I said, Jock has become a cultural icon in this part of the world. There's even a statue of Jock outside the Barberton city hall in Mpumalanga, South Africa."

"I still think it's eerie," she said, closing the book and setting it carefully back in position under the photo. "Stefaan looked like you when you were a boy, if that's you in the hunting photo over there, with your father?"

A wry smile twisted over his lips, but there was a sadness around his eyes. "Yeah, that was me. Lost my dad when I was twelve."

"How?"

"Lion."

Dalilah waited, but he said nothing more, and she didn't press, not now.

"How about that wine," she said with a smile.

With a view of the setting sun, Brandt poured their drinks at an outside table.

"A Buiten Blanc, from Buitenverwachting," he said, pouring. "It's a vineyard near Cape Town—the name means Beyond Expectation. Cheers," he said, raising his own glass, and she chinked hers against it.

"Beyond expectation," she whispered, meeting his eyes.

They sat side by side on lacquered wicker furniture watching animals come down to the pond to drink. Monkeys squealed in a tree above the water hole, and Dalilah's thoughts drifted back to that night in the *lapa.* She turned to look at Brandt.

"Did you watch me for long, in that *lapa,* before the attack?"

A slow smile curved his mouth, and this time a lightness did reach his eyes.

"I thought you were a flame to those diplomatic moths around you." He paused. "I thought you were a tease."

She fell silent as his eyes held hers, a sudden tingling heat low in her belly.

He got up suddenly, taking his glass to the railing. "Come here," he said, holding his hand out to her.

Dalilah joined him at the railing with her glass. The sun was blood-orange and going squat on the horizon, as if resisting the end of the day before being pushed under.

"I positioned the house and veranda so you could see

the watering hole at sunset and catch the last rays of the evening sun. This is my favorite time of day, when everything is magic. Anything seems possible."

He took her glass from her hand, set it on the railing and tilted her face to his. As the sun slid below the horizon, the last rays caught the rugged planes of his face, and his eyes darkened.

And suddenly she wanted him. All of him.

"I need you, Brandt," she whispered. "I need you, now."

He carried her to his bedroom and laid her on the bed. Here, too, glass sliders were open to the evening air. Outside in the dusk the bush noise grew loud.

But Dalilah froze suddenly as she caught sight of what was hanging on the wall opposite Brandt's bed—a poster-size photograph of *her*. Naked under a waterfall, droplets like jewels spinning in an arc from her wet hair as she tossed her head back, sunlight glancing off the emerald in her navel. The hair between her legs was dark and wet, her nipples tight and pointed. A look of pure joy on her face, her eyes closed.

Dalilah's jaw dropped and she quickly pushed herself back up into a sitting position. She stared at the image—a stunningly artistic shot, more about form than a naked woman, the curves of her body being echoed in the contours of the smooth red rock.

Her gaze shifted slowly up to meet his.

"Why?" she said.

"Touchstones," he whispered, watching her intently. "To capture something of your spirit and bring it home."

And hang it where he could lie and look at her every night...

He lowered himself to his knees in front of her, taking her hands in his.

"I never dreamed I'd be lucky enough to actually bring you home, Dalilah." He drew her closer on the edge of the bed, parting her legs around him as he spoke. "So I stole something I could keep, just for me. Do you mind?"

Her vision spiraled as he pushed up the hem of her dress and slid his hands up the insides of her thighs. She couldn't even think of words to answer him with. His hands went higher, fingers hooking into her G-string as she stared at the photo of her naked self, thinking of how she'd caught him in his own state of arousal. She didn't feel affronted by the photo—it speared heat into her belly, made her breasts ache. She lifted herself slightly as he rolled her G-string down her thighs, and a soft sigh escaped her, her eyelids fluttering low as he drew her right to the edge of the bed and opened her legs wide.

She felt his tongue, teasing, warm, slick, the rough stubble of his jaw rubbing against the sensitive skin on her inner thighs. Dalilah couldn't breathe. She arched her head back, widening her thighs, giving him more access. She felt his tongue entering her. Dalilah groaned, her entire body going white-hot as outside the birds screamed, jockeying in a tree for best position for the night.

He went in deeper, and her pulse started to race so fast she thought she might faint. He grated her with his teeth until pleasure built so raw and wild in her chest she thought she'd burst, scream. Her hands fisted in the sheets, head going back as she grew wetter, aching, desperate for him.

Suddenly he stopped, yanked off his shirt and dropped his pants—no underwear, his arousal evident, powerful. Perspiration glistened over his muscular body.

He lifted her dress over her head and gave a soft inhalation as he saw she wore no bra.

Gently he eased her back onto the bed, his tongue,

wet, teasing slowly up her abdomen, circling the emerald jewel in her belly button. She arched her pelvis, clawing the covers, desperate to have him inside. Now.

But he was taking his sweet time, torturing her, making it last. Sweat broke out over her body, desperation growing unbearable. She reached down, cupped him between the legs, massaged the hot, hard, quivering length of him, writhing her hips up to him with a need and instinct as old as time.

He grabbed her good wrist suddenly, held her arm up over her head, pressing her into the bed with his body as he kneed her thighs open wide. Her breathing was fast, breasts rising and falling, eyelids heavy, mouth open—all she wanted was him, in her, all of him. She was going to implode.

He entered her with just the smooth tip of his erection. Dalilah went dead still, blood pounding loud in her ears. He pushed slowly deeper, then pulled out. Then again, this time going even deeper. She arched her spine, trying to get more of him, but he pulled out again, and then suddenly reentered with a sharp, hard, long thrust. She gasped, her world spiraling into shades of scarlet and black as a sweet, sharp pain seared up through her abdomen and caught her in the throat. Tears flowed from her eyes.

He stopped, a look of concern suddenly in his features. But she shook her head, pulling his body against hers, wrapping her legs around him, holding him in tight. He held still for a while longer, and she could feel him, quivering and hot inside her as her body accommodated the size and delicious feel of him. Then Dalilah began to rock her hips, stroking herself against him, breathing light, fast, faster. She moved harder. Then suddenly she stilled, long fingernails digging into his back, and she shattered around him with a cry, her body besieged by rolling contractions as her muscles spasmed around the length of him.

Brandt's control cracked. He grasped her hips, yanking her against him as he thrust hard, deep, fast. And almost instantly he released, the pure pleasure, the pain of restraint too much to hold on to. Tears of release filled his eyes as a feeling of indescribable warmth rolled through his body. He gathered Dalilah into his arms, and they lay there like that, in the velvet dusk, still joined as they listened to the bush readying for the night, feeling the warm African air on their hot, damp skin. He stroked her hair back off her brow and loved the smell of her, the sensation of her thick curls against his cheek.

"I believe I'm the luckiest man alive right now," he whispered against her skin

They heard the hyenas, a rising *whoop whooooop whooping* call as they started on their night hunt.

"Do they come close?" she asked softly.

"Right up to the house sometimes—you can see their prints in the morning. They're the top predator on my land. They ousted the lions."

"Tautona has no lion pride?"

He laughed softly. "No. There apparently was a pride here before I bought the place. But some really dominant hyenas challenged them. There was a huge bloody battle. The lions were defeated and moved out of the territory. The hyenas control the place now."

Silent, the two of them lay naked, side by side, time stretching out before them.

"Do you ever think of starting your own safari business out here, Brandt?"

"No," he said quietly.

"Why not?"

"I told you. I don't like people."

"I do."

He was silent for a long time and when she said no more, Brandt thought she might have fallen asleep, but she said suddenly, "We do make a good team, you know."

"You say that like you were having doubts."

"I was just thinking, I could handle the people side of things."

He grinned, found her hand, twined his fingers through hers. Truth was, Brandt had started thinking about a way to keep her busy out here. Because then he might find a way to keep her.

"I love you, Princess," he whispered.

Dalilah smiled in the dark, squeezed his hand. Then she heard his breathing change. She propped herself up on her elbow, hair falling over her breast, and she watched his face in the shadows.

Finally, she thought, *Brandt sleeps. Now that he's secure, when the job is done.*

She watched him for a long while, his chest rising and falling, naked. So strong, yet so darn tender it cut right through her heart. She breathed in the scent of him, the scent of their sex, and mingled with it was a fragrance of wild honeysuckle that grew below the window.

"I love you, too, Tautona," she whispered, and kissed him softly in his sleep.

Epilogue

They married eighteen months later—the mercenary and his princess—under a baobab tree over a thousand years old. The base of the tree was wide enough to hide an elephant, and its top tapered to form a perfect bottle shape, branches clawing up to a clear blue, infinite sky.

The tree had a magic about it—it had become a favorite spiritual place of Dalilah's. She liked to sit under it and imagine what the baobab might have witnessed roaming these plains over all those thousands of years—herds of elephant, now-extinct rhinos, humans moving in as cattle herders, great prides of lions.

It was the perfect place for an informal church, and informal was what Dalilah wanted, as far removed from her long-planned royal wedding with Haroun as possible.

And seeing that they were defying convention, Brandt had decided he wanted two best men—Omair and Jacob.

Omair stood to his right now, Jacob proudly at his left.

Jock sat obediently at Jacob's heels, as always, but today the dog sported a special wedding bandanna around his neck.

Jacob had been officially hired by Brandt as his tracker, and Tautona Safari Expeditions was into its second season as a fledging safari outfit. This was all a result of Dalilah's prodding—she'd insisted she wanted to run a business, and she'd insisted on providing substantial seed financing. She'd also set up an arm of ClearWater in Gaborone, and Brandt flew her to the city once a month to check up on staff and the office. He also flew clients in and out of the new bush camp they'd established not far from this baobab. The camp was constructed around a giant old nyala tree and consisted of Meru-style tents with en suite bathrooms open to the sky. The camp could accommodate a maximum of forty guests—a boutique safari outfit Dalilah had called it. He'd raised his brows, but she'd soldiered on.

Brandt had meanwhile bought and outfitted new jeeps, hired two guides, brought Jacob and Jock on as full-time trackers and game spotters, and he'd hired staff from the tiny village nearby as cooks and other help. He'd also built a pool and an outside bar and *lapa* near the main house.

Brandt couldn't be happier. He loved seeing Dalilah energized whenever a new group was due to fly in. He'd sometimes even do some guiding himself, and he liked to sit back at the end of the day, by the outdoor fire, and watch Dalilah laugh and tell stories around the bar.

She'd never be bored, Brandt had thought when both the business and ClearWater Botswana really started to flourish. Their camps were booking out well over a year in advance now, and that's when Brandt decided she really might be happy to live permanently with him out on this farm—she'd never be isolated. Not Dalilah. She was a vivacious, exotic creature who brought the party to her.

And he'd finally felt secure enough in her happiness to ask her to be his wife.

So the planning had begun—more Meru tents had been flown in, the bush camp expanded, invitations sent out to family and very close friends. Small, intimate and informal.

Brandt waited for his bride now, under the tree. Nervous.

In front of him, filling the chairs that had been placed in rows under an awning of reeds to shade guests from the sun, were a few of Brandt's pilot connections, a group of Dalilah's closest friends from New York, including colleagues from ClearWater, and of course, the immediate Al Na'Jar royal family. Blonde Queen Nikki sat in the front row along with her extensive brood of children, the kids—apart from Solomon, the eldest—fidgeting and poking at each other as she fussed with them to be quiet. Tariq and his wife, Bella, had also flown out from the States, and Omair had brought his wife, Faith, and their young son, Adam. It was a time of reunion, happiness and peace for the Al Arif clan, thanks to Brandt and Dalilah—a time of celebration.

They were all going to stay in the bush camp tonight, where the wedding feast was already being laid out—traditional African style, under the giant nyala tree hung with lanterns, music provided by locals from the village.

One of those locals hit poignant notes on his xylophone now as Brandt waited. He checked his watch, wondering if it was written in law somewhere that grooms should fret over whether or not their bride would show.

Omair leaned over to him. "You look after my sister well now, or else."

Brandt's face cracked into a grin. "I have no doubt," he

murmured, but his attention was suddenly solely on Dalilah as the jeep with white ribbons drew near.

The guests rose. The xylophone and traditional instruments started up in an African rendition of the wedding march, and the voices of three women rose in haunting song. Then, just as Dalilah stepped out of the jeep with her oldest brother, blind King Zakir taking her hand, the music shifted into a loud and joyous rendition of a traditional southern African favorite—"Mama Thembu's Wedding Song."

Brandt's heart twisted as he saw Dalilah laugh, her black eyes glittering with delight at his surprise. Her dress was white silk, strapless, and her hair was done up with a sprig of white flowers, showing the lines of her shoulders and neck to their most beautiful advantage. She led her brother slowly down the aisle, her gaze fixed on Brandt. He swallowed as King Zakir placed his sister's hand in his.

Everything fell silent—as silent as the bush can fall—and an old African Zionist priest began to preside over the ecumenical ceremony in Setswana, a language Dalilah had been learning over the past eighteen months. And when Brandt slipped the simple platinum band onto Dalilah's finger, and kissed his bride under the African sun, he knew—he really, finally, had come home.

"I love you, Stryker," she whispered into his ear as the music rose joyously around them again. "I'm glad you came for me."

"Me, too," he whispered.

He might have regretted that one phone call from Omair, but it had changed his life. And hers. All of theirs.

Later that night, Omair rose from his table and clinked his champagne glass, getting ready to make a speech. The prince looked dark, handsome, like his brothers—an exotic, strong family all around, thought Brandt, and they'd embraced him fully.

But before Omair could toast the bride and groom, Jacob appeared like a shadow behind Brandt, and placed his gnarled hand on his shoulder, leaning forward to speak in his ear.

"What is it, Jacob?"

"The lions, Mr. Stryker." His eyes gleamed. "They are back. I saw the pride this evening, down by the river."

Dalilah met Brandt's gaze and something raw and powerful passed between them. She reached for his hand under the table.

"It's supposed to be," she whispered. "They've come home."

* * * * *

HARLEQUIN® ROMANTIC SUSPENSE

Available January 22, 2013

#1739 BEYOND VALOR • *Black Jaguar Squadron*
by Lindsay McKenna

Though these two soldiers face death day after day, their greatest risk is taking a chance on each other.

#1740 A RANCHER'S DANGEROUS AFFAIR

Vengeance in Texas • by Jennifer Morey

Eliza's husband has been murdered, and she's in love with his brother. As guilt and love go to battle, Brandon may be the only one who can save her.

#1741 SOLDIER UNDER SIEGE • *The Hunted*
by Elle Kennedy

Special Forces soldier Tate doesn't trust anyone...especially the gorgeous woman who shows up on his doorstep asking him to kill a man.

#1742 THE LIEUTENANT BY HER SIDE
by Jean Thomas

Clare Fuller is forced to steal a mysterious amulet from army ranger Mark Griggs, but falling in love with him isn't in the plan. Nor is the danger that stalks them.

HRSCNM0113

REQUEST YOUR FREE BOOKS!
2 FREE NOVELS PLUS 2 FREE GIFTS!

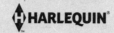

ROMANTIC suspense

Sparked by danger, fueled by passion

YES! Please send me 2 FREE Harlequin® Romantic Suspense novels and my 2 FREE gifts (gifts are worth about $10). After receiving them, if I don't wish to receive any more books, I can return the shipping statement marked "cancel." If I don't cancel, I will receive 4 brand-new novels every month and be billed just $4.49 per book in the U.S. or $5.24 per book in Canada. That's a savings of at least 14% off the cover price! It's quite a bargain! Shipping and handling is just 50¢ per book in the U.S. and 75¢ per book in Canada.* I understand that accepting the 2 free books and gifts places me under no obligation to buy anything. I can always return a shipment and cancel at any time. Even if I never buy another book, the two free books and gifts are mine to keep forever.

240/340 HDN FVS7

Name	(PLEASE PRINT)

Address		Apt. #

City	State/Prov.	Zip/Postal Code

Signature (if under 18, a parent or guardian must sign)

Mail to the Harlequin® Reader Service:
IN U.S.A.: P.O. Box 1867, Buffalo, NY 14240-1867
IN CANADA: P.O. Box 609, Fort Erie, Ontario L2A 5X3

Want to try two free books from another line?
Call 1-800-873-8635 or visit www.ReaderService.com.

* Terms and prices subject to change without notice. Prices do not include applicable taxes. Sales tax applicable in N.Y. Canadian residents will be charged applicable taxes. Offer not valid in Quebec. This offer is limited to one order per household. Not valid for current subscribers to Harlequin Romantic Suspense books. All orders subject to credit approval. Credit or debit balances in a customer's account(s) may be offset by any other outstanding balance owed by or to the customer. Please allow 4 to 6 weeks for delivery. Offer available while quantities last.

Your Privacy—The Harlequin® Reader Service is committed to protecting your privacy. Our Privacy Policy is available online at www.ReaderService.com or upon request from the Harlequin Reader Service.

We make a portion of our mailing list available to reputable third parties that offer products we believe may interest you. If you prefer that we not exchange your name with third parties, or if you wish to clarify or modify your communication preferences, please visit us at www.ReaderService.com/consumerschoice or write to us at Harlequin Reader Service Preference Service, P.O. Box 9062, Buffalo, NY 14269. Include your complete name and address.

HRS13

"How *did* you find me, Eva? I'm not exactly listed in any phone books."

She rested her suddenly shaky hands on her knees. "Someone told me you might be able to help me, so I decided to track you down. I'm…well, let's just say I'm very skilled when it comes to computers."

His jaw tensed.

"You're good, too," she added with grudging appreciation. "You left so many false trails it made me dizzy. But you slipped up in Costa Rica, and it led me here."

Tate let out a soft whistle. "I'm impressed. Very impressed, actually." He made a tsking sound. "You went to a lot of trouble to find me. Maybe it's time you tell me why."

"I told you—I need your help."

He raised one large hand and rubbed the razor-sharp stubble coating his strong chin.

A tiny thrill shot through her as she watched the oddly seductive gesture and imagined how it would feel to have those calloused fingers stroking her own skin, but that thrill promptly fizzled when she realized her thoughts had drifted off course again. What was it about this man that made her so darn aware of his masculinity?

She shook her head, hoping to clear her foggy brain, and met Tate's expectant expression. "Your help," she repeated.

"Oh really?" he drawled. "My help to do what?"

God, could she do this? How did one even begin to approach something like—

"For Chrissake, sweetheart, spit it out. I don't have all night."

She swallowed. Twice.

He started to push back his chair. "Screw it. I don't have time for—"

"I want you to kill Hector Cruz," she blurted out.

Will Eva's secret be the ultimate unraveling of their fragile trust? Or will an overwhelming desire do them both in? Find out what happens next in SOLDIER UNDER SIEGE

Available February 2013 only from Harlequin Romantic Suspense wherever books are sold.

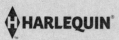

NOCTURNE

They never expected to fall for each other…

She's a committed sergeant in a top secret military unit.
He's a reluctant recruit—and a shape-shifter. But sparks fly
when Kristine and Quinn masquerade as honeymooners on a
beautiful island in search of Quinn's missing brother and his
new bride. Can the unlikely pair set aside their differences
in order to catch a killer bent on destroying Alpha Force?

FIND OUT IN

UNDERCOVER WOLF,

**a sexy, adrenaline-fueled new tale in the
Alpha Force miniseries from**

LINDA O. JOHNSTON

**Available February 5, 2013,
from Harlequin® Nocturne™.**

NOCTURNE

Discover

THE KEEPERS: L.A.,

a dark and epic new paranormal quartet
led by *New York Times* bestselling author

HEATHER GRAHAM

New Keeper Rhiannon Gryffald has her peacekeeping
duties cut out for her. Because in Hollywood, it's hard
to tell the actors from the werewolves, bloodsuckers and
shape-shifters. When Rhiannon hears about a string of
murders that bear all the hallmarks of a vampire serial
killer, she must unite forces with sexy undercover
Elven agent Brodie to uncover a plot that may forever
alter the face of human-paranormal relations....

KEEPER OF THE NIGHT

by **Heather Graham,**
coming **December 18, 2012.**

And look for

Keeper of the Moon by Harley Jane Kozack—
Available March 5, 2013
Keeper of the Shadows by Alexandra Sokoloff—
Available May 7, 2013
Keeper of the Dawn by Heather Graham—
Available July 1, 2013

NOCTURNE

Secrets, Suspense and Seduction…

Deep in the woods, wolf-shifter Nick Jenner is compelled
to help beautiful Mia D'Alessandro after she's bitten by a
feral wolf—a bite that could destroy her unless she bonds
with a pack in time. But Mia's not all she seems….

In a race against time, can they learn to trust each other
and their fragile new bond in order to overcome the evil
that threatens to destroy everything they hold dear?

FIND OUT IN

THE WOLF'S SURRENDER

by

KENDRA LEIGH CASTLE

**Available March 5, 2013,
from Harlequin® Nocturne™.**

www.Harlequin.com

HN88566